G000125280

Praise for

A delightfully original and
pockets of forgotten past
loves to new beginnings.

Namita Gokhale

Love shared cannot be erased. Yesterday's and today's Belfast
and Salamanca meet in an intriguing novel in which the dead
and the living help one another discover the truth of those
words. A confidently bold approach to the ghost story, *The
Sandstone City* explores love for family, lover, and country and
what it takes to reconcile present and past. A multi-generational
story of demanding journeys towards healing and happiness.

Angela Graham

Elaine Canning is a new and original voice whose wonderful
novel seamlessly links the living and the dead to powerful and
moving effect.

David Park

Whether read as a page-turning mystery or as a magical
exploration of the ways in which the present is haunted by the
past, *The Sandstone City*, is a tremendously accomplished literary
debut, blessed with wonderfully memorable and engaging
characters, both the living and the dead.

Alan Bilton

This rich, haunting novel had me completely engrossed.

Francesca Rhydderch

A dazzling debut. Elaine Canning's words sing with grace and
a quiet, glowing energy as she inventively fuses the real and
the fantastic.

Prajwal Parajuly

THE SANDSTONE CITY

THE SANDSTONE CITY

Elaine Canning

Aderyn

First published in Great Britain in 2022 by Aderyn Press
Gweledfa, Felindre, Swansea, Wales, SA5 7NA

www.aderynpress.com

Copyright © 2022 Elaine Canning

1 3 5 7 9 10 8 6 4 2

The moral right of the author has been asserted in accordance
with the Copyright, Designs and Patents Act 1988.

All rights reserved. No part of this publication may be reproduced,
stored in a retrieval system, or transmitted, in any form or by any means
(electronic, mechanical, photocopying, recording or otherwise),
without the prior written permission of both the copyright
owner and the publisher of this book.

A CIP catalogue record for this book is available from
the British Library

ISBN 978-1-9163986-2-7
eISBN 978-1-9163986-3-4

Cover design: Kari Brownlie
Text design: Elaine Sharples
Printed in Great Britain by 4edge Limited

For my mum, Geraldine,
for everything you have done and continue to do.

And for my grandparents, Joseph and Lena, the greatest
storytellers I ever knew whose light forever shines bright.

Day 0: Mahogany Overcoat

I'm lying in the box waiting for them to open the lid. I know full well they've positioned me next to the bay window of our cramped front room. My Annie will have given the orders, though she'll say they come from a 'higher place'. Never met a woman like her for her faith.

This isn't a space I normally inhabit – nor is the box, of course. Annie always kept me away from the window; she said it was for the best, for prying eyes only gave rise to tittle tattle. I never understood whose eyes she was talking about: whether she was more concerned about me seeing, or being seen, but I knew better than to question her. God knows I knew better. I also knew better than to ask what she was doing hanging about in front of the window when it took her fancy, all those times over the years. From my chair by the hearth, I could always see out into the street painted black with marching mourners, or blazoned white with the day's bride, or snuffed grey with bonfires or someone's burnt out vehicle. It never mattered whether her slender frame was in the way or not. Sometimes it was better that my Annie didn't know everything.

Today's a special day, however. Today, in death, it's imperative that I'm on display. I am so thankful that my eldest daughter Chrissie was the one who picked out my clothes and it wasn't left to the other two. Mary and Catherine, not an ounce of sense between them. I know I will be in my best grey suit, the one Maginty knocked up for me a few years back.

Knocked up. Jesus, what a term. Almost enough to make this stiff, useless body recoil. Implies some desperate botched job, the kind I used to fall for, especially when it came to the house or business. Always when I was trying to give some young lad a turn. But Maginty knew people, proper tailors like.

'I'll keep you straight, Michael, don't you worry yourself,' he'd say.

I've always been fond of a good suit, certainly since my twenties. I'm sure it comes from my days in the war – nine months of being forced to wear a filthy, louse-ridden, ill-fitting uniform is more than enough to make you crave a well-cut jacket and decent pair of trousers. My daughters always said I had some sort of compulsive disorder, sitting about the house all dressed up with nowhere to go. Now that sounds strange, talking about the girls in the past tense.

I feel different. Pain-free, thank God, in the physical sense, though not so sure about responsibility-free. Does responsibility ever leave any of us? And this oul' heart of mine, its beat might have ground to a halt, but there's still plenty of love in it if I'm given half a chance to share it.

The trickling shush of my Chrissie's voice coats the air like dripping butter. I know she'll have matched my grey suit with a starched white shirt and one of my nice silk buttonhole hankies, even though I didn't have time to instruct her. I didn't expect to go so soon when it came down to, you know, *actual dying*. She knows me inside out, that girl.

I'm lying here feeling all regal-like in a top-quality mahogany overcoat, courtesy of O'Halloran and Sons. Their parlour is just a stone's throw from the Estate. I called to check them out almost a year ago, several months before the awful poison took over my entire body. Poison, aye, that's what I've always called it. No point in trying to give it some fancy medical term, dressing it up when it's stripping the life clean out of people. Poison pumping through me that was too much for doctors, consultants, even prayers to control. But sure, I mustn't complain. Poor kids eaten up by it when they're only small. No life at all. And then there's me: Michael Doherty, eighty-eight years of age – a decent oul' number – and my three girls and

Annie all healthy, thanks be to God, and the five grandchildren already up and the wee great grandchildren doing well.

It's the youngest of the O'Halloran lads whose face I see as they lift the lid. Martin, I'm sure he's called. God help him, he can't be more than sixteen years of age, wearing a look you might call compassion that's probably been forced into him. Unless he takes after his mother – not a kinder soul could you meet than Sissy O'Halloran. She was with Annie the first day I laid eyes on her. 10th June 1941, it was, the two of them bathed in a golden sunlight that couldn't do a thing to salvage the eyesore of a factory behind them. That dungeon of a place was as dismal on the inside as the outside, though I didn't know that then. Nor did I know that Sissy and Annie had been cooped up in it all day, shedding and picking yarn. I'd no idea that for every imperfect product, management docked their wages. All that would come later. All I knew in that moment was the sight of the slim copper-haired beauty sharing a cigarette like a Hollywood diva was doing something to my heart. Something I'd only experienced once before – in another place, another lifetime.

'Nanny, sure c'mon and see our Granda. Look how handsome he is in his suit.'

Our Declan, my Cormac's eldest, always the same, always looking out for his grandmother. Always looking out for his own mother and aunts too, despite being a soft touch of a lad. He'd only just become a man, hit the big eighteenth birthday, when his father was taken, God bless him.

I listen for the familiar lilt of my Annie's voice, but I know it won't be forthcoming. Even grief can't unnerve her, not when the house is rammed. She'll save her tears and talk for the middle of the night when – if – we're alone. Sixty-five years, two Annies, one reserved just for me.

'Lads, you lot go ahead, the family'll follow,' Declan says.

Charlie Chuck is first, his ashen features scarily close as he leans in and dangles a Miraculous Medal in my face. Jesus, what happened to respect for the dead? A wee bit of personal space, please. And then I'm confronted with the flecked grey-brown crown of his head – I can only assume he's fiddling with a pin to attach the medal to my lapel. Next up it is 'Dirtbag', heart of corn, feet like dung. Thank Christ I can no longer smell him.

'For you, Sir. Always a gentleman. The team signed it for you,' he says.

The green and white hoops of the Celtic scarf tilt and fall as Dirtbag tucks it in somewhere. God, what I wouldn't give to be able to touch it.

'Hello, Da. It's almost time. Don't be afraid to say your goodbyes. I'll look after you.'

I instantly recognise the deep, soft tone of the voice of the son I cannot see. It belongs to my Cormac, unchanged since I last saw him. Can it really be nineteen years? He only got half the life I had; I'd have cut off my limbs to save him. What made me more entitled? Where's the fairness in that? Just as well Annie can't hear me or she'd be chastising me for questioning God's plan for us all. Well, fuck the plan. No parent should have to bury their child.

'What are you doing here, Son? Why can't I see your face? It's so good to hear your voice.'

'I've come to take you home. And you'll see me very soon.'

'Listen to him, Michael. This loitering malarkey is doing you no favours.'

'Waiting for you, Mickey. Knew you'd outrun the lot of us.'

'Venga, compadre.'

I try to ignore the broken voices I don't recognise, as well as those I'm afraid to admit I know – some belong to men long dead and drag up memories I've long tried to bury.

'Sure, would you look at him? There's one fine gentleman. Always the same.'

Tank McGinty stares down at me, jaw like concrete. 'Muffler' McInerney, eyes like slits, hovers next to him.

I hear a soft *thwack thwack* under the window – must be our Catherine's wee grandchildren with their skipping ropes.

The ceiling begins to sway back and forth, dips to lap my chest, rises and retracts into darkness. This space seems so familiar and yet so alien, my place of residence, now rest, until they lower me into the ground.

I heard them talking the other night, Mary and Catherine. Chrissie was there too, though she didn't say a word. Assuming I was asleep when I was merely resting my eyes, the cheek of them.

'Do you think Da has any regrets?' Catherine said.

'He'll be riddled with them,' Mary scoffed between gulps of what she said was water. 'Always was a bit of a mouthpiece.'

That's my Mary alright, speaking ill of the dead before I was even pronounced. To be fair, I didn't always do enough. Certainly said too much sometimes when Satan's spit made me fierce-tongued. And yet, I was hardly about when they were growing up – Mary was barely a year old and my other two girls were in primary school when I went on the boats. As for Cormac, he was in the throes of puberty, a pencil-thin fourteen-year-old with a mouth that could do with a good scrubbing out. It was my Annie who did all the grafting and lifting and laying.

I like to think I was less stern with the grandchildren, though I've always been careful about being seen as sentimental. Too much emotion on show never did anyone any favours. Yes, I'm only human – *was* only human, Jesus wept – and so I've had my moments. Fatherhood softened me up a bit – you know, that warm ache of a love that kicks in when your first born arrives. But it wasn't until my grandchildren came along that I let my guard down just a little, shook the lads' hands and allowed the girls to give me a hug at Christmas.

There is so much I'll miss about them. 'Friday pay day', when they were all only small, was always particularly special. I would put on my best serious face when they lined up before 'Cracker Jack', pushing and shoving each other while I got out my bags of twenty-pence coins. I always kept them in a red cash box in what the grandchildren called 'Granda's special cupboard' next to the hearth. As soon as they had their 20ps in their hands, it was a mad rush to the shop at the top of our street. The five of them would bolt to get their forty half-penny sweets, then rush back for the comfiest cushion on the floor in front of the television. I say five because that is how I like to imagine those Fridays, but really there were only four. My Sarah, my youngest granddaughter, came much later when Cormac's children had outgrown the tradition, but she's always there in the pay day line-up when I think of them. If I could turn my head now, I might be able to picture them all, sprawled out down there on the rug.

'For God's sake, Chrissie, why can't your Sarah just come down and pay her respects? Bloody ridiculous, she is, behaving like that at her age. Needs to wise up.'

Mary, at it again. I don't need her interference to know my youngest granddaughter isn't in the room. Her absence seeps through the familiar faces that touch, kiss, cross me, through the ethereal bodies that beckon me. My heart hurts.

'C'mon, Da. You need to prepare yourself, or there'll be consequences.'

The clock chimes three times, slower each time.

***

Sarah is curled up in a ball on the floor, wearing one of those oversized hoodies her mother, my Chrissie, can't abide.

We're in the box room, right above the living room – my bedroom of twenty plus years after Annie decided it was best to have separate rooms. I can hear the murmurings downstairs, the slam of the front door as someone else arrives and another person leaves and the wind catching it unapologetically. I'm sure Sarah can hear it all too, even with her hood up and her hands over her ears. I wish I could see her face.

I didn't expect her to be downstairs. She told me straight one night at the hospital when it was just me and her left in the room. 'I know you're going to die, Granda,' she said, in that matter-of-fact way she has of speaking when pretending she is alright with the world. 'But there's no way I'm going to your wake.' I'd semi-squeezed her hand with the last bit of strength I could muster and whispered a thank you for her support.

'You don't get me, Granda,' she said, 'I'm doing this for you. I'm not going to sit there like I'm okay with you on display like some fucking ornament.'

I wanted to tell her off for her language, but the words didn't come. Probably best to cut her some slack anyhow – there are worse things that grief and sadness do to us all. God, I know.

I'm not a fan of wakes myself – been to far too many over the years. There's something awful unsettling about being left with a freakish puppet image of someone you shared a few weekly pints with. Worse than that, though, is the closed coffin wake. I know not everyone gets it, but it's not the done thing around here. A closed casket means that your best friend, your neighbour, someone's child is too damaged to be presented. Even the skills of a top mortician cannot rescue them. No, thank you. No to those horrific images that assault your thoughts in the dead of night, no to that thick mesh net that quivers and descends upon your semi-conscious body.

'I'll definitely be at your funeral, though,' she said.

There's nothing left in the box room except the bed that is expecting me for my afternoon nap, or my night's sleep. It doesn't look like it's been touched since I last made it. No one else knows how to tuck in the duvet cover like that, to make its dogtooth checks expand way beyond their original size.

I bet it was Mary who put everything away, who emptied out every trace of me. I'm sure she couldn't wait to get rid of me, even though I like to imagine she loved me in a strange sort of way. Don't we all have to love family, even if we can't stand the sight of them? I wish I could laugh. Mary hadn't given me so much as a kind look in years.

Sarah pulls down her hood and looks straight at me. Straight through me. Christ, I need to catch myself on. Of course she doesn't look at me or through me, it's all just wishful thinking on my part. She looks at nothing, or perhaps at a push she gives the back wall a once over. Her hair is pulled tight into a strangled nest on top of her head, last washed God knows when, the copper tones she gets from Annie's side dulled through neglect. Even her eyes aren't right; they look stained, a muddy brown.

'Sarah, love, would you come down for a wee minute? Say a prayer for your grandfather?'

Chrissie's voice floats into the room, gentle, non-judgmental. I know she's hurting and yet I know she'll be putting on her best face, meeting and greeting, making endless cups of tea, listening to Charlie Chuck tell the same story on repeat, trying to get a few words out of Tank McGinty. She deserves a medal, that same girl.

'Maybe later,' Sarah says.

Her right hand reaches for the silver crucifix at her chest, the one I just gave her for her twenty-fifth birthday. She has a collection of crosses in matt and shiny silvers and golds, presents from family members to mark special birthdays and milestones. I should have given her this one – my one – some time ago.

'Rest in peace, Granda. Love you always,' she says.

I love you too, I say, or think I say. *Everything will be okay.*

Sarah pulls her knees inside her hoodie and rocks gently, her right hand twisting, untwisting the necklace. The sobbing comes in anguished fits and starts, clawing the walls of the box room, threatening its emptiness.

I'm here and I see you and please don't cry.

8

Day 1: The Boneyard

The gloom that arrives in the dead of night folds around me. It's the same oul' gloom that I used to dispel with the flick of a light switch. No such thing as control now. But at least she is here, my Annie, her face soft as a whisper in the pitch black. There's no sign of anyone else.

'Are you alright there, love? Bet you're loving all this attention!'

Annie dabs the outer corners of her eyes and attempts to catch her fragile teardrops in the pleats of a tissue. Her tears are too light to dew her lashes, yet laden heavy with anger, with guilt at being angry. I want to reach out and pull her, close enough for the blue sapphires of her eyes to illuminate mine.

I remember the first time I touched that face – it was just a few minutes after I'd seen her standing outside the factory with Sissy. I had followed them, her and Sissy, slipping along behind unnoticed. So engrossed were they in some gossip or other, so invisible was I, that I was tempted to quicken my step, not to eavesdrop but to inhale the scent of Annie. I thought if I could get close enough to do that, to fill my lungs with the sweet fragrance of her, she'd imprint herself on me, tattoo my soul.

The two women continued talking without drawing breath all the way down Kennedy Street before reaching the front door of The Claddagh at the bottom of the Estate. A heave and grunt of the panelled wooden door and Sissy disappeared inside, while Annie spun around suddenly, as if she had been expecting me.

I was the last thing on her mind, of course. She was desperately trying to light the cigarette hanging out of her mouth. With her free hand, she pressed a loose auburn curl behind her ear; a delicate floral perfume pinched the air.

'Don't suppose you've got a light?' she mumbled, without looking up.

'I'm sorry, I don't smoke. Does awful things to your lungs, that oul' stuff.'

Annie sighed deep into the back of her throat and raised her head. Then something happened, a proper one-off, which she still denies to this day – the stones of her eyes scoured the length of me with a mix of measured impatience and disdain before she stared at me hard and told me where to go in words I've never heard her use since. I asked her if she was sure, and before she could answer, before I even knew what I was doing, I leaned forward into the spell of my girl and brushed an eyelash from the rosed arc of her cheek.

***

My Annie's eyes are lowered; I know she is tinkering with my tie. I know she is re-pinning Charlie Chuck's medal so it doesn't fall inside my jacket. I want to ask her: *do you remember what you said the day I met you?* I want to ask her: *do you remember how I quickly got the measure of you, my sweet girl?*

'Ach, look at you, all handsome now. You'll do me proud today,' she says.

I want to feel her hand; she hasn't let go of mine. I want to take both her hands and protect the smallness of them within mine; I want to caress the length and curve of them one last time. I want to twist her wedding ring the way I used to and tell her again that in death, we do not part.

'Right then, best get myself ready, love. Don't want to let you down.'

Her face fades away and I can't stop it – please let it stop – and then there is nothing only black, deepest black.

***

The tapping is coming from the windowsill next to me, I'm certain of it. It doesn't sound like the knocking of one of our Sunday visitors, or the lash of the children's skipping rope; it's more like an annoying drip, drip. Bloody rain. Could it not have kept itself at bay, today of all days? This is the last thing my family needs, getting soaked to the skin at the boneyard. Wasn't it at Liam Donnelly's funeral when we had that torrential downpour? Several of us nearly ended up in the grave alongside him, earth crumbling away at our feet. Jesus. Almost eight for the price of one.

'How are you this morning, Mrs Doherty? Did you manage any sleep at all?'

Tank is back, ready to take charge. He knows his stuff, that lad, he'll give me a decent send off. Big on respect, he is. He'll make sure there are plenty to carry me from the gate to the chapel doors.

'And how are you today, big man?'

Tank stares down at me; I want to tell him I'm not ready, it's not time yet.

'Father Murphy'll be here soon, he'll say a wee decade of the rosary before we leave.'

Thank God for Father Murphy. Annie knows how I feel about that other one, the McMullan fella. Sure you wouldn't know if the rumours were true.

And somehow Father Murphy is present, making the sign of the cross on my forehead, blessing himself. I understand now what my Sarah was referring to – I'm lying here making an exhibition of myself, like some desperate museum piece.

'It's time,' the youngest O'Halloran lad says.

I catch nothing more than a glimpse of my Annie leaning in to kiss me and now the lid comes down and I hear them locking it and there's deepest black again.

***

My front garden is rammed with people clustered under golf umbrellas in a variety of colours. Who'd have thought the rain would bring my mourners closer together? Sarah is in the middle of the crowd, the rain lashing her bare legs. I bet Chrissie told her to put on a pair of dark trousers; they will have had words this morning. Too late now. Stubborn that one, like her oul' grandfather.

There are plenty of strangers here. Must be friends of our ones, work colleagues, friends of friends. People who mean absolutely nothing to me, nor me to them. And then there are others out on the street, different kinds of strangers. Take the O'Connells, for example. There they are, a few doors down, huddled like a dark blanket around the front gate. They haven't spoken a word to us in, must be five or six years now. Not since the row between our Mary and their Saoirse. Odd things, these funerals. Still, at least the crowd amounts to a great turnout — nothing worse than an empty chapel.

'He was a gentleman,' someone says.

'Always a decent fella.'

'The Estate won't be the same without him.'

'Never would've passed you on the street.'

'Look, here he comes.'

My coffin leaves the house, nobly elevated in the arms of our Declan, the O'Halloran lad and a few others I can't make out. The rain continues to hammer down, making the brass plaque and cross glisten; you'd think it was sacred water gifted by the Holy Spirit.

Tank puffs out his chest and leads the lads ceremoniously through the guard of honour that lines the length of the path. In the street, there's a small group waiting for the changeover — I recognise 'Muffler' and Dirtbag. Looks like they've scrubbed up well for the occasion, kitted out in black double-breasted jackets with white lily buttonholes. Someone helps Tank unfold the tricolour and he lays it gently across the top of my coffin, as if he's afraid of disturbing my slumber.

In the chapel, they place an old photo of me from about twenty years ago in a fancy new silver frame on top of my coffin. I can't quite remember where it was taken, but it was definitely at one of those big family dos. Big smile plastered across my face, teeth showing, unusual for me. Never was one for smiles and teeth. They've cut away my Annie, leaving only a phantom strip of arm next to mine. The white roses next to the photo are a lovely touch; I'm sure my Annie must have organised those.

'Now then, Da, enough's enough. Come on.'

'Cormac?'

'You have to let go.'

'But I'm not ready.'

'Yes, you are. Get back in your box, let them bury you in the dirt.'

'I can't.'

'I know it's hard. But Ma'll be grand.'

'It's not Ma I'm worried about.'

'Who is it, then?'

'Our Sarah. Just look at her.'

Sarah is kneeling at the end of the first pew, her head bowed. Chrissie taps her on the shoulder and indicates the aisle. She files out slowly, trailing her cousins, and takes one of the white roses from the top of the coffin. She grips it tightly with both hands and turns to the choir in the upper balcony. She doesn't regard them; she's nothing to give. Life's been bled out of her, as if she is a ghost of herself, her body boxed away next to her grandfather's.

'She needs me, Son. There's something not quite right, hasn't been for some time now. You understand, don't you?'

'I left this world a long time ago. I know very little. But talk about leaving it until the last minute! I'm here for you, to take you home. If you refuse, there are risks.'

'But I'm not ready.'

'Don't dally, Da. Do you know what that might mean?'

I know exactly what it means. Linger too long, get caught in some in-between place. Lose loved ones, living and dead. Become nothing, nowhere.

***

Tiny bullets of hail assail my coffin as I descend. I hear the straps slide around the outside of my box, hear them slap the earth as they lower me. I wish my heart would swell with pride – they did a great job, all of them. And fair play to Tank. I'm not justifying any of his shenanigans, of course not, but they happened a long time ago now and he can be a gentleman when he puts his mind to it.

I listen to the final blessing of Father Murphy, to the prayers of those gathered that rustle like faint sighs. I hear the thuds, one by one, as the white roses hit my mahogany box. I wait for my Sarah to speak.

I'm going nowhere.

Day 2: The Estate

Sarah is swathed in a blanket of sleep as slithers of sunlight filter through the gaping blind. She thinks of her poor grandfather lying buried under a heap of drenched dirt. It is not her first thought of him since the funeral – visions of him have plagued her all night: a fresh-faced Michael Doherty she never knew; the Michael Doherty she knew only too well sitting reading in the scullery; a fully alive man; a cancer-ridden flake of a man. With her eyes still closed, she feels sick to the pit of her stomach wondering if the graveyard sludge has leaked inside the coffin and stained his good suit. As if any of that matters now.

She has always been her grandfather's blue eye – everyone said so and neither she nor he ever denied it. That is why his illness and death have hit her so hard, they all said, apart from Mary who told her to drop the 'poor me' act. Mary is the sort of woman who begrudges anyone having anything more than her, even grief.

But there is so much more to Sarah's outpouring of grief. No one knows the silent suffering that has crippled her for the last six months; no one knows how she is haunted by the sight of a man her own age lying lifeless in a faraway hospital bed, hooked up to bleating machines. *Bleat, bleat, bleat.* No one knows how her grandfather's death has suddenly given her licence to mourn two men – the Michael Doherty they all love, and another man Sarah alone loves. A man who may or may not be dead.

Sarah pushes back the dead weight of the duvet and places her hand over her grandfather's crucifix. The metal, ice cold against her fingers, sends a shiver through her whole body. Her insides throb, as if she has been someone's punch bag.

'Sarah, love, are you up?'

'Yes, Mam. Coming.'

The aroma of woody cinnamon and warm buttery sponge drifts onto the landing, reminding Sarah that she has not eaten a bite for days. Like a starving animal, she tilts her head this way and that to sniff the air and follows the scent trail down to the kitchen. Her mother is busy pressing a fork around the edges of a large apple pie while humming a song Sarah does not recognise. Baking is her mother's answer to everything – exam pressure, boyfriend drama, wardrobe disasters, death. She feeds others to alleviate their pain, never her own.

'What do you fancy, love? The traybakes are just coming out of the oven. You'll have to wait for the apple pie.'

'But it's just gone 9am.'

'Never too early for a sweet treat. Your nanny used to send to the bakery for her box of buns at first light. Do you remember? Here you go, love.'

Her mother sets down a steaming cup of coffee and kisses her on the cheek. Her russet bracken hair, infused with spice, brushes Sarah's face.

'It was a lovely send off, wasn't it, Mam?' Sarah puts the cup to her lips and then thinks better of it, pushes it away. It's still Lent and she still has much to repent.

She buries her hands deep inside the pockets of her hoodie as her mother sits down opposite her. Despite the first chinks of spring sunlight and the warmth enveloping the kitchen, Sarah cannot get heat into her bones. Lack of sleep, or food, or a combination of both have left her stone cold.

Or perhaps it's nothing to do with hunger or fatigue. Perhaps her body is responding to her conscious decision to shut herself down, to distance herself from reality. She might as well be dead inside. Trembling, she looks out through the patio doors.

A small brown bird hops across the sun-striped decking and stops momentarily to observe her. There is something about his gaze that taunts her, reminding her that the world is not done judging her yet. All she did yesterday was step back from her grandfather's grave a few moments before the end. The usual lot could not help themselves, spouting their opinions as she walked back to the car. She heard them all, their vicious words mumbled under their breaths. God help her if they were ever to get wind of what happened in Spain.

Her mother does not notice the bird; she is too busy smoothing the tablecloth with the heel of her hand, her brow creased in concentration.

'I said it was a lovely send off for Granda, don't you think?'

'Even a good iron couldn't get the creases out of this bloody thing.' Her mother pushes down hard, sending white half-moons shooting up her freshly manicured nails. Catherine had insisted on doing them specially for the funeral after she had sorted her own and Mary's. Michael Doherty's daughters couldn't turn up to say goodbye to their father in a state, she'd said.

'What was that, love?'

'Did you sleep alright?'

Mam lets go of the cloth, looks up and locks her hands on the edge of the table as if to steady herself. 'A few hours, yes. Sure that's all I need.'

Sarah can tell she has not been to bed. The shadows under her eyes hang heavy like stuffed coal sacks and lumps of mascara cling to her upper lashes. She has seen it before, when Uncle Cormac passed away, when her father died a couple of years later from a heart attack. It's strange the things you remember from your childhood, the images that stick hard and fast in your mind. And now her mother is raging her personal war against sleep after losing her own father, as if self-inflicted deprivation can fix anything and everything.

Sarah slides her chair across the smooth glossed tiles to join her mother at the other side of the table. She puts her arms around her and shrinks into her, snug as a bug. Her mother begins to cry, softly at first, before the room lashes with the sorrow of days of funeral preparations, of weeks of hospital visits, of years of asking why her brother, why her husband. Sarah pulls her closer, desperate to withdraw the heartache, to pile it on top of her own dishevelled state of sadness. She wishes they both could remember the women they have forgotten to be.

***

Sarah was just five years old when Uncle Cormac passed away. No one had expected him to die, not really, not even his sisters. He was their anchor: the sensible, level-headed one once his teens were firmly behind him. He was the all-seeing, honest, trusted big brother.

They had taken turns to cover the overnight hospital shifts. There was plenty of talk of him improving, of things looking up, of holidays they would book once he was back on his feet. There were candles and prayers and special masses and offerings. And then, out of nowhere, he was dead, aged forty-four, with a son and daughter on the brink of adulthood. It was as if he decided enough was enough and the man they always knew as a fighter had no fight left. Ursula, his wife, was distraught, blamed herself. She fretted that he did not have enough to live for. The things we tell ourselves in mourning.

Cormac's death was Sarah's first proper experience of grief; at five years old, she thought she had it all worked out. She remembers being sad that Uncle Cormac was gone, but wasn't he a big man, an old man who had lived a long time? By the time she was seven and left fatherless, she was not so sure if she'd ever work out life and death. She still does not think she has it in her, to fully appreciate every waking moment, to let go of regret and to forgive, especially herself. If only she could forgive herself.

Her mother never fully recovered her spirit after Cormac's death. She spent most of the time talking about the injustice of it all – how he was never meant to be in Castle Street that day; how cruel life was, him being the victim of some random attack. The rest of the time, she talked about them growing up, thick as thieves, climbing yard walls, falling off them and getting into all sorts of trouble. That was when a fleeting burst of her spark would resurface, the same spark that was very quickly quelled when Sarah's father passed away.

'Are you feeling any better now, Mam?'

'Yes, love. Sorry about all that. I don't know what came over me.' Her mother unwraps herself from Sarah's embrace and gets to her feet, wiping down the pristine skirt of her apron, dusting off her vulnerability.

The sudden vibration of Sarah's phone startles them both.

'Who's that, love?' Her mother assumes the voice of a carefree young woman while staring at the window, wiping away jagged streaks of ash from under her eyes.

'No one … just Amy. I'll phone her back later.'

'Right you be.' Her mother sighs. 'I'm sure she misses you. You really should start thinking about getting back to your flat, your routine. Back to some sort of normality, away from this place.'

'Anyone would think you're looking rid of me!'

'You know what I mean. I think we've all had enough of this Estate for the time being! Living in each other's pockets, listening to the same drivel from the same ones, it's no good for anybody. Now, what would you like to do today, love? Visit your grandfather's grave, maybe?'

A vague sort of anxiety prickles the back of Sarah's throat.

'Actually, Mam, if it's alright with you, I'd like to go and visit Nanny.'

Her mother's face brightens as she smiles and nods in agreement. She then turns away and starts scrubbing her hands viciously with a small nailbrush. It's a habit she picked up from her father when she was only little, she'd told Sarah many times before. There were never any flannels in their house because, according to Michael, what actual use were they?

Sarah imagines her mother as little more than a toddler, her reddish-blonde pigtail pinned to the lower leg of a tall, suited man as she pushes up on tiptoes to see what he is washing in the scullery sink. It is the same suited man Sarah remembers, 'the gentleman' as everyone called him, who took great pleasure in retiring to his 'library' at the back of the scullery to tell her stories. He only ever shared them with her, his youngest grand-daughter, usually on a Sunday after Mass when the living room became too crowded, or if he had a minor disagreement with Nan and was keen to make himself scarce.

Sarah knew then that she was special, that her grandfather had been storing up years of tales of mermaids and ice queens and enchanted sailors for her ears only. She never asked why he had saved them all up for her. It was like magic; if she asked why, she might break the storyteller's spell.

To call her grandfather's range of books a 'library' really was pushing it. The scullery had nothing more than a few old shelves packed with a mishmash of battered books from local charity shops and the odd new hardback Michael received as a present. Her grandmother despised the look of it all and said so to anyone who would listen. For her, the second-hand books were filthy cast-offs, nothing more than dust collectors. She had never read a book – postcards, menus and greeting cards were the extent of her reading material – and she would often threaten, half-jokingly, to set the kitchen on fire.

'An eye sore the lot of it,' she would say, usually when she was cleaning something – anything from a crumb-strewn worktop to a frying pan that had seen better days. 'And Michael Doherty should know better than to be filling his grand-daughter's head with nonsense.' She always referred to him in the third person when her temper was frayed.

Sarah and her grandfather learned to exchange a look and say nothing until Annie retired to the living room. They would then pick up where they had left off, playing word games, reciting some Heaney from memory and flicking through the books her grandfather had bought or been given since they last sat down together.

'What shall we have today, then?' he would ask, skimming the shelves with the back of his hand, knowing there was only the slimmest chance there would be a children's book amongst the offering. If he ever picked up a children's classic, he always gave it to Sarah right away to take home for bedtime.

'Please can we have one of yours?' she would say.

Whenever she was with him, even as she grew older, Sarah's preference was always for one of the stories deposited in his mind like hidden treasures. She imagined them as delicate parchment scrolls, slightly scuffed and rough at the edges.

The silver crucifix at Sarah's neck suddenly begins to pulse a slow, steady heat. Confused but desperate for the first trace of warmth filtering under her skin, she pushes it hard into her flesh, ignoring the scalding sensation prickling her fingertips. It makes her crave the arms of a loved one, being locked into someone's core, even if it is on borrowed time.

'Of course that's alright, love. I'm sure she'll be glad of the company.'

'Sorry, what?'

'Your nanny, I said of course we can go see her.'

'Right.' Sarah tries to imagine the touch of Raúl's hand against the small of her back, but all she can see is his bloodied face. She lets go of the crucifix and attempts to shake off the sight of him. 'Let's go, then,' she says.

With the heat from the cross ejected from her body, Sarah attempts to distract herself by watching her mother, who massages a tiny amount of cream into her roughly dried hands and slips her wedding ring back on, her arm movements as graceful as a ballerina's. It wouldn't surprise Sarah if her mother was repeating her vows in a hush meant only for herself and her dead husband.

Sarah had never asked — it's not the sort of thing you ask

your mother – but she wonders if the flaunting of the ring is her mother's way of making sure no one takes Sarah's father's place; if it's her way of projecting herself as forever betrothed. Perhaps that's why she is standing here now, arm outstretched, her hand gently moving from side to side, the ring's small diamond catching parcels of light. Her mother admires it, not like a veteran widow, but more like someone newly engaged, loved up. Sarah wonders if she will ever feel the same durability of romantic love. She's not sure if she even wants it.

'Right you be, love,' her mother says suddenly, her tone uncharacteristically abrupt. 'You know, it's awful hard when the house suddenly empties, even in a place like this with plenty of people about you. They say that's when real grief comes knocking. We've got to hang onto the things that matter for as long as we can.'

***

The Estate is a bit of a strange place, takes a bit of getting used to. It's the sort of place that always looks cast in shadow, even when the Belfast sun makes a rare appearance. Its rows of grey terrace houses with black painted railings form a neat, dark grid and the community moves around like counters on a gameboard. Same streets, same movements, same façades, same faces.

Sixty-five years, I had, of 'sameness' – I consider myself very fortunate. It was work that brought me to the Estate initially, and my Annie who kept me there. When I arrived back from Spain in 1937, I'd no idea what to do with myself. I wasn't quite nineteen years old and I was broken, inside and out. They say war opens your eyes, makes you stronger. That's what my superiors drilled into me: every time a comrade got injured or killed; all those times when I lay petrified, face in the dirt, listening to enemy boots trample and kick the dry or sodden earth. Even on the nights when I couldn't control the tremors wracking my body because of fear or hunger or solitude, the mantra was always the same.

Home – it's one of those words that we bandy about and take for granted. There was no home and no family for me when I got back. Not a sinner to welcome me with open arms – I'd have settled for a nod or a handshake. But enough of all that – Christ, the last thing I want is sympathy. It was the reality of having nothing that traced my path to Annie – some might call it fate, others coincidence. Whatever it was, it started with me drifting from one labouring job to another, working my way across the city. I didn't stay long enough in any place to feel part of it. I had no interest – not in fitting in, nor in being with anyone.

Then I came here to this Estate. Spring 1941, it was, when the crisp days lengthened and the city was being devastated by German bombs. I should have been petrified, but I was strangely immune; it was like watching myself from above, looking down on a rake of a lad working twelve-hour shifts to rebuild the streets. The Estate was mayhem at the time – a big awful mess of smoke and rubble.

Eventually, I found some sort of inner peace, almost a reconciliation with myself. It happened as soon as I saw my Annie, a few months after I arrived on the Estate. I knew I'd found a soul to connect with, perhaps even a community to belong to.

I know my Sarah's never felt the same about the place – she used to tell me often enough. From no age, really, she was adamant that she'd make a life somewhere else. I tried the being somewhere else; it didn't work out for me. Wartime doesn't permit new beginnings in new places, however much you might try to convince yourself otherwise. Not ones that endure anyhow. I know that now.

***

Sarah closes the gate and puts her hand into her mother's pocket. She's always done that with my Chrissie, ever since she was tall enough to reach.

They head up Strathearn Street, tackling the hill with brisk uniform steps. Theirs are the steps of youth, long snatched away from me. Tank is on the other side of the street, hosing the suds off his red Mondeo, soaking himself more than the car in the process. He'll never learn, that same fella. He gives a sort of half wave with his free hand but my girls don't see him. The street is fairly quiet otherwise – there are a couple of boys playing kickabout on the road in expensive-looking trainers which are probably new for Easter and shouldn't be near their feet yet; Mrs McGivern is washing her front window, arms twirling like the sails of a windmill; and Frankie McAuley is sitting on his front step turning the pages of yesterday's *Irish News*. Always one day behind everyone else, Frankie, anything to save a few pence.

'Mam, do you think Nanny'll be alright?'

Sarah doesn't look at her mother as she waits for her to answer; she's busy scouring the pavement for anything that might ruin the soles of her new ankle boots. The streets are well kept for the most part – the neighbours look after them – but Sarah insists on checking. It's not her fault; she can't be blamed for something she took after me. She was only small when we started walking back from chapel on a Sunday morning and she'd count how many times I jumped or side-stepped onto the kerb.

'It'll just take time, love. Same for the rest of us,' Chrissie says, squeezing her arm.

'But they were together for such a long time, her and Granda. I can't imagine being with someone that long.'

'Me neither. They had their moments, of course.' Chrissie's laugh is tender and Sarah looks up, smiles, and removes her hand from her pocket to hug her.

My Chrissie doesn't know the half of it. Our house – or

should I say, my Annie's house — is visible now, just a little further up the street. Will Annie still call it home without me around? I can't imagine the place without her. I'm sure it would feel like an awful shell, a mere stop-off where I'd eat and sleep and bide my time. Thank God I've been taken before her.

'Look, Mam, Nanny's out front.'

Annie is kneeling with her back to us, her body tilted forward towards the white rose bush. One of her gloved hands rests gently on the branches while the other cuts the canes. I know her expression will be serious, concentrated.

I'm outside the gate, looking in, every bit the stranger. Suppose I should count my blessings that I'm even here; God knows what lies ahead of me.

'Ach sure, look who it is. Are you both feeling a bit better today? What about you, our drama queen?'

Mary points at Sarah and holds back her shoulders to fill the frame of the front door. That one has every intention of making a nuisance of herself, as usual.

'Yes thanks, Aunt Mary.'

Mary nods, looks my Chrissie and Sarah up and down, and checks the street as if she's expecting someone. Maybe she's waiting for one of her fancy men. Nearly fifty years of age, she is, and still hasn't managed to settle down. I know Annie prays every day, both for her union with a decent man as well as some peace for herself. I won't miss Mary's daily antics.

The same one is so distracted checking out who's parking where that she doesn't notice Sarah throw her one of her looks.

'And what about you, Aunt Mary?' Sarah tries, not out of concern for her aunt, but in the hope that it will break the silence and make her get out of their way.

'Sorry? Oh, I'm grand,' she says, a little flustered. 'So's your nanny. Aren't you, Mammy?' She waves a finger at Annie, feebly trying to reassert her deluded sense of authority. 'Up with the lark, blinds and curtains open. Sure you wouldn't even think Da's body was still warm yesterday.'

Annie swivels round and scrambles to her feet, her face chalk-white with horror.

'What in God's name, Mary? Just keeping busy, that's all!' There's a tremor in her voice that she'll be fighting hard to smooth over. God forbid anyone but me should have access to how she really feels.

Mary laughs and folds her arms, defiant. 'Whatever you say, Mammy.'

'Don't rise to it,' I hear my Chrissie whisper to Sarah, 'you know she's just trying –'

'Still warm, Aunt Mary? Don't you understand the definition of a corpse?'

'Ach, look who's got her voice back. We thought you'd taken a vow of silence when you lost your granda.' Mary scrunches up her face like a moody child, making her eyes disappear.

'Come on in, love, just ignore her. Fell out of the wrong bed this morning.'

'Nanny!'

'What was that, Mammy?'

My Annie manages a half-smile while Chrissie and Sarah have the same tight-lipped look about them, one I know well – mother and daughter in cahoots, both trying to stop themselves laughing. For even a morsel of laughter certainly wouldn't go down well in the street the day after my burial.

Annie takes off her gardening gloves, links arms with Chrissie and Sarah, heads towards the front door. Although I can't see her, I know the expression on her face is plenty to make Mary shift out of the way.

I watch the three of them enter the hall, disappear into the living room, become blurs of themselves sliced by the venetian blind. Mary continues to hang about the front step, tutting and chewing her mouth, pressing her ear every so often against the living room door.

'Hello, Da. I've got an update for you.' The voice is crisp, too close, the body still absent.

'Christ, Cormac! You'd have given me a heart attack if I wasn't dead already! Can't you show yourself? What are you talking about, an update?'

'You said you weren't ready to leave. You said you couldn't leave Sarah.'

'That's correct, Son. I'm not budging.'

'But you have to remember, Da, that's not exactly your decision to make, is it?'

'Why not?'

'Well, for one thing, you're dead now.'

'Rub it in, why don't you, Son?'

'And if you're not alive, free will doesn't quite work in the same way.'

'I'm going nowhere. Look, I know not everyone crosses over right away, I know there are exceptions. I'm not saying I want to stay forever; I just need a bit more time.'

As a dead man, it's hard to count how long the silence lingers, harder still when you can't even read the face of the man you're speaking to.

'Let me ask you something, Da, before I run through the conditions of your temporary stay,' Cormac says finally.

'Conditions?'

'You know there are people whose loved ones let them back in once they've … once they've … you know, crossed over fully. Won't you take the same chance with our Sarah?'

'That's not an option, Son. I need to be sure I can help her. I can't bet on chances.'

'But you said you're close, and I believe you, Da, I wish I'd seen it with my own eyes. Why wouldn't she let you back in?'

'Because, Son … because she's like me. I never let anyone back in, including you. And Christ, I wish I'd behaved differently. I was too afraid of getting hurt, made sure I kept my walls up. I heard your whispers, though. Yours and a few others. You tried, didn't you, to reach me?'

'I understand,' Cormac sighs eventually. I just wish you had.'

'Your mother let you in, didn't she? She never said a word about it to me, but Annie always does – *did* – the right thing. Didn't she let you back in?'

'She did, Da. I've got a lifetime to tell you about it once you cross over. But for now, if you're sure you want to stay a while, I have to lay out the terms. They don't come from me, of course. I'm just the messenger.'

'Work away.'

'Right then. You've got forty days –'

'Forty days? Jesus! Biblical-style?'

'You're no prophet, Da, trust me. Forty days, so long as you don't overstep the mark.'

'You're not making any sense. How am I fit to overstep anything?'

'Sarah won't be able to see you. There might be times when she hears you, but you can't advise or push her. Encouragement is alright, if she's willing to listen. No heavy duty hustling.'

'But if she can't see me, might not even hear me, how the hell can this work? I'm not being awkward, it just sounds a bit … impractical. Christ almighty.'

'Practicalities aren't your concern. You're not some holy Joe on a mission.'

'More's the pity. And don't you forget who you're speaking to, Son.'

'Two people, possibly three, from your past will be appointed to engage with Sarah.'

'Why are you talking like that? Engage indeed! Who, Son? Tell me.'

'I don't know, they haven't been chosen yet. Depends on the path you set Sarah on. You won't be able to negotiate with them, but I can act as an occasional intermediary for you, pass messages on. And you won't be able to see everything all the time. You'll have to learn to hand things over.'

'It all sounds a bit overcomplicated. Is there any other way?'

'Those are the terms. Non-negotiable, I'm told. And one final thing – you must be prepared to confront certain things from your own past – some situations might require it. Plus, you've already had two of your forty days.'

'Excuse me?'

'You should've been dead and buried when they took you to the boneyard the other day. What do you say, Da?'

'Are you sure there's no other way?'

'This is your only option. Or you cross over with me now.'

'I'm going nowhere. Tell them I accept.'

'Right you are. I'll confirm right away. No going back now, Da. So first things first. What do you want for Sarah?'

'Six months ago, Son, she returned home from Spain, completely out of the blue, and wouldn't utter a word about it to any of us. Just sank into an awful state of silence, a sadness hanging over her I've never seen the like of. She was meant to be starting a new life out there. Wouldn't even confide in me about what happened, that's how bad it was. I think she needs to go back, Son, as soon as possible.'

'Okay, let's see if we can set that in motion. Anything that can help us?'

'There's a box I want her to have, some oul' things of mine, haven't shared them with anyone else.'

'Not even with Ma?'

'Not even with your mother. Stuff from before I met her.'

'Are you absolutely sure now, Da? Once we start, that's it.'

'We're doing this, Son.'

'Alright. Here we go. I'll see you soon – *we'll* see each other soon, Da.'

It's strange how silence descends, how I know Cormac has gone without seeing him depart. It's just me and Mary again, me in the street as temporary spectator. What does 'soon' mean in these circumstances? How long do I have to wait to see my son, to see Sarah open the box – my box of memories? Patience, oul' man, for virtues must still count for something.

Day 3: Scraps and Titbits

None of the family know how the box ended up in Sarah's old bedroom. Or so they say. It was just there, a hump of a thing taking up too much space on the floor next to the bed, waiting to be opened when she got back from her grandparents' house last night.

It is still there, still waiting to be opened. The sight of it is causing Sarah much annoyance, never mind the cloggy, fusty smell of it.

Her first name is scrawled in red ink across the lid in bulky bleeding letters, the handiwork of a hulk of a man. Or so you'd think. Her grandfather's handwriting was the one thing about him that was untidy and never suited his slim body or twig fingers. The scrawl is the same as the one he used to imprint on Sarah's gym bag, on the label of her coat, on the front of her exercise books every September.

'I didn't know Granda left me something,' she said to her mother the previous evening. Sarah was standing next to her on the landing, regarding the box suspiciously.

'Oh, it's not much, love; he had lots of you to get round,' her mother said. 'He'd wanted to leave you all a few extra pounds more, but wasn't able. Said so each time he reviewed his will.' She paused to catch her breath, oblivious to the presence of the box, or only pretending not to see it. Sarah reckoned it was the latter – one more reminder of the dead man she didn't need.

'I'd take no heed when he started getting on like that, couldn't handle the morbid small talk, never wanted to think of him as somebody capable of dying. Stupid, isn't it?' Her mother stared at the floor, her shoulders rocking gently under the pull of tears she refused to shed. 'Do you think he knew, love, how much I cared?'

'Oh, Mam, I didn't mean to drag all that up,' Sarah replied, not touching her mother in case the contact broke the older woman's composure. It might set Sarah off, too. They were the same, two fully-armoured women, able to take on all sorts but easily shattered by a kind touch. 'I just meant that, in there,' Sarah said, pointing at the box this time.

'Ach sure, that'll be nothing. Just a few scraps and titbits.'

'But Mam...'

'But nothing. You can rummage through another time. C'mon, let's watch one of our programmes for half an hour.'

She took to the stairs before Sarah could respond and disappeared along the hall. Sarah removed her phone from her back pocket and texted Tank, Aunt Mary, Aunt Catherine in quick succession – she couldn't think of anyone else who might know something. The television droned beneath her like an invasion of cicadas, intercepted by the purr of her mother's voice rolling out her running commentary. The sweetness of the morning's baked feast stalked the air like a bad influence, pressurising her growling stomach to give in to temptation.

She cursed the box, cursed herself for overthinking everything. Then she gave it a sharp kick, unsteadying the lid, and decided whatever was inside could wait.

***

Night is settling like draped velvet in the corners of the bedroom when Sarah heaves the box onto the bed. She intakes a deep breath to steady her quivering hands. The lid is lifted, flicked face down – a false self-distancing of no value at all; no hiding the roughly scribbled name can make Sarah forget the contents are meant for her. She is not one for surprises, her grandfather knows that. What is he playing at? An unusual loathing for him latches onto her – she'll be damned if she'll repress it.

31

The box is packed with roughly cut newspaper clippings, yellowish-brown in colour, crimped with age, corners torn or lost. Sarah sifts and drops papers in anguish and expectation, words in English and Spanish colliding like dark clouds transiting the same sky. There is a 6d memorial souvenir with a faded quote from Byron – something about a banner like a thundercloud. Poking out underneath there is a staged image of a curly-haired young girl, eyes sealed shut, mouth wide open, holding up an illegible rectangular placard while fighter planes invade the blurred expanse of sky above her. Sarah thinks it must be a drawing ripped from the cover of something or other and wonders why her grandfather would hold onto it.

Anxious to learn more about the girl, Sarah resolves to keep the drawing for now. She carefully lifts out a random article on the Spanish war, then another, close to where the girl first appeared, as if she has breathed her whereabouts into the faded inky recesses of the pages.

It is only then that she notices an image of another female, a young woman. A photo this time. Her eyes, silk black, almond-curved by the force of her smile, stare straight at her. Sarah's heart thuds, drumming her thoughts as she tries to unravel what she is experiencing – surprise, fear, wonder at the beauty of this woman? The muse of her photographer, hair panther black and tightly curled, the dip of her neck modelling a pretty oval brooch fastened to a crisp white blouse. What others might call a vision.

With trembling hands, Sarah removes the photo and attempts to disperse the worst of the dust. She draws the picture close to her face, despite the unease tearing into her flesh. She wonders if she is meant to recognise her, but how can she? She is a non-entity – her beauty can't change that – hidden inside a box Sarah never knew existed, a remnant of someone else's past. Whose past? Whose sibling, whose child, whose lover is she? *Whose lover is she?* The words stab her in staccato screams. Sarah knows damn well whose past is in the box and whose lover the woman is not meant to be. Cannot be. Like the dust that brazenly coated her image, the woman herself has no place there, not in Sarah's family home. Her existence would kill Annie.

Sarah must be mistaken. She lays the photo on the bed next to the drawing of the girl and feels the room close in on her, silently mocking her.

A group of petrified soldiers sketched in pencil look up at Sarah from inside a dirty trench, their bodies shoved together, bleeding into one another, rifles butting partially obscured faces and limbs. Next to them is a pencil drawing of a soldier propping up an injured comrade as smoke bellows from a burnt-out village in the background. *El herido / The Wounded Man*, the caption reads. Sarah can taste the soot and blood like wet gravel weighting her mouth. Is this what betrayal does to you? Or the threat of it?

What's all this, Granda? Sarah throws the drawing of the girl back into the box, rules her out. She should have trusted her initial instincts: there's no way she's real. There, she's done with her. Not with the woman, though, no, she's a different matter altogether. Sarah raises her hand to the crucifix at her neck, chokes it inside her clenched fist. For what? Clinging onto an old scrap of metal cannot resurrect the dead man and force him to explain himself. No, the cross won't explain the woman nor the interred men in splintered, smudged reproductions, alienated from the country Sarah had wanted to call home.

Sarah waits in Madrid's Chamartín station, her heavy cases stamping the thick yellow warning lines at the platform edge. She gently massages her wrists, brittle as honeycomb after dragging herself and her belongings through Barajas Airport, through the dank, sweltering corridors of the Metro.

'Can I help you with those?' A skinny dark-haired boy in black jeans and a mauve-coloured shirt is standing next to her, his head raised just the fraction shyness permits, not enough for Sarah to see his eyes. He points at her luggage as the train pulls up, his stance and smile competing awkwardly for most embarrassing pose.

Exhaustion makes Sarah nod robotically. She's not in the habit of just handing her things over to a stranger, but she figures he's about her age and harmless.

'Great. Let's go,' he says, relaxing his shoulders a little. 'This is my carriage, too.'

Sarah watches him wrestle the oversized cases with his undertoned arms through the narrow gap of the train door. Two flights, a stopover in Amsterdam and the crush of the underground have left her feeling out of sorts: a strange dizziness hangs listlessly over her. Perhaps that's why she continues to watch the boy struggle with her things and doesn't offer to help. Perhaps that's why she stands like a petulant brat in the middle of the aisle, every wheel and turn of Aunt Mary, blocking everyone's way. People begin to mutter, quietly, quickly; '¡venga, chica!' echoes in a strangled chorus through the carriage. Someone nudges her in the ribs; she flinches and yelps before begrudgingly slipping into the nearest empty seat.

'Disculpen ... disculpen,' she murmurs with no heart. No one seems to notice her false apology. People file past her, flicking their hands dismissively into her face, tutting and saying things she doesn't understand. She can't explain the attitude; she won't care until hours later when, alone in the *hostal*, the thought of it will make her turn a ridiculous shade of scarlet. For now, she pulls her hair up into a defiant ponytail so anyone can see her face properly.

'Gracias,' she says as the boy approaches her. His cheeks are blushed with exertion or shyness, she cannot be sure.

'You're welcome. And listen, English is fine. Plenty of time for your Spanish once you get to Salamanca. Come on, let's find a seat before the rest of them get on.'

'How did you know?'

Sarah walks behind him, sizing up the grey lopsided

rucksack that stretches across his back. There can only be room in it for a change of clothes, a few toiletries and a couple of books.

'You've got that look, I've seen it so many times before,' he shouts back before stopping abruptly. 'Here. These two are unreserved. Window or aisle?'

'Is that where you're going? Salamanca? Window, please.'

Sarah moves into the seat, unzipping her jacket as she goes and passes it to the boy with no name. The train starts to move and the boy sits down, wraps her coat inside his. It seems a little too personal, too intimate maybe, but Sarah is too far gone to protest.

'Yes. I'm a third-year student. English literature.'

'Me too. Third year, I mean. Spanish literature and history.'

'Great.'

For the first time, Sarah sees the marine green of his eyes, translucent like sea water. She is about to comment but forgets what she wants to say; instead, she rests her head against the cool glass of the window and thinks about nothing.

***

'Hey, we're here, look.'

For a moment, caught in the vestiges of a half-sleep, Sarah has lost her bearings. But then it hits her and she bolts upright, loosens her hair and redoes her ponytail to buy herself some time. Can she really have slept three hours next to a total stranger, her bags lying unattended for all to help themselves? She can picture her grandfather rolling his eyes in exasperation.

SALAMANCA sprawls across the window in shiny cared-for capitals as the train comes to a standstill.

'Can you pass me my jacket, please?'

'Sure. Listen, Sarah –'

'Wait.' She raises her hand defensively, forcing the boy to recoil. 'How the hell do you know my name?'

'Sorry?'

'My name. How do you know what it is?' The raised volume of her voice surprises her; she wishes she could disappear through the window, extend the gap between them. She gives him the once over for the second time and wonders if he's really as innocent as he looks.

'It's on your luggage tags.'

'Oh, yeah. Right.' She imagines herself shrinking into oblivion as she tries and fails to fan away her embarrassment. Discretion is not her forte.

'Do you need help finding somewhere to stay?'

'I'll be fine, thanks. Gracias, you've done enough.'

Okay, if you're sure.'

The train has emptied by the time the boy removes Sarah's luggage from the rack. 'So much easier when no one's watching.' He laughs and Sarah smiles back at him, grateful for the unsolicited kindness. She isn't accustomed to it.

'Here, just in case you need anything, or change your mind.'

The boy holds out a piece of paper, its side shredded by the cut of a spiral notebook.

'Just ask for Raúl.'

***

Sarah gently nudges the box under the bed with her foot, knocking its lid to the floor. Only then does she notice something pulsing at the bottom, like an abandoned heart desperate to be reunited with its rightful owner. Whatever the something is, barely wrapped in flimsy writing paper freckled by shards of lamplight, she is not ready to see it. Not yet. Christ, she's seen enough for one day.

She won't bend down to pick up the lid in case she marks the photo tucked away inside the front pocket of her jeans. It's no one else's business, that box, that woman. Definitely not one for family; their hearts are broken enough. She'll have a word with Amy, though, if she can force herself. Strange how she can contemplate telling her best friend some partial story about her grandfather in Spain – a story currently without a beginning, middle or end – but her own remains firmly censored.

God almighty, Granda, you don't do anything by half! She can't say the words out loud. Her mother says there's never any excuse for speaking ill of the dead, however dead or bad they are.

I see you, Sarah. Can you hear me? Please don't hate me, love. It'll all make sense. Christ, have I done the right thing?

'She can't hear you, Da. She's shut herself down, needs some space. Can't you tell? Not really a surprise. Hard enough for me having to take all of this in. Look, Da ... here, to your right.'

'Jesus, Cormac! Giving me directions when I couldn't tell left from right when I was alive! Running joke on the boats with the lads. *Don't leave Mickey in charge,* they'd say. What am I meant to see?'

'Keep going, Da. That's it.'

'Right ... Right ... Holy Mother of God, is that you, Son? Christ, my heart is doing somersaults. You look just like ... just like ...'

'Myself?'

'Aye, that's right, yourself. Exactly the same as the last time I laid eyes on you ... no, not the last time, not when you were lying in that coffin dead to the world. Before all that tragedy came knocking – I couldn't cope at all, Son. I mean, before you headed into town that day. Look at you, not a scratch on you, thank God. Jesus, Mary and Joseph, I can see it now, what they all said: you're a picture of me. Why did I never see it before? Same glint around the eyes, a decent nose, wide mouth like our ones. A picture of the man I used to be, not this decrepit oul' fella. Is that how you see me, Cormac? An oul' withered mess of a man?'

'Ach, Da, I see the man I last set eyes on all those years ago with a wee bit more grey round the temples. And a touch more frail.'

'You're some storyteller even in death, God bless you.'

'I didn't get it from a peddler! But enough of that oul' talk. Back to business, Da.'

'She despises me, doesn't she?'

'Aye, she does alright, but sure it'll pass.'

'I pray to God in heaven you're right.'

'It's time for one of your assistants to make an appearance. Jesus, I've only known the man five minutes and I know he'll go through me for a short cut, calling him that.'

'Bloody right. A man, you say? Who is he, Cormac?'

'You'll find out soon enough. Our Sarah has to meet him first. And in the meantime, you have to tell me about that woman of yours.'

Day 4: Shipyard and Holyland

Sarah rereads her last message to Amy, the fourth one of the morning. She drums her fingers on the freezing cold seat of the bench, steadies her nerves. She knows there's no way Amy will reply. It's 10:30am on a school day for a start, and she'll be focusing on the thirty or so pupils bunched and slumped around her classroom. What will she be up to? A French vocabulary test, maybe? A game of bingo? Or maybe one of those ancient listening comprehensions about a penpal's visit to Ireland. Christ, she hated those. She'd be doing something similar with her Spanish classes if she were back at school.

But she's not. She's sitting on an ice-cold bench the colour of pea soup under her grandmother's front window, tormenting herself with the thought that her friend might be ignoring her. Sarah Cassidy, today's window display; Michael Doherty's substitute after him doing the honours for a few days. People will be talking – *there she is*, they'll say – *isn't it great to see the young ones?* Young life after death, how overrated.

She wonders if it matters that the last time she and Amy spoke was on the day of the funeral. A brief hello, hugs and goodbye as if Amy were a mere acquaintance. But that's what everyone was that day: it wasn't about anyone else, apart from her grandfather.

10:32am. She rereads her first text to Amy. The charge in her phone plummets another 5%. She really needs to sort that out.

Some people don't get them, her and Amy. She can't imagine why anyone would think real friendship only exists if you shared a first encounter with the school nurse and cried, God knows why, in a corner of the yard afterwards; if you were both picked last for a game of rounders. Sarah couldn't care less about other people's ideas – friendship isn't something she's ever measured by length of service. It's something that pulls you from the gut, knots you together; when you know, you know.

10:34am. She considers texting Amy a fifth time, then thinks better of it. She opens her list of contacts instead, scrolls to 'Granda Doherty'. She'd never have called him just 'Granda', a man with no name. And calling him 'Michael', well, that made him sound like a million other Michaels: generic, common.

His name is logged there, against her grandparents' landline number. You could argue that it was his number, not theirs, since her grandmother never used the phone. She had no interest whatsoever unless it was an emergency – an oul' anti-social contraption is how she has always described it. She prefers face to face – or, these days, ear to ear to make sure she doesn't miss a single word.

The only time her grandmother ever called her was on 17th March, 9:33am, when Sarah was in the middle of packing up the last of the bags in the boot of Amy's car. They were heading to Donegal for the long weekend. She'd assumed it was her grandfather phoning to wish her a Happy St Patrick's Day when she saw his name flash up on the screen. She was sure he'd also want another word with Amy about being careful on 'those oul' roads'.

Her grandmother's breathing was broken like a cracked record, sporadic between sobs. Sarah managed to make out that her grandfather was going into hospital for some tests. 'Only they must be important because the doctor called an ambulance,' she'd said. She'd asked if Sarah could follow them to the hospital and said that Chrissie and Tank were already with her. Mary was on the missing list and Catherine was trying to get cover in the shop.

Sarah remembers the short drive to the Royal, the silence punctuated by the occasional rattle and slide of items in the boot that she hadn't finished packing properly. She didn't know then that it would be the first of many hospital visits in the weeks that followed, that she and Amy would never make it to Donegal, that her grandfather wouldn't make it out alive. Why hadn't anyone told her if Raúl made it out alive? Anyone meaning María, the sort of girl who couldn't put differences aside, even in an intensive care unit.

'Low battery' notification. Another 10% gone.

'Are you coming in, love? You'll catch your death out here.' Her grandmother stands halfway between the hall and front step, wrapped like a boiled sweet in a tartan shawl.

'In a minute, Nanny.'

Sarah looks down the bleach-scarred path into the street. A fine thread of sunlight grazes the damp pavement. Hardly anyone is around. It's that odd time of the morning when kids have gone to school, people have left for work and morning Mass has already finished. Mrs McKinney glides past in a royal blue trench coat with a cloth shopping bag folded under her arm. She raises a gloved hand in a graceful flourish like the Queen Mother and bows her head. Sarah waves back as the bite in the sharp spring morning air cuts through her. Mr Delaney, who lives in the house opposite, is trying to shoo away next door's cat from the tiny patch of grass he calls a garden.

The soft vibration of the phone grazes Sarah's palm.

'Jesus, Sarah, what's with all the text messages? What's wrong?'

'Amy, thank God. I didn't expect you to ring, not until lunchtime anyhow.'

'What's happened?'

'Oh, sorry, I didn't mean to worry you. I just wondered if you'd meet me for a drink after work?'

'Bloody hell, is that it, Sarah? I mean, Jesus, I'm out of my mind here. I thought somebody was dead.'

'Not funny at all, you'd be as well catching yourself on. Say 4pm, usual place?'

***

'Would you look at her, Cormac? Sitting there, no distance from where they laid me out. Christ, I'd give anything to breathe the same air. My Annie's right, though, she'll be foundered from the cold. Actually ... forget that. To hell with standing there freezing.'

'You're a ticket, Da. And don't you think I know what you're at? All the small talk, anything to avoid talking about your woman from Spain. Who in God's name is she?'

'You can't rush these things.'

'What's she got to do with us, Da? With Sarah?'

'Now's not the time, Son.'

'Now's precisely the time. And time isn't on our side, or have you forgotten already? C'mon, Da, give me something. You owe me that.'

'Fair enough. But if you really want to rake up the past, we have to start long before all that.'

'What do you mean?'

'Listen, Son, there are things you didn't know ... don't know ... and all I can say is I had my reasons for not going into them. Hindsight is a powerful thing, but at the time I thought I was doing what was best for everybody. If I got that wrong, I'm sorry.'

'Just tell me, Da.'

'Right then, give me a second. Christ, where do I begin? Are you sure, Son? Like I said, you can't rush these sorts of things. They might rip our souls to shreds.'

'If we'd anything left to rip up ... Yes, Da, I'm sure. I think I've waited long enough.'

'Alright, Son. Look, we lived in the west of the city. Me, Ma and Da, the McBrides and Tommy. Tommy's parents and mine were very different people, rest assured of that.

'We shared a tiny terrace, the six of us on top of each other. Ma always said we were the lucky ones. Just us two boys with the adults, in our own space, sharing special occasions like Christmas and birthdays. On those days, we'd all sit around the table like one big family, Tommy and I balancing on stools made from a few wood cut-offs Mr McBride found lying in the street. Ma said there were whole families still stuck in the parish hall with the bare essentials, trying their best to get by. 'Two years is an awful long time,' she'd say. I was only four then, in 1922, and days and hours and years meant very little to me, unless I was counting sleeps til Christmas.

'I don't remember when the riots started. I remember the glass in our front window being shattered often enough for us to keep some thick cardboard tucked away at the back of the scullery. And the smell ... Christ, I remember the smell alright. Horrific, like petrol poured on burnt food. And I also remember Da giving off about someone taking away his job at the shipyard; I had no notion who.

'We lived in one of those residential side roads round the corner from the pub and spirit grocers owned by Mr McBride ... Danny McBride, his name was. The business was a favourite on the hit list. Alcohol and a Catholic proprietor, a lethal combination. Mostly the hit on our house was deliberate; only on the odd occasion was it accidental.'

'Why are you telling me all this, Da? Why now?'

'You were the one who asked, Son. And these are the sorts of things that shape us. We mightn't know it at the time, but life throws odd stuff at us to make us who we are. Back then, I wanted nothing more than to be just like Tommy. Tall and broad-shouldered, not short and thin as a rake. And before you say it, yes, I shot up as I got older, made up for lost time. I hope you don't mind me telling you all this now, Cormac.'

'No regrets, Da, that's what you taught us. What else is there?'

'Back then, everyone had to make do, pull together. I ended up with Tommy's hand-me-down clothes: shorts which sat too far below my knees and his oul' woollen jumpers with sagging sleeves. But sure, I didn't want his clothes; it was his attitude I was after. Opinionated, fearless, he was, and it got him far on the streets for years. The riots came and went – though there were always clashes of some sort or other – and Tommy was constantly in the middle of it all. It wouldn't have been like him to be anywhere else. I'd have given anything not to be hiding behind him, hanging off him like some reprobate, hanging on his every word.'

'And now, what's all that got to do with Sarah, with that woman?'

'Everything and nothing, Son. God, it's complicated. Look, do you recognise that pub? Never set foot inside it myself.'

'Aye, Da, there are a fair few good memories connected with that place.'

***

Sarah scans the bar just in case Amy is there already. Wishful thinking on her part. She knows only too well the joys of escaping the classroom and beating the traffic at the end of the school day.

There's no one there apart from a decently attractive middle-aged couple sharing a bottle of red and an elderly man in the corner nursing a small whiskey under one of the place's fancy mirrors.

She thinks 'elderly', though she has little to go on. She can't see his face, but he looks small in the chair, his shoulders are hunched, and his hair ripples in even grey ridges glossed by the orange ceiling lights. He twists a silver pen between his thumb and forefinger. Every so often, he dips his hand to write in what appears to be a small leather-bound notebook. His overcoat looks expensive: a tailored garment in a quilted gold fabric, streaked copper by the overhead lights. The man seems a little too sophisticated for this place. He takes a sip of the whiskey.

'Who's that over there?' Sarah asks the barman, whose name

badge tells her he's called Andy. She props herself up onto one of the two bar stools opposite the till. 'I'll have whatever he's having, and the wine list too, please.'

'That gentleman?' Andy nods in the direction of the man in the gold coat. 'He's a regular who's been in all week, used to come here before but haven't seen him for a few years. A very modest, polite fella. Keeps himself to himself. Writes away in the corner, always on his own.'

'Is that right? Seems a bit overdressed. I don't mean for here … I mean, generally. Don't you think?'

Andy shakes his head, confused, as Sarah takes the whiskey from him. She barely lets it touch her lips before she sets it down on the counter. 'Maybe I'll start with the wine. Anything in particular you'd recommend?'

'Oh, all the house wines are grand, and the special offers are on the front page.'

Sarah scans the list and tries to disregard the gentleman to her right who is now writing furiously and whispering to himself.

'Take your time,' Andy says, 'I'm just nipping out back to change the barrel. If anyone comes in, tell them I'll be back soon.' He disappears as the slow shuffle of the well-dressed man announces his approach to the bar. Sarah turns to regard the stooped, glinting outline of the figure whose head is inclined.

'Hello, young lady. May I?' The softly accented, unexpected clip of the man's voice surprises Sarah. He indicates the bar stool next to her while still looking at the floor.

'Um, yes … I suppose so,' she mumbles, removing her bag to make room. The gentleman is indeed gentle, shrunken under the weight of his heavy coat.

'Thank you, young lady,' he says, looking straight at her now: his face is glass-like, eyebrows hunkered in almost invisible mounds, his eyes absent. 'Christ!' Sarah gasps, knocking the whiskey across the counter. 'I'm sorry. Are you alright? What happened to you?' She nudges her stool away from the man and curses herself for doing so.

'My apologies, young lady,' the man says, wiping his face with a handkerchief, 'I did not mean to startle you. Please, may I have a moment.' He presses the handkerchief down hard on his eyes, their shape stitching itself onto the fabric. 'I forget they disappear sometimes,' he mutters, 'though it doesn't affect my vision. I'm sorry to have frightened you. There – is that better?'

'Yes, yes, much better,' Sarah says, though she is standing now and has moved a little further away still. The man is too unsettling to look at, his eyes waxing and waning between this world and another. 'But why do they do that? Your eyes ... were you in an accident of some kind?'

'I'm very pleased to hear that the sight of me is no longer so alarming, though surely that is a polite exaggeration on the young lady's part.' He looks down at the floor and assesses the increased distance between them. 'Yes, you could say I had an accident of sorts; and now that I'm travelling around, I'm also mal-adjusting at times. As you can clearly tell, young lady.' He laughs softly.

'Where are you from, then? And how have you ended up here, in Belfast? And why the coat? You need to be careful wandering the streets, dressed like that.'

'You have many questions, young lady. Please, let me try to answer.' The man sits up poker straight and his diminished frame fills every inch of the overcoat.

'First of all, I'm from different places,' he says, setting his notebook on the bar. 'Cities, I mean, though you could say I inhabit different worlds too. I wasn't always able to choose where I ended up. Do you understand?'

'I suppose so,' Sarah says, though she doesn't.

'Second, I'm just here helping an old friend. Someone we both know.'

'I doubt that.' Sarah scans the bar frantically for any sign of Amy – or Andy, even Andy, the barman she's only just met, will do.

'And the coat ... it's part of me, filled with memories I like to hold onto. I didn't always have it; now I've got it back, I'm determined not to let it go.'

'That's ... that's nice for you,' Sarah says, wishing the man would stop talking.

'May I show you something, please?' The man points at the notebook. 'It will only take a moment.'

'That's probably okay, as long as it's just a few seconds,' she says reluctantly, not wanting to appear rude. 'But my friend will be arriving any minute.' Her voice sounds quiet, as if hushing a prayer.

'Who, Amy? You're very close, aren't you?'

'How...?'

'Don't be scared, I promise you're safe. I promised your grandfather.'

'What? How?'

'Please, don't be frightened. I won't harm you. Here, watch this.'

The man lifts the notebook off the bar, turns the cover to face Sarah and begins flicking through the pages at speed.

'Keep watching.'

Sarah doesn't see it at first because she doesn't want to; she wishes she could temporarily impose blindness upon herself. But then it's there, her grandfather's signature, in the process of being written across the top and bottom of each page, over and over, by an invisible hand.

'Holy Jesus, what is that thing?' She jumps forward, snaps the notebook from the man's hands and flicks the pages at speed.

'Please don't be scared.'

Her grandfather's signature is gone, cruelly lost, any trace of his hand swallowed by the blank pages. She shakes her head violently. 'No, no! What have you done with it? Who are you?' She's pacing up and down the bar now, swearing under her breath, conscious that the middle-aged couple are staring at her, judging her. 'Who are you?'

'Won't you sit back down? Please. I told you, I'm helping an old friend. Come on.' The man attempts to direct her back to the stool but she shakes him off, pushes him away.

'No! I won't! Just tell me!'

'What's all the shouting about? Are you okay?' It's Andy leading her back to the stool this time. 'Like I said, you don't need to worry about this man here. Does she, Joseph?'

'Are you in on it too?'

'Settle yourself down ... that's it. Joseph will explain now.'

She won't look at the man; she won't give him the time of day. She hears him clear his throat and wonders if Andy sees him as she does.

'Sarah,' the man says meekly, 'don't you know what it's called?'

Panic steals her voice; she will not speak.

'It's what they call a God incidence,' the man whispers. 'And it's nothing to be scared of.'

'How do you know?' asks Sarah, swallowing back her tears. 'Who are you?'

'Because I know,' the man replies, sipping from the tumbler Andy has set down in front of him. 'And believe me, it's the living we should be scared of, not the dead.'

The thump of the door makes them both jump. It's Amy, bounding in in a fluster, her jacket halfway off, her face half-hidden by strands of her long blonde bob.

'I'm so sorry,' she says, throwing her coat and bag onto the bar counter, hugging Sarah. 'A school thing. You know what it's like.' She glances at the man, unsure what to make of him, and turns back to Sarah. 'Hey, what's wrong?' She grabs a tissue from her bag, passes it to her. 'Who's that man? Has he upset you?' She turns to the elderly gentleman. 'Listen, Mister, I don't know you from Adam, but you better not have upset her. Do you hear me?'

The man says nothing and offers Amy his stool. He then gathers the notebook and tumbler and walks slowly back to the table, shrinking into the floor under the pull of his coat.

'Jesus, what happened? Can't leave you on your own for a moment. Have you ordered yet?' Sarah tells her no and Amy orders a bottle of house white.

'Now, tell me what happened.'

'Have you ever heard of such a thing as a God incidence?'

'You come off with some stuff, Sarah, you really do.' Amy laughs. 'Are you having withdrawal symptoms from the Holylands?'

'What?'

'Our flat in the Holylands. Are you ready to come back now?'

'Actually, that's exactly where I need to be,' Sarah says, turning to face her. 'Away from all of this, away from every-thing. She indicates the man who sits with his back to them, scribbling notes.

'Maybe he was just looking for a bit of company?' Amy offers. 'You have to feel sorry for him.'

'So you see it too? That business with his eyes, the coat?'

'Ach, yes,' Amy says. 'Major bags under his eyes and that wee grey trench coat has seen better days. Sure it can't even be waterproof anymore, raindrops sticking to it there like fairy lights.'

'You're right,' Sarah says, not taking her eyes off the man, 'nothing but tiredness and a trench coat.'

Day 5: *Something or Nothing*

I've no idea what I was expecting from all this – this damn situation, which I take full responsibility for – but it certainly wasn't this. No word from Cormac; no sighting of Sarah. Have I messed it up already, secured my place in some awful limbo? Perhaps I've locked myself into an eternity of nothing. God only knows. Nothing is what I couldn't ever abide, what I won't be able to stand for.

If this is my permanent nothing, please, God, have mercy on my soul and put this oul' lad out of his misery. Throw him back in the dirt where he obviously belongs. Give him half a chance at some sort of redemption.

The audacity of me to be asking for anything else when I was well warned by Cormac. But sure, if you don't ask, you don't get. No point in hanging about here all mealy-mouthed pretending I'm okay with it all.

Imagine an oul' dead man like me having a time limit. I suppose when Cormac mentioned it, the forty-day grace period business, I assumed I'd have some natural indicator – imagine that. Imagine me thinking I'd know the difference between day and night, between one hour and the next. I thought Cormac would keep me straight. I wonder what Sarah makes of me now.

So here we are, me taking full responsibility for instigating my current – what? State? Moment? Take it as my metaphorical putting up of the hands and admitting I've made a mistake. I can imagine what our ones would say, buckled in two at the very thought of it. That's not the way Michael Doherty normally works. He's more of a 'hope nobody noticed' sort of fella, while he scurries about behind the scenes trying to put something right. But our ones always knew; Christ, it was impossible to hide anything from them. You couldn't bless yourself without one of them asking what was up.

And there it is again – me making out that I'm something, a presence in this strange … 'present'. This 'present' in which I don't know what I've got left to hold onto. Even a blackout would be an improvement: let me deep dive again into blackest black.

Sarah's never pushed me out before. It was close, very close a few times, but thanks be to God it never came to that. There was that time when she'd just turned fourteen and she'd got her eye on young Thomas McKinney, Brigid McKinney's grandson. He wasn't from the Estate – his mother and father had touched lucky in one of the pools draws and had bought a small two-bedroom semi a few minutes' walk away. But the very same Thomas McKinney might as well have been. A lanky, scrawny lad, he was, never out of Brigid's house. And never out of our garden, calling for Sarah after school, though he wouldn't set foot inside the house. Aye, that's just how the kids were then, they'd pass themselves with you in the street, no bother, but God forbid they'd have to sit down and have a conversation with you. Anyhow, one afternoon around that time, Mrs McGinty, Tank's mother, God rest her soul, turned up on our doorstep. She said she didn't want to cause any trouble and she'd love a cup of tea but couldn't stop; she just wanted a quiet word about our Sarah. 'Good as gold, that child,' she'd said, 'but I think she's running about with the wrong crowd.' I asked her what she meant and she said she was sure she'd seen her hiding under her neighbour's parked car. 'Those boys were at it, too,' she said, 'but I know your Sarah isn't like that.'

Do you remember, Sarah? You were mortified when I confronted you; you said you weren't involved, then stormed off and locked yourself in the bathroom. I went after you and told you I'd sit outside on the landing until you were ready to talk. I told you that you didn't need to be scared, that everything would be fine. When you eventually came out, you couldn't look at me, but I knew your eyes were thick with tears. We squeezed onto the top stair and you told me it was Thomas' new version of hide and seek. Do you remember, Sarah? I didn't have to tell you not to do it again because I knew you wouldn't.

I'm still here, Sarah. Just ... waiting. With all these memories or stories or imaginings or whatever they are. God forgive me for my weakness, for asking to be put back. I don't mean a word of it. I'm here waiting, Sarah, offering you every pearl of love I'm capable of. Waiting, going nowhere.

Day 6: Palms

This has always been her favourite time of day: when a skim of moon barely lingers; when the first tendrils of light dab the sky's dark overcoat of clouds; when the amber haze of the streetlights flickers and slowly slips into sleep; when the oak tree on the corner of the street stands sentry-like, guarding the pavement drizzled with dew. When no one else fills the frame and all of this is hers.

It's only been one day, away from everything. But being in her own space, this flat she rents with Amy, makes it easier to breathe. Not to forget or ignore. No, she doesn't want that. She doesn't want to forget the gentleman and the so-called 'God incidence', the sign from her grandfather which she was too afraid to acknowledge in the moment. She just needs a chance to pause, that's all; to slow it all down.

There are things in the flat she's thankful for. Small things, comforting distractions that probably no one else would even notice. The plush cream eyelet curtains her mother hung in the lounge when they first moved in because she said they'd go with anything; the feature wall flecked in gold spirals; the oversized table lamp complete with taupe satin shade her mother was going to give to charity anyway. Memories of her mother fixing what she called 'the dungeon of a place' seep out of the walls, through her skin, deep into her bones. They are the sorts of memories she can manage right now.

And then there are the photo albums, lined up in alternate blocks of blue and red on the oak unit behind the sofa like giant lego bricks. They've always been there. The plastic index squares on the spines are empty, deliberately so, but Sarah knows exactly what's in each one. No label means no giving away the contents to anyone else. She reaches for one of the blue ones, flicks on the table lamp and settles on the sofa.

She runs her index finger along the words inside the cover – 'Old Family Photos' – as if reading them for the first time.

Every page is carefully arranged; her own handiwork, though they're Mam's photos. There are photos which capture Sarah's youngest years: her eyes stoked with terror during her first visit to Santa; her strange smile dressed as a flower girl at a family wedding; her face drenched in embarrassment when forced to pose next to her thirteenth birthday cake in the shape of a pink butterfly. Every photo in neat rows like old negatives, every photo captioned and dated, though not always correctly. Photos which captured a beat of her life when everything was so much less complicated.

She slowly peels back the plastic film and removes the flower girl photo. She can't abide this doll-like version of herself, the artificiality of her expression, the fussiness of the dress. God, she wishes she could bin it. Her mother said it was taken in June 1987 at some cousin's wedding and instructed Sarah to print the date in small letters on the album page. Sarah is still convinced it dates from a year later when another cousin got married, the year she lost both her front teeth. She remembers practising her smile in the mirror for weeks before the big day, lips welded shut in a lopsided arc. She remembers feeling sad that there were far too many cousins and not enough teeth. She wonders why her mother would hang onto such a monstrosity of a picture. 'Nostalgia' was the answer her mother gave, even if she didn't know which wedding it was taken at.

Sarah is in the centre of the photo in the same white lace ruffle dress she wore to both cousins' weddings. Her parents are crouching either side of her, holding her hands, joining theirs in a static version of ring-a-ring-a-rosie. Grandparents are relegated to the background, their faces expressionless, looking straight at the camera. Was it a generational thing, did all grandparents wipe the smiles off their faces before the photographer struck? Or was it for a more morbid reason, to make them look less like themselves so you'd miss them less after they'd gone?

What is actually wrong with me? Why do I suppose the worst? She contemplates how her own grandfather doesn't look anything like himself, yet the knowledge that it's him makes her loathe his box a little more. *Bloody man.* She covers the length of his image with the sleeve of her dressing gown to ward off a new wave of grief. She checks her neck to make sure she's removed the crucifix. Tiredness does this to her, plagues her with self-doubt, makes her check, double check, triple check.

She diverts her gaze to her father, recalls how he'd convinced them to recycle their outfits, given that the weddings were just seven months apart. Always the sensible one, never missed a trick. 'Now don't be telling your daddy,' her mother would say when the postman arrived with another catalogue order. 'He won't even notice, he won't remember we didn't already have these,' she'd say, pulling dresses and flouncy skirts from the box, holding them up against them, telling her to twirl round, the two of them laughing until they hiccupped. 'We're like two models,' she'd sputter, 'the belles of the Estate.' That was normally Sarah's cue to twirl even faster, to shriek at the dizziness curling around her, and then she'd imagine she was one of the perfect tiny ballet dancers they watched on a Saturday evening. She'd twirl and twirl until she lost her balance and tumbled onto the rug. She loved those days when it was just the two of them. She never expected they would become a permanent feature so early on, dampened by the dark veil of mourning.

'But you did always notice, Dad,' Sarah says, smiling down at him. 'And you always told Mam to send it all back and she'd just look at you with her big chocolate button eyes and you'd say *alright, but that's the last.*'

Sarah doesn't remember how her father got his way with the weddings, but she recalls the sameness of them both. It wasn't just the outfits: there was the same ceremony at St Joseph's; same hymns; same bouquets; same receptions at The Claddagh. Even the same 'English visitors', as her grandmother called them, all the way from London and Liverpool. Formal-looking, posh versions of her grandmother who never fancied a dance and only drank sherry from sherry glasses.

Is this all her family members are, a series of duplicates, at best reconstructions? She'd left the Estate to try something new, to be a better version of herself; instead, she'd managed to self-destruct and obliterate the life destined for her. She wonders what happened to her grandfather; if he, like her, was too terrified of judgment to confide in anyone. She wonders if he too might have hurt someone.

She inhales deeply, exhales slowly, repeats, stares hard at the image. She'll make herself disappear – it's something she's perfected with other more recent photos, to block herself out, especially the ones with Raúl. The ones she just couldn't part with and filed away in one of the red albums, the ones she takes out every so often to check if the agony has eased. If only it were so easy to permanently erase painful memories and start again.

She tapers her gaze carefully so it captures only her. The image fades slowly, blurs and flakes to cinders. She shuts her eyes to hold onto the undoing.

The soft whistling of a song she vaguely recognises coasts the room, disturbing her concentration. She puts the photo back inside the album, slams it shut and walks over to the bay window overlooking the street.

The whistling gently brushes the glass, seeking permission to come in. Sarah cautiously obliges, opens the blind halfway, releases the window just enough to welcome the cool spring breeze that tingles her face, her hands, the dip of her neck. Through the wooden slats, she glimpses the slim frame of a faceless man backlit by the dying streetlight. His overcoat billows behind him in soft golden tones and his steps are slow, deliberate, as if he's counting every single one.

She wants to ask him what he's doing there, if he's following her, how he knows where she lives. She counts his steps – one, two, three – but he's still in the same spot, his walk motionless. His notebook balances in the crook of his right arm. She wants to ask if there'll be any more God incidences, how long he'll stay for, if he's seen her grandfather yet.

'Pinch, punch, first of the month!'

'Ow! Jesus, Amy, what are you doing?'

'And good morning to you too! First of the month – the first of April, remember?'

'April? Sure it's Palm Sunday.'

'Yes, that too,' Amy says. She laughs softly, pads to the fridge in her thick slippers. 'But there's nothing stopping Palm Sunday also being April Fools, is there?'

'I suppose not,' Sarah mutters, leaning out the window again. The street below her is deserted. 'Great!' she says under her breath and begins to pace back and forth.

'What's got into you?' Amy yawns as she pours herself some milk. She puts the mug into the microwave and turns the dial. 'Do you want one?'

'No thanks, you're alright.' Sarah's voice is strained, small, as she stretches her arms above her head. 'I might go for a run in a bit, try to get myself back into some sort of routine. What has you up at this time of the day?'

'Nothing,' Amy says, her back to Sarah. I mean, I'm not *up up*. I woke up, fancied a warm milk and I'm going back to bed. You should do the same. Maybe after your run? That might help you sleep a bit better.' She takes the mug out of the microwave, blows around the rim. 'What time are you meeting your nanny? It's not until later on, is it?'

'No.' Sarah sighs, scouring the street one last time for the slightest contour of the man, curses it as if it's the street's fault. Disappointment raps her chest.

'I mean, yes, later, after Mass and dinner. I couldn't coax her out for lunch, you know what she's like.'

'She's a wise woman, your nanny. I certainly wouldn't sacrifice one of her roasts for a toastie!' Amy stands next to Sarah, her arm draped lazily across her shoulders. 'Anything exciting out there?'

'Not at the minute.' Sarah reaches into the pocket of her dressing gown, takes out the photo of the woman and holds it out to the light.

'Do you think I should just forget all of this?' She tilts the photo so the natural beauty of the woman's face is illuminated and turns it towards Amy. 'Honestly, now, what do you think?'

'I think you don't really want me to answer that.'

She's right. Amy's always right. Always the more cautious one, goes out of her way not to get hurt. And look where that got her. Still didn't stop Peter from doing what he did, the bastard. After five years together.

Amy takes the photo out of Sarah's hand, examines it for a moment. 'We can't ever make ourselves forget what we're desperate to find out, can we? Come here.' She hugs Sarah tightly. 'But listen, how about ... it's only a suggestion ... how about I hold onto this for you, just for a little while?'

Sarah can part ways with this woman for a little while; yes, she can do that. She turns her gaze back to the street, to the spot where the man stood. If she concentrates hard enough, she can make him reappear. No one believes she's got this gift, so she's given up talking about it. Even those who used to humour her told her it would all stop as soon as she got over whatever it was. *Whatever it was. Whatever they were* is what they should be saying. They know nothing.

Sarah focuses hard on the man's spot and closes her eyes. When she opens them, it isn't him she sees. It's Raúl, her Raúl, staring up at her through a crop of thick dark hair. He's wearing dark jeans, a white shirt and black jacket, the same outfit he used to wear when they were going for a proper night out. And there he remains, Sarah doesn't know how long for, the perfect version of his imperfect self: pre-accident, pre-trauma. He fills the street in the city he never got to visit, stands on the pavement where Sarah's family and friends have often stood. He never came, not after that first year when they met, not when she came back home for her final year at university, not when she got her first proper teaching job. 'Because it's always good to have a back-up,' her grandfather would say, 'even if you're planning on moving away.' Raúl was like her, always thought they had plenty of time for introductions to family, to friends. There was no rush to share what was theirs. No time limit. If only.

She knows it's time to let him go, to allow the breeze and first light to carry him away, to let her heart think it's stopped beating. She hugs Amy back. 'I'm freezing,' she says, pulling her tight, closing the window, inhaling the creamy steam from Amy's mug. 'Go on, then,' she says, pointing at the cup, 'make me one of your gourmet drinks.'

**

The café feels unusually warm after the brisk ten-minute walk from the flat to Botanic Avenue. Sarah unbuttons her coat and releases one arm, then another as she manoeuvres her way past tables occupied by students, tiptoeing through pushed-out chairs, trying not to listen in on morsels of conversation. Her mother and grandmother are already there, sitting next to each other in the far right hand corner. They've got dead men to contend with – husbands, fathers, brothers – but no complicated relationships, not as far as she knows anyhow. Sarah doesn't know if she has the strength to take on her grandfather's past.

'Sorry, I'm running a bit late.' Sarah flops down in the seat opposite Annie and hangs her coat over the spare one. As if they've both rehearsed it, Chrissie and Annie extend their arms in perfect unison and each take one of her hands. Her grandmother plants a kiss on the one she's holding, then lets go of it hurriedly and checks her scarf is still positioned correctly across her shoulders. Sarah remembers picking that one out for her last birthday at her grandfather's request, avoiding the list of patterns and motifs he'd explicitly forbidden — *no butterflies, no birds, no stripes, definitely none of that sparkly rubbish.*

Sarah had settled for a pale orange neck scarf with a gold hoop design that matched her grandmother's favourite earrings and complemented her skin tone.

'How have you been, love?' *Is her mother actually trying to read her palm for answers?*

'Yes, love, how have you been? We've been missing you.' Annie smiles broadly but refrains from showing her teeth as she passes Sarah a menu.

'God, anybody'd think I'd run away. It's only been a couple of days!' Sarah half-heartedly returns the smile, her mouth managing no more than a stitched line. She frees her hand from her mother's and turns over the menu.

'Are you both sure you won't have anything to eat? The desserts look good, Nanny. And how have you two been, more like?'

'We're fine ... your nanny's fine, love. Aren't you, Mam? Plenty of people still popping in. Nice when that happens. Good neighbours, thank God.'

'Yes, aha,' her grandmother says, distracted by the glasses which refuse to stay on her head as she attempts to read the small print on the card.

'Oh, hi, Sarah. It's good to see you. So sorry about your grandfather — Amy was telling me.' James is holding a small notepad and pen, his flour-dusted purple apron clashing with his royal blue tie. He's worked there for as long as Sarah can remember, making his way up the ranks — waiter, supervisor. It was Amy who told her he was now managing the place.

'Thanks. This is my mam, Chrissie.' James nods knowingly as Chrissie extends her hand. 'You might have already met before. And this is my nan.'

Annie shuffles in her seat and places the menu card close to her face. It's been a long time since she was introduced to someone new. The faces and talk of the Estate suit her just fine.

'My deepest condolences, I'm so sorry for your loss.' James lowers his head, waits for Annie to respond. Sarah sees how his neck blotches with embarrassment. James clears his throat. 'So, then, what can I get for you ladies? Tea for three, is it? A few desserts? My treat – to say, you know, so sorry again.'

'Just the three teas will be grand, thanks,' Sarah says, taking the card out of her grandmother's hands, passing it back to James.

'Actually, can I just ask you something, Son?' Annie indicates the specials board. 'Would you say your plain scones with butter don't count as sweets?'

'Sorry, Mrs...?'

'Doherty. Plain scones with butter. They don't count as sweet stuff, do they? It's just that, well, it's Lent and I'm off desserts but a wee plain scone wouldn't do any harm, would it? Save me making some tea later.'

'You're fine with a scone, Nanny,' Sarah says, offering James a complicit half-smile. 'Actually, can you bring us two, save Mam cooking later too?'

'No worries at all.' James looks at Sarah with comfortable familiarity. 'Coming right up.'

'Well, he's a nice young lad, isn't he?' Annie helps herself to some milk before passing it to Sarah. Chrissie titters softly and keeps stirring her tea. 'How long have you known him, Sarah?'

'We went to uni together, so a good few years now. It's no big deal.'

'Really? So how come he's working here now? And how come I've never met him before?'

'Leave it, Mam, come on now,' Chrissie says, sipping her tea. 'They obviously weren't that close.'

'Well, there's a first for everything. And you could do worse than seeing a lad like that. At least he's got himself a steady job.'

'Jesus, Nanny, could you please stop? He'll hear you.' Sarah tuts loudly and checks the coffee area directly behind them for any sign of him.

'Looks like a bit of a grafter. Just like my Michael was, God rest his soul.'

'Yes, Granda was quite the grafter,' Sarah says, pushing her cup to one side. 'And since you've brought him up, do you mind if I ask a few things?'

'Sarah, a bit too soon, don't you think?' Her mother gives her one of her looks.

'Told you there was no such thing as a free pot of tea.' Annie nudges Chrissie expectantly. 'What is it you want to know?'

'Go easy, love,' her mother says, reaching for Sarah's hand again.

There are so many things Sarah wants to know, so many things she is desperate to ask. So many questions hammering her thoughts. And so much anxiety, so much doubt about her ability to cope.

'So, you know that box, Nanny? Do you really not know where it came from?'

Annie sighs and a slight scowl threads her brow. 'I'd tell you if I did, love, but why are you worrying yourself unnecessarily? I mean, it's obviously for you, your granda went to the trouble of putting your name on it. What's the problem, do you not want it? And besides,' she says, touching up her scarf, 'the house hasn't stopped, you know what the Estate's like, everybody chipping in, trying to get everything squared up. Any number of people could've sorted it out. You know what it's like, doesn't she, Chrissie?' She nudges her daughter again, hoping she'll say something.

'But how did it get to —'

'Your mam's? Someone'll have dropped it in. Tell her, Chrissie.'

Sarah's mother lifts the lid off the teapot and peers inside. 'Do you think young James would fill this up with a drop more hot water? The teabags'll do fine ... Yes, sorry love, somebody must have dropped it off, sure there's a few of the neighbours there with spare keys.' Her mother catches James' eye and waves him over to their table. 'Can you do us a top up, please? Thanks very much.' She pushes the pot into his hands before he has a chance to respond.

Sarah looks from her mother to her grandmother, wanting to believe them. Although they don't resemble one another, apart from the varying shades of red hair – her mother has Michael's build and facial features – they both share the same traces of grief: charcoal circles etched under their eyes, new crease lines across their foreheads, the pallor of mourning. Christ, she can be so selfish sometimes, wading in, momentarily forgetting the suffering of the two women she adores.

'I'm really sorry, I didn't mean...'

'Oh, it's fine, love,' her grandmother says, 'just say what you need to say.'

Sarah pauses. 'Do you mind if I ask ... there's just one more thing.'

'Ask away.'

'Remember what I said, Sarah.' Her mother's gaze is kind but firm.

'Did Granda ever tell you he went to Spain?'

'He did, love, yes.'

'What? Did he? What did he say?'

'That was about it: that he went and came back before he met me. He was always a very private man, as you know.'

'But didn't you want to know more?' Sarah struggles to retain the calm in her voice. 'Didn't you want to know where he'd been, why he was there? Why didn't he tell me?'

'It wasn't my place to ask.' Annie shrugs unapologetically. 'He shared what he could, what he thought was proper. Who was I to ask for more?'

'But you were his wife,' Sarah says quietly.

'Indeed I was. And his best friend. And now I'm his widow.' She averts Sarah's gaze and lifts her bag off the floor, removes a tissue.

'I'm sorry, Nanny, I didn't mean to upset you.'

'Where's that young lad got to with our tea?' Her grandmother dabs her eyes and looks around the café, folds the tissue and presses it into her palm. 'I think I might have to take back what I said … you know, about him being a grafter.'

'Poor lad, no chance being measured against Michael Doherty, has he?' Her mother smiles, but her expression is pensive.

'God, no, no chance.'

'Come here.' Chrissie leans across to straighten Annie's scarf. She smooths the edges gently with her fingertips. 'That's better, all gorgeous again.'

'Thank you, love.' Annie turns back to Sarah. 'And you know, dear, you can ask me anything, anything at all. No secrets, okay? I just can't promise I'll have all the answers.'

'Thanks, Nanny.' Sarah replays her grandmother's words in her head, wonders how she can now withhold what she knows. Surely guilt will trip her up. But any secrets she chooses to harbour will be for her grandmother's own good, for the good of the family.

'Here we are, ladies, sorry to keep you waiting.' James sets the teapot in the middle of the table. 'And there's a few extra tea bags and a fresh jug of milk.'

'You're a fine lad,' Annie says, 'you'll have to come over to our house one of these days. Sarah tells me you were at university together.'

'Nanny! Ignore her. Sorry.'

'We'll see,' James laughs. Sarah mouths another *sorry* and covers her reddened face with her hands.

'And you, young lady,' her grandmother adds, removing her hands from her face, 'why don't you come over tomorrow and check there's nothing in the attic you might want? No secrets in this family, okay?'

'No secrets.'

No secrets.

Day 7: Tank

'Are you sure it's not too heavy, love?' Her mother lifts the box into the air and carefully sets it back down onto the coffee table. It's as if someone has warned her about the fragility of what's inside, of lives broken and lost.

'Not at all,' Sarah says, running a thick strip of brown postal tape across the top of the box to secure it, patting it into place. 'It's only a few bits of paper and clippings.' *Documents and photos fastened to her grandfather's heart.* She holds up the box, lowers it, raises it up again. 'See? Light as a feather.'

'If you're sure,' Chrissie says, opening the front door for her. 'And what if there's anything else in the attic?'

'Then I'll get a taxi home. Now stop worrying.' Sarah skims a kiss across her cheek and steps onto the path. 'I'll phone you as soon as I get back to the flat.'

A white Audi flashes past Sarah before she has time to check out its driver. 'Fancy so and so!' she murmurs to herself, watching as it indicates left at the top of Strathearn Street and disappears around the corner. She asks herself what the car is doing in the Estate and hopes one of the neighbours has had a windfall. God only knows the people round there could do with a break.

She crosses the street to find Tank standing outside his house nursing a stepladder. 'Right on cue,' he says, 'your nanny says you're a stickler for punctuality.'

'Right,' Sarah replies, confused. She stares at the ladder. 'What's that for?'

Tank lets out a deep, rough laugh. 'Your nanny asked me to bring it up, says one of her own borrowed hers and never brought it back. Let's go and have a look at this attic.'

65

'But…' *God, the embarrassment.* 'I'm so sorry, Tank, I didn't mean for her to ask you. I can manage the attic perfectly well. There's no need —'

'I'm not taking no for an answer, love.' He hitches the ladder onto his shoulder, sticks out his chest and starts walking alongside her. 'What on God's green earth would your grandfather say?' His pace is quicker than she expected; she speeds up a little. He reaches for the box but Sarah shakes her head and pulls it tight to her chest. 'And besides,' he adds, running his free hand down his side, placing it on his hip, 'an extra bit of exercise always does wonders for my svelte figure.' He attempts some sort of jig on the spot.

'You're not wise,' Sarah says, laughing hard as he tries to flick his legs left and right, holding the ladder at arm's length to maintain his balance.

'Did you notice that Audi in our street just now? Someone's doing well for themselves!' Sarah pushes open the gate and finds her grandmother's key waiting in the lock of the front door.

'Oh yes,' says Tank, letting them in, 'the state on that, eh? Powerful! They're saying it belongs to Saoirse's new man, you know, Saoirse O'Connell? The one your Mary had the row with?'

'Our Mary? Rowing with someone? Which one would that be?' Sarah rolls her eyes and places the box on the hall floor.

'I'll just leave this here for now,' she tells Tank, aware that he's watching. 'I'll take it upstairs with us.' She pauses. 'Anything to avoid any potential drama in there, you know? I'm really not in the mood today.'

'Good plan!' Tank walks ahead of her into the living room, holding himself in just in case his bulk disturbs the many ornaments. 'Understood.' He turns round, nods in agreement, winks.

'Only us, Nanny!' Sarah shouts through to the kitchen and sits down on the edge of the sofa closest to the hall door. The room smells of coffee, mints and furniture polish.

'Good morning, Mrs Doherty, and how are you keeping this fine morning?' Tank's gruff formality makes Sarah laugh; she's not even sure if he knows her grandmother's first name. Annie appears, delighted to see him, and totters over with a tray laden with plates.

'Here you go, Son, your favourites. Got to keep your strength up.' She holds out a mix of biscuits and cakes: custard tarts, bourbons and custard creams.

'Did you make all those, Nanny?'

'Ach, no, too old for that now, love. Sent up to the wee bakery at the top of the road. Prefer the garden to the kitchen if I'm feeling up to it.' She turns to Sarah and holds out the tray. 'And ... before you say anything, love, Tank's only down the street. Aren't you, Tank? And he didn't have any other work on today.'

'That's right,' Tank says, his mouth thick with custard. 'Always happy to give a hand.'

'You've them all spoiled rotten, Mammy!' Mary emerges from the kitchen cloaked in a drift of thick cigarette smoke and sits down on the sofa between Sarah and Annie.

'And what are you hoping to find upstairs, love?' Mary breathes into Sarah's face, knowing how much she hates the stench. She must already have had a dozen or so this morning, Sarah thinks, covering her nose and mouth with her sleeve.

Tank gets up, sensing her unease. 'Will we head on up, then, see what's there?' He holds the door open for her. 'You go on ahead, love, I'll bring the stuff we need.'

Sarah nods and makes for the hall. She can hear Mary tutting behind her, striking another match, filling the room with her agitation and nicotine.

'I'd really prefer to go up first.'

'You know your grandfather would turn in his grave if he heard you getting on like that.' Tank opens the hatch from halfway up the ladder and feels for the light switch. 'What do you think he'd say if I was standing down there holding the ladder like a first-class idiot, letting his granddaughter crawl about up here? I'd never hear the end of it.'

'That's true,' Sarah says, and for a moment she visualises him sat in his chair by the hearth, ranting about this or that. No one has sat in his chair since he passed; it's there in the same place like a sacred theatre prop.

'How about we make a deal, then?' she shouts up. 'We'll go together, sort of. You go first, then I'll follow and stay at the top of the ladder, give the place a quick scan. Deal?'

'Stubborn like your oul' grandfather. Okay, deal!' Tank climbs awkwardly through the hatch, sucking in his stomach; he swings himself around and peers down at her. 'Maybe we should invite your Aunt Mary up, too, just in case she thinks she's missing something?'

'Over my dead body,' Sarah says, pulling herself up the ladder. Tank begins to laugh and the harshness of his features relaxes; it's rare to see his face like that.

'Right, go on then.' She jabs him in the ribs. 'You start moving. That way, I'll have a bit of room to see what's what.'

Tank crawls towards a small pile of boxes neatly stacked in the corner. Sarah surveys the rest – apart from an old toy chest directly in front of her and a crate of dust-covered vinyls to her right, there's nothing else there.

'I thought your nanny said this place was full of stuff?' Tank starts unstacking the boxes, placing them in a row in front of him.

'Yeah, she did,' Sarah says, making an ungraceful sudden turn to face the other side. Hanging from the beams are a couple of badminton rackets, an old wooden tennis racket, a thick skipping rope they used for swinging round lampposts, and a rounders bat. It must be at least ten years since she and her cousins played with them.

'So that means there can only be a couple of explanations.' Sarah twists herself round again, bangs her kneecap, yelps.

'You okay?' Tanks asks.

'Yep, fine,' she murmurs, regaining her balance. 'As I was saying, I reckon that either Mary or Catherine cleared it out when they did Granda's room. Or...' she feels her throat thicken with tears, 'or Granda knew more than he was letting on and cleared it himself.'

'What are you saying, love?' Tank places two of the boxes in front of her and crawls back towards the others. 'Do you mean that your grandfather was making preparations way in advance?' He sets the last two boxes next to the others, kneels beside them. 'Because that wouldn't be hard to believe. You know he always liked to be organised.'

'I know,' Sarah says, pulling herself up through the hatch, kneeling next to him. 'Do you want to do the honours?'

Sarah leans in to inspect the contents as Tank removes the lids one by one. There are books, lots of them: poetry pamphlets, a few Brian Friel plays, three or four cookery books which make Sarah smile, knowing what a philistine her grandfather was when it came to cooking. They were definitely his, though – her grandmother would never have laid a finger on them. The box closest to Tank has the old board games they all used to play: snakes and ladders, draughts, ludo, monopoly. Monopoly – the one game Sarah could never figure out and the only one she ever had permission to bail out of. She'd draw or read in the living room while her grandparents and cousins played in the scullery.

'What's in those two?' Sarah says, pointing at the ones she can't quite reach.

'Looks like old clothes and blankets. Come here.' Tank gives her his hand, guides her as she crawls behind him around to the other side of the hatch. He's right – it's mainly baby clothes: crocheted cardigans and booties in pastel colours, a few bonnets, knitted blankets and gloves, christening robes carefully wrapped in tissue paper.

'Do you think these were Mam's? Aunt Mary's and Aunt Catherine's?' Sarah smooths one of the tiny pink cardigans at the top of the box.

'I would imagine so,' Tank says. 'Right then, love, may we confirm there's nothing else here you want to keep?'

Sarah quickly rummages through each of the boxes again, then crawls over to the old toy box and crate of vinyls, just to make sure.

She doesn't know how much time has passed – a few minutes perhaps – when she turns round to face Tank again. He is sitting patiently at the top of the hatch, humming to himself, his legs resting on the ladder. It's probably the longest break the poor man has had in years. He's a workaholic, they say, always wanting to make her grandfather proud. Even now.

'There's nothing else here,' Sarah says. 'Let's go.'

***

Tank switches off the engine in the residents' bay where Amy normally parks.

'So, this is how the other half live! You've done well for yourself, girl.'

'It's not all that,' Amy says, blushing. 'It's only a flat, it's rented and it's tiny. Still,' she says, opening the passenger door, 'it's mine and Amy's – for now, anyway. Feels strange to be living all the way over here, though. Still getting used to it.'

Tank stands in front of the car, assessing the street. 'Your grandfather was very proud of you. You know that, don't you?'

'I do,' Sarah replies quietly. 'Listen, thanks for the lift, Tank, I really appreciate it. I better get this upstairs.' She indicates the box.

'Yes, about that,' Tank says, lighting up a cigarette. 'It's not my place to say, but your grandfather would only want the best for you.' He inhales and puffs out slowly. 'I know it'll sound strange coming from a big awkward fella like me, but he sorted me out, was awful good to me. Pulled me out of many's a hole. I miss him.' He takes another draw of the cigarette, then throws it onto the road and stamps it out. 'Awful habit, need to give it up. It's worse when the oul' nerves get the better of me.'

Sarah stares at the ground, overcome by the sadness she's been trying to keep at bay. It rises rapidly through her, heart to head, and she can't look at Tank; she won't. She's frightened of what she'll see in him, of what it might set off in her.

'Thanks again, Tank.' She rushes to the front door, taking the steps two at a time.

'If you need anything at all, don't hesitate to give me a ring.' She waves at him as he pulls out of the bay, then slams the door behind her. She slides down onto the hall floor next to the box. She doesn't yet know how long she'll stay there.

***

The sweet perfume of the roses blankets the cool air of the garden. Sarah contemplates how much she's missed this, how long it's been since she sat amongst the laces of pink, red and gold petals. She used to come to Botanic Gardens at least a few times a week when she was a student, sometimes with the girls, sometimes alone. Sometimes she'd hide herself in the rose garden, like today, trying to switch off from the rest of the world; on other occasions she'd sit opposite the glass curve of the Palm House and watch people passing by, imagining who they might be.

'Good afternoon, young lady. How are you?'

God, no. Not today.

'May I?' The man's clipped accent sounds more pronounced than before. He sits down next to her before she has a chance to say anything. Sarah has no desire for conversation, but she can't let him disappear again.

'What are you doing here?' Her voice is stippled with apprehension.

'I could ask you the same thing. Actually, I'm not planning on staying here much longer; I'll be leaving soon.'

Thank God, she thinks, *but not before I work you out.* The gentleman proceeds to unfasten his overcoat, extending the sides to blanket the bench they're sitting on. The coat gleams in the pale light of the afternoon and the roses seem to raise their heads in reverence.

'Oh,' is all Sarah can manage as she assesses his skinny frame draped in a neutral-coloured army uniform. He doesn't strike her as the military type. 'Where will you go?' she asks finally.

'Wherever they send me,' he replies, reaching into his pocket. His eyes are a soft blue this time and gaze warmly, steadily at her.

'But first, I must keep my promise.'

'Promise?' Sarah asks nervously.

'About this beautiful coat, yes. Have you ever seen anything quite so exquisite? It's my memory coat. I said I'd tell you all about it.'

'Ah ... I see ... But only if you must.' *Who is this person, what's he trying to do to her?*

'I'm fortunate to wear this garment,' he says, smoothing it down with the delicate touch of his fingertips. It's like a protective cloak, filled with memories of my loved ones. Are you following me, young lady?'

'I ... I think so.'

'So when I first saw you, the granddaughter of my dear friend –'

'No, stop. Enough.' Sarah leaps to her feet, moves a few feet away. 'Please, that's enough.'

'Please, young lady, don't be alarmed. I'm on your side. Let me show you.'

'I really don't want to see anymore –'

'Just let me show you. One moment, that's all I'm asking for. Look.'

The man traces his hand along the stitching of a gold panel next to his breast pocket, all the while reciting what sounds like a solemn chant under his breath. He tracks the stitching again, anti-clockwise this time, and covers the panel with his hand.

'Now,' he says.

Sarah watches as the golden panel detaches itself from the coat and settles in the man's hand.

'What the ...?'

'Look again, in there.'

Reluctantly, as she tries to control the stop-start of her breathing, Sarah leans in to look under the panel. There, emblazoned on the lining of the coat is his name – MICHAEL DOHERTY. Below it: 26.03.2007. *Date of death.*

'No! Who the hell are you? Please, please tell me this isn't some sick joke. Because ... because my heart wouldn't be able to take it. Please.' *Please let it be true, whatever this is.*

The man reaches for her arm, but she moves away, sheltering within her own grief and doubt. The blue of his eyes begins to drain into pools of white and Sarah forces herself back into the present. *He can't go, not like this.*

'Please, tell me you knew him.'

'I'm sorry, young lady, I don't mean to cause you distress.' The man smooths the panel back into place and pulls the coat tightly around him, owning his memories again.

'You must know I'll never hurt you. I'm here for your grandfather, Michael.' His eyes flash blue again at the mention of his name. 'His name is here, close to my heart, because he's a dear friend in need; he hasn't passed over yet.'

'But he's dead,' Sarah says. *Dead. DEAD.*

'It's not so straightforward,' the man says. 'Please follow me. Please come to Spain.'

It is then that Sarah sees herself sitting on the bank of the River Tormes next to Raúl, a modest picnic of *manchego*, black olives and *sangría* laid out in front of them. Her head rests in his lap; he reads to her from Márquez's *One Hundred Years of Solitude.*

'I'm sorry,' Sarah says, jumping to her feet again. Thank you. I'll think about it. There's somewhere else I have to be right now.'

She turns and walks decisively in the direction of the exit, feeling lighter, more alive than she has done for quite some time. She can't think of the detail of it all, not yet, but she knows what she needs to do. She doesn't look back; she knows the stranger is no longer there. It's just forward steps now, back to España.

Something isn't quite the same. Cormac, Son, tell me! Please come back and please God, let it be what I hope it to be. Is there such a thing as sensing the presence of someone you can't see or touch or hear? Sensing an emptiness that isn't quite empty anymore? Or sensing a place, a time you can't distinguish, but you know it lingers somewhere? Christ, I hope I'm not deluded. Something isn't quite the same and please God, let it be her. Let this be her.

I'll see her soon; I know I will. She's coming.

Day 8: Beneath the Daffodils

The picnic by the Tormes was what you might call their first proper date. They'd done other things before then – walked home together from lectures on balmy evenings; had a drink in *Camelot* and a dance in the early hours in *Morgana* nightclub. They'd met each other at the mailboxes in the hall of their building, bumped into each other in the supermarket just around the corner. But all of it was unplanned. Or so Sarah thought. It was only later, after they'd been together for a few months, that Raúl confessed their meet ups weren't as coincidental as Sarah had believed. He'd watch her head for the supermarket from his balcony overlooking the street and would rush out to 'casually' find her there; he'd figured out which nights she went to *Camelot* and which days her classes finished at the same time as his. Not in a creepy way, he'd hastened to add.

It was a gorgeous bright day in the middle of March when he finally plucked up the courage to invite her for a picnic. He'd found her by the mailboxes, sifting through coloured envelopes all marked 'airmail'.

'Hola, Sarah, how are you today? Is it your birthday or something?' he'd asked, hiding behind the open door of the family mailbox, rooting inside to buy himself some time, too nervous to look at her.

'Hola. Oh no, nothing like that,' she'd said, laughing, 'they're St Patrick's Day cards from friends back home. They promised to send me some ... a little bit of home since I can't be with them.'

'How lovely.' Raúl closed the mailbox, swallowed hard and dared to look at her. He watched how she turned one of the envelopes over and inspected the address on the back; how she smiled to herself distractedly, how she slid the letter into the middle of her pile.

'I don't suppose…' He stopped. He couldn't ask, couldn't bear it if she said no.

'¿Cómo? What is it, Raúl?' Sarah was all too aware of his shyness, even after they'd known each other for several months. They'd had plenty of conversations, short ones, granted, and she'd led most of them. But wasn't he the one who'd approached her on the station platform, not the other way round? Wasn't he the one who'd offered his address and contact number first? There was a time when she thought he was potentially interested in being more than just friends, but she'd abandoned that idea as the months rolled on and nothing happened. He'd had plenty of opportunities, took none of them up. And now she didn't know if the feelings she'd had for him a while ago were still even there.

Raúl took a step closer. 'I don't suppose you'd come to the river with me?'

'The river?' Sarah looked at him, confused. 'What's with the river?'

'A picnic, by the river. Will you come?'

'Okay,' said Sarah, her heart warming. 'Let's catch the lift together and you can tell me more.' She reached for his hand and he let her take it.

They decided that St Patrick's Day was as good a day as any to have their picnic. Sarah wore a short-sleeved green midi dress and a denim jacket with limp shamrock pinned to the lapel. Her mother had sent it over from Belfast, carefully wrapped in tinfoil inside a padded envelope. The dress she'd chosen for the 'date' was a little less casual than her usual jeans and top but not too formal, not too showy.

Raúl was already waiting for her in the hallway wearing a pale green scarf.

'It was the only green thing I could find,' he said, brandishing it in the air like the string of a kite. 'Too much, do you think?'

'Not at all,' Sarah said, threading her fingers through his, relaxing next to this new version of him. She liked it, the easy manner with which he was beginning to carry himself. 'I might have to borrow it myself if the wind picks up like it did yesterday.'

'¡Sí! Of course! And you look so beautiful.' He stepped back to take all of her in, then moved towards her, kissed her lightly on each cheek. 'Let's go.' He let go of her hands, picked up his rucksack. 'We'll take a different route to the centre today,' he whispered, burying his head into her auburn hair, grazing her neck lightly with his lips. 'A quieter route. I want you all to myself.'

Sarah feels the stillness of the graveyard envelop her like a crocheted shawl. She likes it here, the peace of it, the solemn respectfulness that permeates every headstone. The love that seeps through every stone, every flower laid, every prayer said. She picks at the withered rose heads on the mound of earth in front of her, the dirt under which he's buried. She gently tears the brown brittle leaves from the dozens of garlands that line the perimeter of his grave. She unties a bunch of bright daffodils and places them in the glass vase under the wooden cross Tank has made. *Precious memories of Michael Doherty*, she reads, *loving Husband, Father and Grandfather.*

'And great-grandfather, Tank, you forgot great-grandfather.' Her smile is faint, her tears abundant. She clears her throat. 'Trust you not to be left unidentified while they prepare your headstone. Trust you, Granda.'

She kneels down next to the cross, feels a light rain brush her face and hair. 'Where do I even start?' she says, reading the inscription on the cross again. 'Where do I even look?' She glances down at the clods of earth, tries to imagine she can see through them, attempts to tunnel her vision down to where he lies. 'No, not that,' she cries, 'not that!' *Please God, not that.*

She raises her eyes to the cross again and settles on his name. Fear stalks her, but she knows she must try. Just this once. *Just once*. She focuses hard, filling her thoughts with nothing but him. His crucifix pulses at her neck and she repeats his name over and over. *Michael Doherty. Michael Doherty. Michael Doherty.*

She sees him. Kneeling on the other side of his grave, dressed in the navy suit he wore to his last wedding anniversary meal. She holds him there, misted in a haze so fragile, so fleeting.

'You oul' fool,' she says, not taking her eyes off him, 'I should have known you wouldn't go quietly. Still up to no good, even when you're not around.' She wipes her tears, joins her hands together. 'Now you listen to me,' she sighs. 'You can't start this and then abandon me. Do you hear? I don't understand and ... Jesus, I'm scared as hell ... and the last thing I want right now is to go back there.' She inhales, exhales slowly. 'Promise me you won't abandon me. Promise me!'

She stares at the other side of the grave, at the haze drifting and evaporating, at the heads of daffodils looking skyward. She removes one of the yellow flowers and watches the soft drops of rain frisk its petals. 'I know these were always really your favourites,' she says quietly.

I see you run your fingers across the inscription on the cross, I see you ruffle the heads of the daffodils. I see you, Sarah, and all I want is to extract your fear, for you to know you're not alone.

'None of us really are, though. Are we, Da?'

'Son! Praise be to God, Cormac! I'm relieved, delighted ... anxious. What was all that? I just want her to find her way, to heal. Can't you see? I have a chance now. I thought I was trapped, that she'd given up on me. I've never felt so alone.'

'But you weren't, Da.'

'What do you mean? Of course I was. I didn't have any of ... *this*. It was all taken from me...'

78

'There are always those looking out for us, even when we feel at our loneliest.'

'That's very profound, Son. I'm not sure I understand.'

'All this,' says Cormac, his tone serious, 'all of this is the workings of many. Didn't I tell you? You won't always see everything. But Sarah is ready now. Tread carefully.'

'What are you saying, Son?' I see her distant form pale, slip back into focus. 'Are you saying I can go back to that damned state, that I can lose her again? Because I can't, I won't.'

'I'm saying that you also have to navigate your way, Da. And you must guide each other. There'll be things you're scared of too.'

'I'm ready now,' I tell him. '*We're* ready now.'

I'm not afraid of the past anymore.

Day 9: Checklist

Sarah lays everything out in piles on her bedroom floor – long and short-sleeved tops in one; skirts and dresses in another; jeans, underwear, pjs. *Is that it?* It's the most haphazard form of packing she's ever undertaken, even by her standards. Her mother has prepared a checklist – *of course she has.* God forbid if she were to forget a few items of clothing, or worse, a few toiletries. She's obviously heading into the wilderness. Who knows how she ever survived when she was living and working out there? Imagine that, making her way all on her own. *Gratitude, Sarah, basic gratitude.* Still, she's thankful for the few hours to herself before her mother gets home from work.

How do you pack for a trip with a dead man, possibly two? How long does it take to revisit the site where your heart was broken, how long to unravel whatever your dead grandfather has thrown at you? There isn't a guide or manual for that. Perhaps it would have been easier for her to pack at the flat, shed some of the drama. No, that wouldn't have been the right thing to do. The speed with which the decision has been taken, the uncertainty about how long she'll be away for, all of it is taking its toll on her mother and grandmother. And besides, her summer wardrobe is still here, vacuum-sealed inside a suitcase under the bed, along with her passport, health-card, leftover euros. Pieces of her are dotted between the flat and here, the house she grew up in. She'd never given any of that much thought before. Perhaps it didn't seem fair that she should settle anywhere, considering what happened to Raúl; what she – *she* – did to him.

'Here we are, love.' Chrissie hurries in with a few plastic carrier bags and sets them on top of the bed. 'These are the bits you asked me to pick up for you.'

'You're home early,' Sarah says, sounding as upbeat as possible. She rummages through the bags. 'Great – thanks.'

Her mother fans her hot, flustered face. 'I told Mr Hennegan you were leaving tomorrow and he said I could finish up a bit earlier, make up the hours next week. Wasn't that nice of him? He's alright, you know.' She's walking up and down, not knowing what to do with herself. 'Let's get a bit of fresh air in here.' She rattles the window latch, unable to release it. 'Jesus!' It's not like her to roar, or flop onto the bed with her head in her hands.

'It's okay, Mam.' It's been a long time since Sarah's mother lost her temper, years in fact. The last time was probably when Sarah was in her teens. What can she do? Invite her to go with her, maybe? God, no, that definitely wouldn't work. And she'd never leave the family, her own mother, not now. Sarah's cheeks warm with guilt.

'Listen, Mam, I'll be back as soon as I can,' she says, hugging her tight. 'It won't be for long. And you understand why I have to go, don't you? I'll only be a phone call away.'

'I know, love.' Chrissie coughs lightly. 'I'm just being silly, a little overemotional. Don't mind me.' She straightens her shoulders, regains a little composure. 'You know I'll always support you. Now, let's get this damn packing sorted and we can have a nice evening together.'

***

It's just gone six when Amy and Annie arrive. 'How did you both time that so well?' Chrissie ushers them in from the pelting rain.

'I wasn't going to let Annie walk down in that downpour, was I, Annie?' Amy hands Chrissie her coat and helps Annie with hers. 'Not jealous at all of you, Sarah, leaving all this atrocious weather behind!'

'Oh, I know, it's almost as bad as the day of Granda's funeral out there. Isn't it, Nanny? You'd think he was having a go at us for partying without him!'

'Aye, you better believe it, and my hair got ruined that day too!' Her grandmother laughs, giving herself the once over in the hall mirror.

'Come on into the heat; Tank will be here any minute with the food.' Chrissie hands them each a small tumbler with a drop of brandy. 'Get that down you, that'll certainly warm you up!'

'Good oul' Tank,' her grandmother says, knocking back the brandy in one go. 'Our poor Catherine can't make it, working and babysitting as per usual.' Annie taps the bottom of the glass, checks she's drunk the lot. 'And I know nobody's asking, but our Mary won't be coming either. The same one already had a date lined up with her new fella. I think she's hoping for a rich man, like Saoirse O'Connell's.'

'Thanks be to God! Sure she wasn't invited anyway!' They all laugh and Sarah allows herself to relax a little. *This is all for her, and whatever happens in Spain, happens. They'll all look out for each other while she's away.*

***

I thought I was done with travelling when I got back from Spain. It took me a while to realise that I wasn't, to work out what was consuming me. You'd think a young man's first trip abroad in a war zone would be enough to put him off. And yes, to say I was relieved to get back onto familiar soil is one hell of an understatement, destitute as I was.

Some would say I walked from one conflict into another. They'd be half-right, I suppose. I also had my own business to deal with, family stuff. Christ almighty, that fairly took its toll, even after lying for weeks on end in filthy trenches, starving, fearing for my life. There's nothing as soul-destroying as your personal world being ripped apart. My Annie saved me, no doubt about that, gave me something to live for again. That woman took my carved-up heart and put it back together, piece by piece.

The first woman I ever loved, my mother, was no longer in Belfast; nor was my father. It was a complicated affair, one I haven't the strength to go into right now. Suffice to say my mother couldn't deal with the shame brought on by her son. An awful proud woman, she was, not dissimilar to my Annie in some ways, though Annie would never have disowned her own. My mother could never tolerate tittle tattle, especially when she or those belonging to her were the subject matter. And so, when my father was offered a job with a construction company in London, she was packing their bags before he'd even accepted. Tommy and I had already left for Spain by then.

It wasn't an appetite for seeing the world that took me away again, with my Annie's blessing. When you're locked in conflict, you're in no man's land, a non-place. It was more the not being able to settle, not for years. God knows, I tried — I worked my fingers to the bone on building sites, taking tremendous pride in the trade my father had taught me when I was no age, when he was forced out of the shipyard. I grafted in The Claddagh in the evenings until closing time, fell into bed and fell out of it again for a 5am start. And so it went on.

And then, one Sunday afternoon when we were all having dinner at the table, Annie took hold of my arm suddenly and whispered softly into my ear. 'Why don't you go back to whatever it was you were doing before we met?'

'Jesus, Annie, where did that come from?' Chrissie and Catherine, startled by the abruptness of my tone, dropped their cutlery. Cormac rolled his eyes and kept on eating. Mary, just a baby in my Annie's arms, continued bashing her spoon against the bowl of mash.

'It's alright now,' Annie said, shushing, fussing, 'your daddy just had a wee surprise, that's all.'

It wasn't until later that evening that we picked it up again. I went first.

'But how would you manage, love? And what about our Cormac? Surely this is the time when he needs a man about the house.'

'I always manage,' Annie said bluntly. She took my hands in hers. 'I love you, you know that, even though you drive me to distraction sometimes. But one son and three daughters later and you're still not settled. Christ, what's that all about, Michael? Now, go on, take yourself away, get it out of your system!'

That was typical of Annie, always putting me and the children first. Still the same to this day, looking after everyone else's needs before her own. The sacrifices that woman made, never a word of complaint. Christ, I loved the bones of her, still do. She'd sometimes joke with the neighbours that I abandoned her for Queen Lizzie. 'Can you imagine,' she'd say, 'him choosing to cruise about on some big ship rather than stay put with me? The man's lost his mind!'

I'd come back with some gift or other for her that you couldn't get in these parts and whisk her out to The Claddagh for a few Pimm's. 'You're a lucky woman, Annie Doherty,' I'd tell her often, 'me off expanding my territory to give you the lifestyle you're accustomed to.'

'Away on with you!' she'd say, pretending to push me away while I pulled her close into the groove moulded for her. 'Stop your nonsense now,' she'd protest, 'we'll be the talk of the place!' But she'd rest easy there, in her groove, sipping on Pimm's and lemonade, not a care in the world.

All that wasted time, it took far far too long. Christ, I've got a fair few regrets I could parcel up.

***

'Now that was lovely, thanks Chrissie. Cheers!' Tank moves around the room, clinking glasses with each of them in turn.

'As for you, love,' he sits down next to Sarah, 'are you all set for tomorrow?'

'Not you, too, Tank,' Sarah replies drowsily. *One last glass, then she'll leave them all to it.*

'The practical stuff. Now, have you sorted work?'

'Yes, Tank. Nothing to sort. Sure we're off now for Easter anyway.' She yawns. 'Sorry, it's not you, it's the *vino!*'

'And what about a place to stay?'

'She's going back to Carmina's,' her mother interjects. 'Isn't that right, love?'

'And who's this Carmina?' Tank asks, a little inquisitorially.

'She's got a B&B in the centre,' Sarah says, 'lovely little place. It's where I stayed when I went out there the first time. And she's a Godsend, helped me find my flat. You'd like her, Tank.'

Tank feels all eyes on him and shifts in his seat, conscious his cheeks are colouring. 'And has she got room, with it being Easter an' all?'

'She's fully booked for a few days, but she says there's always room for me.' Sarah gets to her feet, yawns again. 'Sorry, I'm beat out, everyone. Thanks for a lovely send off!'

'None of that saying goodbye nonsense tonight.' Her mother plants a kiss on her cheek and shoos her out the door. 'Get yourself a good night's sleep. You can save your goodbyes for the morning.'

Day 10: Holy Thursday

By the time I fully settled down for good, my Chrissie was almost twenty and Catherine wasn't too far behind her. That's hard to believe, now I think about it. Chrissie was the age our Sarah was when she first left for Spain, but she seemed a good bit older. I think it's a generational thing, the way opportunities are dealt out, what life expected from us then compared to now.

I feel guilty when I think about the amount of time I gave Sarah that I denied my own children. Not that I can take any credit for how she turned out – that was all down to my Chrissie and Martin. I always loved Sarah's enthusiasm, even if it was a touch too naïve for my liking. I loved how she embraced the adventure of going to Spain that first time, without caring about the fact she'd nowhere to stay; how the flight connection in Amsterdam didn't faze her, nor the over-weight cases she couldn't carry. Many a night's sleep I lost those first few days after she left, waiting for the phone to ring or for Chrissie to let me know she was fine. There were only so many lectures I could give the girl before she left.

I tried to give my Chrissie and Cormac a few lectures, too, back then when she was twenty and he was twenty-six. 1970, it was, and different times brought different worries. To be fair, our Cormac kept himself to himself, didn't get involved, probably because he was still living young love's dream. Almost a year married to a nice girl, Ursula, one of the Flahertys from the top of the Estate, and their first baby on the way. I'd known the Flahertys for years.

Chrissie, on the other hand, had been courting Martin Cassidy for a few months. And they were exhibiting their own version of naïve enthusiasm in the form of a terrible habit for disappearing. It caused Annie and I much distress, especially when the Estate was thick with smoke and riddled with glass. And it happened frequently, far too frequently. There were so many nights when the streets were heavy with agitated young lads and the heft of army tanks and sirens and there was no sign of them. Nights when our own house was searched and Catherine and Mary were woken out of their beds. Weeks on end when we barely closed our eyes.

Plenty of people told me I was mad to even consider opening a business at that time. But I wasn't a man to be deterred – their attitude made me even more determined – and I needed to invest in something of my own to keep my sanity. Of course, it was more than that; it was a contract with Annie. My way of showing her that I was back to stay and the running about was over. She's a worrier, deep down, my Annie, so I got much the same from her as I did from everyone else – *you'll be throwin' money away. You'll be an easy target. People don't have anythin' to spend* – but all of that made me dig my heels in even more.

And it was then that I met Tank McGinty properly for the first time. I'd known him as a young lad about the streets, and he was between my Chrissie and Cormac in terms of age. He went to school with them, too. But I wasn't around when my own children were growing up, never mind Tank, so I hadn't had a chance to form my own opinion of him.

There was talk about him going off the rails, getting himself into squabbles and scuffles, and worse. I didn't mention any of it the day Mrs McGinty hauled him into the café at the top of the road, which I was just starting to renovate.

'Any chance you could give my big son a turn, keep him off the streets?' Mrs McGinty steadied her voice and pulled back her shoulders, trying desperately to hold onto a thimble of the dignity her son's reputation had already shattered. I looked at the lump of a lad who wasn't a lad at all – he was a young adult, his polluted soul threatened with burn out. He fidgeted next to his mother, shoulders hunched, broad jaw already set.

'Is there a day's work in you, do you think?' I aimed for firm but fair and ended up sounding callous. A sweep of terror whipped his eyes and his mouth gaped as if he was about to say something. I jumped in before he could, to keep him from saying the wrong thing. 'I mean, would you like a bit of work, young man?'

'I'll do anything, Mr Doherty. I won't let you down.'

I'd say I gained a second son that day. No one was ever going to tame the fella, not completely, and I had to have words with him on several occasions. But a decent amount of labour proved a fair tonic for the big lump with the softest heart. That's what he was all those years ago, still is. I can picture him now – measuring out the café windows, sawing board after board of wood for the tables, varnishing, scrubbing the floors on his hands and knees, sweat beating off him. Not a single murmur of complaint, not when we were pulling the place together, nor when we were building it back up every time we were hit. Graft, sweat and pride – that's what made us, made the business. It was my name above the door, but it belonged to the two of us.

They say what you give out comes back to you in droves. Always been a firm believer in all that.

Sarah's head fizzes with the remnants of the previous night's send off. In a strange way, she's glad, grateful at least for the distraction it provided from the grand farewell in departures.

She clicks her seatbelt into place and holds her head back, a steadying of herself. She's no interest in the air steward's health and safety check. *Crash and burn is fine, especially today.*

It's only the second time she's taken this route – Belfast to London and on to Madrid. Normally she travels from Dublin, but a lift down there seemed too much of an ask after the week everyone had gone through.

She sizes up the empty seats next to her and smiles broadly for her own satisfaction. She wonders if it's strange that she's relieved about not having to look at anyone, hear anyone, smell anyone; not even having to talk to anyone. She doesn't care if it is. To hell with questions from strangers who don't really care what she says. If they're polite enough, they'll feign surprise, perhaps even a slither of curiosity, depending on what she tells them. She's no time for that; no energy to sift the range of responses she might provide.

Here's what she wants to think about – the last time she took this same route. It's July 2006 again, not even a year ago, and it's a sunny, unusually mild Tuesday morning in Belfast. She's sitting in row G in the aisle seat in jeans and a pink t-shirt with frilled sleeves. There's an elderly gentleman in a white shirt and blue pullover next to the window and she offers to place his coat in the overhead locker. The final few passengers file onto the plane and a smartly dressed woman who looks like she's in her early fifties asks politely if she can cross over into the middle seat. The same woman places a taupe square handbag under the seat in front of her and folds a neutral-coloured trench coat over her lap. She fans herself, fluffs her fringe, smooths the sleeves of her dress.

The man says he's going to London for a few days to visit his son and grandchildren. The woman says she's going for a theatre break with her daughter who's studying over there. *Chicago* at the Cambridge Theatre, she's so excited. Sarah says she's getting a connecting flight to Madrid to meet her boyfriend Raúl who's travelling down from Salamanca. The woman says it must be nice to get away for a few days and Sarah says no, not for a few days, this is it, they're moving in together. She says they're going to flat hunt, find something affordable, something decent and his family will help fix it up. She says she's already got a job teaching English in an Academy and some private tutoring lessons. She says yes, she knows the place, she's lived there before. She says yes, the flight fairly flew in, didn't it, and she hopes they both have a lovely stay in London.

She doesn't yet know, in that moment, that in less than two months' time a broken shadow of the woman she was that day will be flying Madrid-London-Belfast.

***

The plane touches down with a slight bump, skims the runway, taxis to gate number three. Sarah gathers her things, thanks the steward and makes her way into the terminal. She checks the board for her connecting flight, calls Carmina and asks if she can try to reserve her an overnight stay in Madrid.

'But, *cariño*,' she says, 'I thought you were coming straight here. No?'

'I'll be too exhausted,' Sarah says. 'And besides, I haven't booked my train yet.'

She hears Carmina sighing down the line, imagines her gesturing wildly regardless of whether any of the paying guests can see her, counts the sweep of the pause. '*Vale*, I'll check out some *hostales* near Chamartín so you're right by the station. Phone me when you land, I'll give you the details. Okay?'

'Okay,' Sarah says distractedly. 'Gracias.'

'*Venga, hija.* I'm so looking forward to seeing you. And promise me you'll go to the station tonight, book your train for tomorrow? It'll be busy.'

'I promise,' Sarah says, a little non-committal. Because before that, before any of that, there are other places she must visit.

Day 11: Solitude

The hushed hum of the half-empty underground train; the gilded letters of the station names blinking at her; the *señora* who removes her shopping bag from the seat to make room when there's plenty of room elsewhere; the young couple who nod hello – all of this is a welcome she doesn't deserve. But they don't know what she did – how can they? How can they know why she fled, drowning in pools of guilt and shame that have only ever shallowed? Why she exiled herself from everything she hoped to be.

And now she's back, and all she knows is that there's a cross pulsing at her neck – *his* cross – and this is where she has to be right now.

The metro stops at Pio XII and a family of four gets on. No one gets off. The doors swish shut, cocooning them within the family's sharp Texan drawl which echoes through the compartment.

This must be their first visit, Sarah thinks, listening to them debate whether Ópera or Sol is the closest stop to the Royal Palace. Beyond the family, there's a couple with their hands intertwined, her head moored to the curve of his neck. What are they – that couple, that family – other than cruel taunts of her own lost past and forbidden future?

As they pull up at the next station, the *señora* sitting opposite her straightens her bag and beams a crooked, knowing smile, as if she can read her thoughts. 'Have faith, *chica*,' she proffers as she slips past, out into the artificial orange glare that rebounds off the platform edge.

It's only now, with the woman gone and her view of the far end of the compartment no longer obscured, that she sees him.

The grey rippled strands of hair breathing on the back of his neck; the gold tail of his overcoat pleated across his lap; his face glass on glass via the screen where the carriage ends. She doesn't know if she's meant to acknowledge his presence, or if he's keeping tabs on her. She can't really explain it; for now, it's enough to know he's there.

The metro sleeks through six further stops until it reaches Ibiza. Sarah disembarks and strides assuredly to the exit, looking for signage for Retiro Park. There's no trace of the gentleman.

Within minutes, she's one of the crowd scrabbling through the main entrance to the park. Strings of cloud lace the denim blue sky and the mid-morning sun beats down to warm her bones. She fills her lungs with heat. She's ready, but for what?

This park is all a bit too grand, too fussy for me. What's with the symmetrical lines of foliage and greenery I can't identify? The bouquets of flowers in colours I can't even describe? Even white isn't white here; I'd probably call it a shimmer.

There's my Sarah, ready to endure whatever she must, while this oul' fool finds himself caught between two cultures, two women – between two separate versions of the self that never intersected. So why are we here now? The war didn't bring me to this particular spot.

My definition of a park is a bit of grass and a playground, a stroll with Annie, the grandchildren flying on swings or shooting down a slide. All this pomp and finery here wouldn't have suited us. I wasn't expecting an assault of unfamiliarity from the country I spent such important months in.

When I was last here, in Spain, I mean, I didn't see any of *this* – how can I describe it? – this warm easy manner with which people go about their business. I remember sweat and lice, cold and fear. And a woman. I found my warmth in her arms. What we had was hardly anything, timewise, but it was everything in terms of love: we were two eighteen-year-olds who didn't even share the same language. I was a different Michael Doherty back then. But love is love, isn't it? The woman's name was Ana.

***

The blue triangles of rowboats clot the inky green of the lake. And oars, lots of them, slice the water into rippled sheets. A group of women in traditional dress stroll back and forth, dropping yellow and red carnations into the hands and pockets of tourists without invitation. By the railings, a statue of a man rubbed in silver leaps every time a coin is thrown into the box by his feet.

Sarah finds a spot on the edge of a bench opposite the monument to Alfonso XII. It is here that she must see herself with Raúl.

Within moments, the two of them appear in the centre of the lake, their blue rowboat eclipsing all the others, manoeuvring to the left. Raúl cries out, 'No! The other way! We're going to hit that couple!' Sarah can't control her laughter and abandons the oars, says, 'I'm not cut out for this, you might as well take over again!' But he takes her hands first, kisses them dramatically as he kneels to play the starry-eyed lover, almost falls overboard, takes up the oars. He rows and he rows, out towards the spikes of the railings and then back, back, into their own reserved section of the lake. And he says, 'You're sure about this, aren't you?' And she says, 'I've never been surer.' And she leans across to kiss him and the boat tilts suddenly and this time, it is she who almost falls overboard. But he catches her, he saves her and now he looks at her in that way that says he loves every inch of her, every speck of her, and always will. And he asks her again, 'Are you sure?' and she says, 'I've never been surer.' And he rows back, a little further back still, until all Sarah sees is a shush of blue on green.

That's what they were like, her and Raúl, a shush of blue on green. Clashed for some, beautifully complementary for others.

***

The dip in light and growl in her stomach tell her she's been walking a long time. Hours in fact, past kiosks with locals buying newspapers and tourists looking for postcards; cafes teeming with customers in pavement terraces; men and women, boys and girls in band uniforms and dark robes. The incessant thrum of drums in the near distance spurs her on and soon she is swaddled amongst hands bejewelled with the pearls of rosary beads, mouths that whisper words she assumes are prayers, faces looking upward. She looks up too, at the image of Nuestra Señora de la Soledad y Desamparo, Our Lady of Solitude and Destitution, surrounded by white roses, held high by white gloved hands. Sarah examines the sober expressions of the carriers and that of the Virgin, her gold heart speared with swords. She permits her own grief to settle there just for a while: shrouded, impaled.

The sky is coal black by the time she finds a free table in a side street cafe. She'll eat and sleep and tomorrow – yes, tomorrow – she'll catch the train to Salamanca.

Day 12: Sandstone City

It's just gone midday when the train pulls into Salamanca station. They're a few minutes late and Sarah's glad of the minor delay, even though it makes no difference whatsoever. It's just another stab at self-delusion, a fleeting thought that she can put off what she's come here for. A shade of anxiety threatens to creep; she won't allow it. She imagines instead that the crucifix furrows gentle waves of heat across her chest and recalls the first time she stepped into the *Plaza Mayor*.

She stands in the shadow of one of its magnificent arches, tense with excitement. She checks her watch – 3pm – and half closes her eyes to allow the shoal of sounds to thrum through her: the purr of conversations; the clatter of glasses against trays; the clack of heels against cobbles; the churning chime of the town hall clock. She contemplates how many students, like her, didn't even know this place existed until it appeared on a list of year abroad options. The sugary aroma of sweet fried bread in a nearby oven makes her salivate and she wonders which café is serving the garlic seafood mix.

She's actually going to be living here: nine whole months away from moody skies and family chit chat. Some individuals start by moving into halls or flats in a nearby city. Not her. She's going straight from the grey concrete of the Estate to a blue cloudless sky in north-west Spain at the age of twenty. A gift, surely a gift, she tells herself, as she tries and fails to navigate the grooves between the cobbles that stretch teasingly across the square. Heels and luggage wheels catch and grind and she chastises herself for not packing smarter.

It's not your typical Sunday in Belfast where nothing is open – except churches and chapels – out of respect for the day of worship. Definitely no sign of rest here. Tourists hum like bees, relaxing in busy terraces or seeking shade on one of the wooden benches between the archways. A group of finely-dressed women, probably in their fifties, gossip and stroll unashamedly across the *plaza* in fake fur coats. She wishes she had the nerve to parade about like that, never mind the stamina to do so in the sweltering August temperatures. Sallow-skinned barmen, neglected by the sun, are reduced to silhouettes against narrow windowpanes and four student musicians serenade a group of girls under the clock. The strained screech of guitars and male voices is bad enough, but are they really dressed up in Tudor kings' cast-offs? Who'd fall for anyone modelling those ridiculous gold and burgundy robes?

She continues tackling the gaps between the cobbles, with little success, cursing her stupidity. Everything aches now.

'You sure you're sure?'

'Not anymore,' she tells Raúl, relief drowning her laugh. 'Pathetic, isn't it?' It's her turn to stand awkwardly, expectantly.

The clock chimes above them. It's quarter past three.

***

The world beyond the carriage window pocked with passenger fingerprints seems unreal; at best, it resembles a blurred cityscape image taken by an amateur photographer. Carmina stands on the other side of the platform in the blur, her knee-length red coat skimming the indent of her slim waist. She holds a small black clutch with both hands, showing off her blood red nails which match her coat. Her thick loose curls have been recently set and are as dark as Sarah remembers them. She hasn't aged at all; she looks no different to the forty-year-old woman Sarah met for the first time five years previously. If anything, the passing of time is rejuvenating her, smoothing out the soft lines around her eyes and mouth, the crinkles in her hands, the fine creases peppering her neckline.

'Come here, *cariño!*' She pushes unapologetically through the waiting crowd and wraps Sarah into the heat of her embrace, settles a kiss on each of her cheeks. Sarah is only too aware of the hollowness of her body as Carmina skims the smallness of her waist, the narrowness of her back.

'Skin and bone you are, *chica*, but don't worry.' Her dark eyes and smile offer coordinated kindness, concern. 'A few weeks with me and we'll have you glowing again. *Vamos.*'

Sarah lets her take her case and trails behind her to the taxi stand. 'Today you rest, *cariño*,' Carmina calls back, her voice chirruping in the still air. 'But tonight ... tonight we celebrate.'

'What are we celebrating?' Sarah plays along, quickens her pace. At least the ease with which the language is coming to her makes her feel a bit more like herself — teaching children isn't the same as everyday conversation. Another step forward, she thinks, one less thing to worry about.

'Life and plenty more of it!' Carmina claps her hands and greets the taxi driver like a long-lost friend, before sliding into the passenger seat.

'You alright, Da? How does all this feel?'

'Feel? Is that what we're still calling it? There's no denying I feel out of sorts. And not understanding everything that woman is saying doesn't help. So that's the famous Carmina?'

'Certainly is. But sure, you know better than anyone, communication comes in all shades and forms, doesn't it?'

'True, Son, very true.'

'What's it like being back here ... back where your life once was?'

'My life? Here? God no, not in this city, Son.'

'What do you mean?'

'This is where my ghosts reside ... the stories of my ghosts to be accurate. Those that haunted me ... still do.'

'Well, get ready, Da. There are old friends here.'

97

Day 13: Shells and Teardrops

'Won't you come with me, Sarah? They do a lovely Easter Sunday service.'

Pale belts of sunlight skip through the slats of the dining room window, striping the table gold. The latch on the main door clicks shut and there is a scuffle of feet on the rusted tiles outside. The radio croons from the kitchen, too low for Sarah to make out anything the presenter is saying. She swirls her coffee, inhaling the strong, nutty smell of it.

'I'm sorry, Carmina, not today.' Guilt, guilt at leaving Carmina to attend alone, jabs at her. It is another brick in the prison wall she is constructing for herself – a wall which will sentence her to a lifetime of solitude and regret if she's not careful.

But she's not yet ready for another church service. She wishes she could hear her grandfather breathe again: even the final rattle in his chest would do. She thinks 'service' and all she can visualise is his absence, the heavy cut of his coffin isolating his decaying corpse. The white roses from the funeral and her more recent gift of daffodils flaunt their blooms mockingly over the waste of the man inside.

She craves the solemn comfort of Friday just past – the sighs of mourning, the prayers of devotion. She needs the warm air of this city to thaw her thoughts and heart.

'I'll make it up to you, I promise.'

'I know you will, *hija*. Take some time out, we'll eat at 3pm. *¿Vale?* I've everything prepared.'

'You're too good to me.' Sarah means every word of it. Who else opens their arms and their home without judgment after six months of abandonment and silence? This woman has waited; she has never probed or questioned. Sarah's own family eventually left her alone, respected her privacy, burdened themselves with worry – *her* worry – without understanding what it was. Who else knows her like Carmina, allows her to shut down temporarily for as long as she needs? Paco probably does, only Paco, the son Carmina never had.

Sarah accompanies her to the door, past the ceramic wall tiles in bursts of blue and yellow engravings that hold a myriad of stories. She wonders if she would have turned out the same if she'd had her own son or daughter.

Carmina slips on her red coat, clips decisively down the steps and waves without turning back.

Apart from the distant lull of the radio, nothing else disturbs the calm of *El Pintor*. The other guests, five in total, have already left for the day, eager to explore as much of the city as possible. The retired banker from Kent, Jonathan, was the last to leave after being the last to arrive the previous night. It had taken him just ten years to get there, he'd said with a half-smile, his eyes globes of tears, after he'd had to cancel his initial plans when his wife passed away suddenly. 'It didn't seem right to come without her,' he'd said quietly, 'because this was the place of her dreams, not mine. But now I'm ready to bring her here, in my heart.'

Sarah considers the other guests – the elderly French couple, the young American student in the middle of her gap year in Europe, the forty-something woman from Edinburgh – and wonders whether they too have made the trip for someone else. She wonders whether this guest house teems with ghosts seeking solace. She senses no trace of her grandfather, nor of Raúl here. Will this be the resting place of her own ghost? She grabs her jacket and steps out into the street.

First, she turns onto Calle Quintana, then left onto Rúa Mayor, walking briskly in the direction of the University and Cathedral Quarter. At Calle Jesús, she makes a slight right turn towards the House of Shells.

Something is pulling her in that direction, off course from her desired route to the Philology building. She's fond of the Shell House with its calm grandeur and its scalloped shells, symbols of penitent pilgrims – humans much more decent than she is.

The street is unusually quiet, ostracised from the Easter celebrations. There are a few tourists having photos taken with the mansion in the background and a few others staring skyward, revelling in the expanse of scallop shells that decorate its exterior. None of them, however, seem to notice the floating man just above the door next to the coat of arms. *Floating. As if she hasn't seen enough already.* He leans sideways into the façade, the sleeves of his white flannel shirt folding into the dip of his elbows as he trowels the wall, securing one of the shells into place. He's the sort of grafter her grandmother likes. There's a scattering of smaller shells balancing on the hawk in his left hand.

'Ah you're here, love,' the man says in a thick Irish accent, pointing the trowel at her like a makeshift wand. Sarah hopes this fella doesn't have eyes that materialise and then disappear; she prays they're only invisible due to the weight of the grey ill-fitting tweed cap he's wearing. She looks about her for any sign that he could be addressing someone else – anyone else but her.

'I'll be right with you.' He descends slowly to the ground, his shirt sleeves flapping in the breeze, the hawk perfectly still in his hand so as not to disturb the shells. *He's no angel.*

Sarah can make out very little of him. The broad peak of the cap casting his face in shadow makes it impossible to determine his age. When he lands gracefully right in front of her like a dove of peace, a shell offered in place of an olive branch, she sees rivulets of tears running down the length of his face, seeping into the collar and front of his shirt.

'I'm glad you came,' he begins, wringing out his shirt onto the cobbles in a steady stream that rises to Sarah's ankles. She winces in dismay. None of the tourists present are fortunate enough to see him or receive the gift of water. Underneath the cap, his red hair is poker straight and sticks to his scalp and forehead. The watery emeralds of his eyes are set deep within his youthful, freckled face. She thinks he can't be more than twenty years old. 'I've something to show you,' he says.

'Show me?' Sarah is surprised by the boldness of his statement. 'But you don't even know me.'

'Ah, now, yes I do,' the man says, setting down the hawk and removing one of the shells to hold it close. His tears fall easier now, lightly, pooling inside the shell, dissolving into tiny flakes of ash.

A memory gatherer and a water carrier. Anyone else, Granda?

The man tips the ash into his hand, blows gently and watches the morning breeze carry it away.

'That's better,' he says, holding out a shell to Sarah for the second time. 'Take it.' The streaks on his face fade to dust as Sarah regards him, trying to get the measure of him. 'Now, where was I?' He clears his throat. 'Ah yes ... what I mean is ... I know all about you.'

'About me?' Sarah is a little flustered now. *What can this man have to do with her?* 'I think you must be mistaken, Mr...'

'... Call me Charlie.' He extends a pale hand to her. She shakes it dubiously and offers the shell back to him.

'You hold onto it for now,' he says, backing away. 'Bring it back whenever you're ready to see what I have for you.'

She is about to protest, but he's gone, evaporated into the swarm that bustles in the street now, or through the walls of the shell house, she's not sure. She turns on her heels and starts heading back to the *hostal*, abandoning her plan to visit the Philology building.

What was that all about, eh, Granda? She passes the restaurant where she celebrated her twenty-first birthday, the *Tabacos* where Raúl used to get his cigarettes, the bookshop where she spent far too much money, the bar on the corner with the best *tapas*.

And what is the point of this thing? She clutches the shell nervously, wants nothing to do with it.

'Cormac, is this for real? Charlie never set foot in this city. What in God's name is he doing here? Jesus, my heart is going to shatter all over again. I don't know how I survived his death.'

'Yes, Da, it's Charlie. He's here to help you, insisted on it.'

'Christ. I loved that man. I don't know why he got taken out and I didn't. Who else is here?'

'The other one's working away; he'll be about soon. But first, tell me about Charlie, Da. You've never mentioned a Charlie.'

'I know, Son. He's another one I had to bury. It's been years since I saw the face of him. And the face is exactly the same – dead youngsters don't age.

'Charlie was always very like me, holding back while Tommy and a pile of the other lads were in the spotlight. It's probably the reason why we stayed so close. We were on a similar wavelength, had no position at all in the street hierarchy. I never said much; neither did he. But, Jesus, he used to shed a fair few tears. I used to joke that I'd get the pots out to catch them in the scorching summer months when the family could do with a drop more water. We milked them too, to get a free something from the shop or a few coins on the street when people felt sorry for him. He could fairly turn them on when he wanted to. God knows how long Sarah will tolerate him.

'On a serious note, though, poor Charlie seemed to carry the weight of the world on his shoulders. Often enough I told him that other people's problems weren't his own and to save his tears for when he needed them most. No talking to him. Still no talking to him by the looks of things. And of course, some of the lads tried to make a fool out of him, mistaking his tears for cowardice. They got their comeuppance when they pushed him too far. He wasn't a bit soft, ignored their taunts and name calling. Where were they when he signed up, like me, for another country's war? He certainly wasn't too soft then. Those same lads, apart from Tommy, weren't such big brave men ready to join the call.

'It's starting to make sense, Son, Charlie turning up here, of all places. He'd have done anything for me. Trust him with my life. And Sarah's.'

'Have you been shopping without me, *hija*?' Sarah doesn't say anything as she hands Carmina the shell. Carmina turns it over, runs her fingers along the ribs of its fan. 'Imagine you going off and getting an Easter gift!' Her laugh is loud, kind. She hands it back and opens the door. 'Come on,' she says, 'you can tell me where you got it.'

Sarah will tell her soon. But first, she needs to find out if one man is dead and reread the letter of another who probably is.

Day 14: Absences

I'm getting more used to the pale moments of reflection when the absences of Cormac and Sarah render me deaf and blind. It's just me, then, and those I choose to recall. No fear, no judgment.

Me and Charlie were always close in a way that Tommy and I weren't. It's hard to pinpoint, however, exactly when us two began to drift apart. Years we spent working alongside each other, honing our craft, tight as ever. Whether it was new windows being replaced, a piece of furniture that needed fixing or a bit of paintwork that needed touching up, we turned up together and shared the work between us. He had all the banter, I wrestled with all the embarrassment. The slightest compliment and I burned with shame. But Tommy, he revelled in it – I laboured away stony silent while he grafted and did all the sweet talking.

I suppose it happened when I stopped heeding him, when I took stock of how often his mouth got him into trouble. There were several things he brought to our door which weren't taken kindly to. I would have been in my mid-teens then, getting to grips with my own principles, with what made sense. Tommy ran with a different crowd, always in the limelight, their unofficial spokesperson. I'd happily hide in his shadow, loved him even when I didn't like him very much.

Who would have thought that another country's politics, not even our own, would have caused the definitive split between us? The war never brought me to this city which has haunted me for years. This was never my city.

It was Tommy who came here with the Irish Brigade, while me and Charlie went to Madrigueras. And then, when Sarah told me she was coming to study here ... here, of all places ... I wasn't sure what to make of it. There was so much I wanted to say but couldn't, so much threatening to throw itself up which I had consigned to the grave. I didn't want to implicate Sarah in a past that wasn't hers. And now, I worry about the extent to which this city haunts her, too.

I've always wondered what happened to Tommy. They told me things and my gut told me something different and I was left forever not knowing. I saw you at Jarama, or at least I think I did, for the head and heart play awful tricks on the battlefield. Did they ever tell you about me and Charlie when it was all over? Did you get to see the end? I sense something of you here, slipping and seeping through the city, through my thoughts, and I don't know what to do about it. I pray you rest easy, wherever you are.

As she stands by the intercom, waiting, Sarah's expression is vacant, her body weak with apprehension. She steps back from the shade of the building into Avenida de Portugal, the soothe of the cool breeze lost on her. The sky is powdery blue, cloudless.

The door buzzes menacingly and she jumps forward to swoop the handle. She cannot miss her chance to enter – it might be her only one.

Once inside, she is haunted by the unsolicited memories of their meet ups in the inner hallway: early starts for lectures, both of them lugging books too big to fit into rucksacks; late returns with overfilled shopping bags; the choking smell of bleached floors; the swish of the lift opening on the ground floor. She rushes to the stairwell: six flights of steps to banish five years of memory-making.

'Hola,' María says bluntly. Only María could somehow turn one two-syllable word into an uncompromising threat. A greeting downgraded to a dismissal, just like that. She looks Sarah up and down, slices through her with the cut of her glacial stare.

Sarah inhales slowly, holds her breath. She and María only ever tolerated each other for Raúl's sake. And now María holds all the cards; she's the one who will break the news about whether he's dead or alive. Sarah steadies herself for the worst after six months of absence.

'Please, María, I just need one moment of your time.' Grief saturates her voice; she knows María will be sensing it, relishing every second of it.

'You've some nerve turning up here after what you did.' María flashes her a look of disgust. 'What have you come for, anyway? To pretend you're sorry, now that … now that he's over the worst?'

'Over the worst? You mean he's alive?' *He's alive, not dead. Alive.* 'Can I see him?' she asks meekly.

María shakes her head violently. 'Absolutely not,' she replies, enunciating each syllable. 'And you mean to tell me you didn't even know? Turning up here, not knowing if we had to bury him? Really? You're something else. Go away, *guapa.*'

'Bloody hell, María!' Without thinking, Sarah pushes her face into hers. 'Since when were you his keeper anyhow?'

María grins callously, measures up every inch of her. She then steps back into the hall, shakes her head in disgust. 'I'll tell him the *irlandesa* called,' she sneers, 'but best if you take yourself off back home. There's nothing for you here.'

'Is that right? You don't get to tell me what to do, *guapa.*' Sarah slams her hand against the wall; the door slams in her face.

***

'I think you need this,' Carmina says, passing her a glass. 'Sounds like you gave as good as you got. And at least you know now.'

Sarah nods, takes the glass. 'Yes, but I don't know everything, I don't know what state he's in. *Over the worst,* she said. What

106

does that even mean? And who the hell does María think she is, anyhow? My relationship with Raúl is damn all to do with her.'

'*Hija.*' Carmina takes her hand and indicates the *plaza*, alight with the soft dance of lanterns flooding each archway. 'Look at all of this ... whatever happened ... whatever happens from this point is not in your control. Raúl is a grown man. You can't force anything.'

'But I can try to speak to him, find out what's going on.'

'Of course. And you can stay for as long as you like.'

'Thank you.' Theirs is a friendship Sarah vows never to take for granted.

'I've enough going on with my grandfather anyway. It's him I'm meant to be here for.' Sarah reaches into her bag and takes out a folded note, thin as tracing paper. The blonde light of the lanterns splices through it, catching the curled black tails of letters which Sarah has already committed to memory. 'There's something I'd like to show you, something that was also in the box,' she says quietly. 'A letter for my grandfather. Here.'

'No, *cariño,*' Carmina says, pushing her hand away, 'you should read it.'

'Okay.' Sarah unfolds it carefully, pauses for a moment to compose herself.

Madrid, Spain, July 1939
My dear Michael,

It's time I write to you to tell you we are safe. We have enough to eat, somewhere to stay and everyone is in good spirits, despite everything.

I will write you again soon.
Regards,
José Luis Hernández López

'That's all there is.'

'Then that's all you need. For now. Your grandfather will pave the way. One step at a time.'

Sarah feels for the photograph in her pocket and looks past Carmina to two figures standing just a few metres away, silhouetted against the butterscotch columns of the clock tower. They stare into the central light of the *plaza*, the first holding a notebook, the second a shell. Between them, Sarah thinks she sees the outline of a young woman, hair curling into the nape of her neck, drifting in and out of focus.

'Yes,' she says, holding the three figures within her gaze and heart; she won't release them, or Raúl. Not yet. 'I have all I need.'

Day 15: Silences and Discoveries

The *plaza* murmurs with goings-on behind closed doors in the low light of the early morning. It's just gone 7:30am when Sarah passes through on her way back to Avenida de Portugal. She knows it's too early for visitors, but this is her best chance of speaking with Raúl. *Her* Raúl. Alive. Isn't he? This can't be one of María's cruel tricks. Even she wouldn't stoop so low.

Perhaps Raúl will be stirring, throwing off the shackles of sleep. María will have already left for work, she's sure of it. Sarah knows she won't have told Raúl about her calling the previous day.

As she crosses the cobbles, her thoughts are as confused and anxious as ever, not understanding the man she's hoping to find. She walks along Calle Zamora, hears the faint whirr of cleaning trucks in distant shadowed side streets. The grey road tiles glittering in pockets of misshapen puddles tell her they've already been here. The street pleats around her, the sleek narrowness of it, the grandeur of its golden façades and iron-grilled balconies, the peppering of old-fashioned streetlamps. She and Raúl had looked at an apartment here, knowing that it was too far out of their league. It was her idea; he went along with it, of course. He'd have done anything for her, back then.

Within moments, she finds herself outside the entrance to the Church of St Mary Magdalene. She runs her palm across the broad sand blocks of its exterior, reacquainting herself with the place she used to visit regularly. Raúl had pointed it out to her one evening when they were walking home from lectures, told her that the building was in fact a church. She'd been walking past it for a few weeks by then and didn't believe him. Nestled between shops with no obvious markings, neglected like a sorry piece of concrete, she'd thought it was some sort of government office. It was only when she'd moved to the far side of the street that she got a view of its twin bell tower. Its name etched modestly in bronze lettering to the left of the entrance had completely passed her by.

Intrigued, she'd stepped inside, expecting to find a plain shell to match the blandness of its exterior. Instead, she'd encountered a marble altar flanked by shiny golden columns and intricately decorated interior windows. A holy theatre of sorts, she'd thought. Something about it captivated her, gave her a sense of belonging within a city she was still learning to be part of. She returned regularly and with each visit, she found a fleeting inner peace, as if something was cloaking her in warmth, kindness. Something was offering her protection, if only temporarily.

When she received the news about Raúl's accident, she stopped going there. Protection and recovery for him were what she wanted, not for herself. Not when she was the instigator of his accident. María had told her he might not make it, and if he did, he might have life-changing injuries.

This church still can't tempt her inside, not yet. It's only been six months and she still doesn't know what's happened to him, not fully. And her grandfather's death on top of that. It's all too much. Time and healing – that correlation makes no sense to her. No one knows her heart.

Despite not knowing for sure, despite the questions and guilt, she feels something akin to warmth, there on the street, something attempting to envelop her. It's as if someone or something has been expecting her; an additional beat of life offering itself, if she'll accept it.

***

Sarah presses the buzzer and steps back to check the balcony for any sign of life. *One last try*, she thinks, moving forward, pressing the apartment number again, stepping back. *Come on, Raúl, please be alive. Please don't shut me out.* She remembers how the buzzer sound used to pierce the apartment walls, disturbing deep sleep and drifting conversations. For a moment she considers trying her old flat, 2H, but she knows that her flatmates, Rocío and Lucía, moved out a few months ago, just after Christmas. There's also 4G, the one that she and Raúl were hoping to buy, the one drenched in natural light with a corner balcony overlooking the street. The one that they were meant to populate with their memories.

In her typically impulsive way, she'd begun making plans before the paperwork had been finalised. They'd paint the frame of the balcony doors daffodil yellow and replace the beige fabric ceiling shades with glass ones. They wouldn't keep the previous owner's warped old bench; they'd invest in a comfortable bistro set for two. They'd get a cat, perhaps a patched tabby like the stray her father found on the frost-thick pavement outside their house one freezing winter's night. They'd give it a Spanish name, or perhaps a double-barrelled Spanish-Irish one.

A serious-looking young woman in a black trouser suit is about to leave the building. Sarah takes in her stare, the puzzled look about her, as she holds the main door open against her slender hip. The woman decides that Sarah has no place there and slams the door shut, shuddering its metal frame.

Furious, Sarah follows her at a short distance, back down Avenida de Italia and into Calle Zamora. *Who does she think she is, playing God!* The woman's stride is assured, the snap of her heels stamping authority where there's no one to regard it. There's no way Sarah will give up on Raúl, not yet, but she'll deal with the situation her way. No snapping, no stamping; she won't be beaten, not by María, not by this woman desperate to make her mark, not by her own demons and obsessions.

Everything about the street is so far removed from life back home. Perhaps when all of this is done, a school trip with her older pupils might be a possibility. If she manages to get her job back, that is – she never told her mother or grandmother that she was only covering maternity leave and her time was up. She'd sacrificed the permanent contract when she left in the summer to make a life with Raúl. That wasn't a worry they needed to bear. Perhaps when she untangles what happened here, whatever the outcome might be, it might make room for her to be herself again.

At the Church of St Mary Magdalene, she stops momentarily, tilts her head upwards and fills her lungs with the sweetness of the air. With her eyes firmly shut, she imagines Michael sitting at the scullery table, smiling at a pile of charity shop books piled on the table in front of him. She imagines Raúl twirling her round in the hallway of their building, his green eyes glowing at the sight of her. No one else had ever settled their eyes on her like him.

She continues down the street, nodding to those who catch her eye and quietly wishing a good morning to silent workers unshuttering windows and doors ready for the day's trade. She's not giving up.

On the pavement outside *El Pintor*, Charlie is hovering a few feet off the ground in the same clothes from the previous day. The passing tourists pay him no attention; Sarah wishes she could not see him. She's not in the mood today, but she won't jeopardise the chance to speak with him either.

Charlie holds his cap outstretched like a begging bowl rather than a tear catcher and sucks his bottom lip nervously, his gaze fixed on the large pool of water by his feet.

'Are you looking for me?'

'Oh, there you are,' Charlie says straightening up, relief in his voice. 'Are you ready?'

'I am,' Sarah says, forcing herself to sound bright. 'I just need to get the shell first.'

'Oh, that can wait. You can bring it when I see you next.' He nods reassuringly and tips his cap back, freeing a crop of auburn fringe to sheathe his eyes.

Sarah says nothing, aware that nothing here is hers to control, and walks alongside him. She notices how Charlie's shirt creases and billows like a ruffled cotton ball in the light breath of morning.

'I don't mean to speak out of turn,' she says eventually, 'and feel free to say no ... But ... do you mind if I ask you a question?'

'Go for it, love.'

She hesitates a moment. 'Why is it ... Jesus, why do you cry so much?'

Charlie bursts into laughter, dimpling his cheeks. 'Just come straight out with it, why don't you? Now, where do I start with that! It's a very long story.'

'I don't mind. I have time.'

'Oh, but you might mind!' Flushes of pink creep onto his neck and he pulls his cap a little further over his eyes. Sarah feels sorry for him and tries to manage her own discomfort at a man shielding his eyes from her, rather than from the first blinks of sunlight.

'I was always an awful worrier,' he blurts out, quickening his pace. 'And now here I am worrying about you.'

'Thanks, but you don't need to do that, I've enough people looking out for me.'

'And I'm one of them,' he says. 'No arguments. Right, this way.'

Sarah follows, though there's much about all this she would change if she could. But it's not hers to tamper with, she knows that. Raúl is a different matter altogether, even with María in the way.

Charlie suddenly veers right towards the House of Shells, retracing the same steps Sarah took the previous day. 'C'mon,' he shouts back, speeding ahead. 'I wanna get you in before the rest of the world descends.'

'Coming,' she says, wading through the golden and silvery streams of water that mark the pavement in his wake. *As if it matters if the rest of the world descends because all of this is just for her. There are certain things she'll share with Carmina, but not the presence of this man, illusion, whatever it is.*

The inner courtyard of the mansion is luminous in the sun's flare. Above it, the spires of the cathedral tip the fluff of light clouds. Honeycomb balconies swaddle the fountain in the centre and nothing breaks the silence, not even breath. A sweet dew perfumes the air.

'Up there,' Charlie whispers, pointing to the upper balcony opposite them. 'Watch carefully. Don't be afraid.'

As if on Charlie's instruction, a black banner secured to three marble columns begins to unfurl itself slowly, inching its way down past the balconies to the matching columns at ground level. At first, all Sarah can see is a panel of red roses stretching horizontally and then dropping vertically. Down, down, the swirl of roses fall before the woman's face begins to appear – her dark curls framing her wide bright eyes, her light smile pausing on the corners of her mouth.

'My God, what is this? What are you doing?' She muffles her cries in the sleeve of her jacket and her body begins to tremble. She won't allow herself to be frightened, she knows this is meant to be. *This is meant to be. But Granda, who is this woman? What has she got to do with you?*

Sarah reaches for one of the rear columns to steady herself and feels for the photo in her pocket. She spins around and holds it out to Charlie.

'I know,' he says quietly. 'Her name is Ana. We both knew her.'

'Who do you mean by both?' *No, no, no.*

Sarah's mind races, not with the possible answers that Charlie might give – she knows what he'll say. She's dizzy trying to determine what this means for her, her mother, her grandmother. She can no longer bury this woman's face, pretend she's not real.

'Tell me about her. I need more, you know I do.'

'Trying to make sense of everything is futile,' Charlie says finally, moving in slow motion towards the image. 'You'll know more soon, maybe even see her, if you'll allow yourself. But sometimes we just have to let things be and know that they'll make sense – eventually. You're not alone, Sarah.'

'I know I'm not.' Sarah's voice is quiet. 'But sometimes I wish I was. It might be easier.'

'I understand.' Charlie pauses. 'But you're here for answers, aren't you?'

He holds the door open for her; a gentle breeze slips through and tousles the trim of the wall hanging. Sarah examines the image one last time, her eyes darting from the banner to the photo. She doesn't yet know, can't know, how long Ana has been waiting for her.

'You're right,' she says finally, making her way to the exit. 'I'm looking for answers and I'm not leaving without them, however tough this gets.' She notices the street is awash with gold and silver twines of Charlie's tears and wishes she could pour out her own worry there too.

'Come find me tomorrow,' Charlie says, drying his cheeks and brow. I have one more thing to show you.'

Day 16: *Old Acquaintances*

'Guess who's arriving today, *hija*?'

Carmina flits butterfly-like around the kitchen in a wraparound dress striped in blocks of turquoise, yellow and red. She turns the radio up, shimmies, turns it down. She sits down, dips a *magdalena* into a bowl of warm milk, takes a bite, stands up again.

Sarah can't help but smile. Her mind burrs with questions and expectations and the sight of Carmina flouncing around is a welcome distraction. She loves how she can make an empty room feel so full of life with the simplest of things; how her love for her nephew runs so deep that it makes her bubble over like this.

In all the years Sarah has known her, Carmina has told her so little about herself. She knows that she came to Salamanca in need of a fresh start thanks to some money inherited from an elderly aunt. She knows that when she saw *El Pintor* was on the market, she figured she had enough life experience to run a *hostal*. It took her a couple of years to refurbish and get the place fully up and running. She knows that the business hadn't been open very long when a twenty-year-old auburn-haired Irish woman turned up on the doorstep looking for a room. But there's much she doesn't know – what Carmina left behind in Madrid, why she never settled down, whether she misses anyone or anything. And she's fine with that. Carmina's unknown past has never prompted her to ask questions and Carmina has only ever listened to what Sarah herself has wanted to share. Theirs is a friendship based on respect for discretion in private matters.

'It must be someone very special for you to be all dressed up at this hour of the day.' Sarah can't help but tease her a little. 'Where's the boyfriend taking you?'

'Oh, *hija*,' Carmina says, swooping round to face her, flicking her hair over her shoulder. 'No boyfriend could be a match for this young man!' She waves a finger at her, laughing.

Sarah's heart skips a little. 'It's not Paco, by any chance?' she asks, playing along, knowing that it can only be him.

'Of course it is!' Carmina says, slapping her palm against the edge of the table. She slides into the seat next to Sarah, rests her hand against her chin conspiratorially and fixes her eyes on her.

'Oh no, not this again!' Sarah laughs, feels her cheeks flush in embarrassment. Carmina and her matchmaking obsession have been constant ever since she and Paco met all those years ago. Even when Sarah was with Raúl, Carmina still joked about what she was missing out on. According to her, no one was a patch on Paco.

It was obvious to Sarah what sort of person Paco was when she first met him: a decent, kind human being; soft-centred. He was like the brother she'd never had, or perhaps she told herself that because she was romantically involved with someone else. He felt the same way about her; he used to call her his long-lost sister, twin even, given that their birthdays were only days apart. Nothing either of them could say could ever convince Carmina.

'You know what they say,' Carmina quips, batting her heavy lashes. 'You won't know until you try. And neither of you are getting any younger!'

'My God, Carmina! We're only twenty-five! And you can talk!' Sarah giggles and wraps her arms around her. 'What time is he arriving? I'll make sure I'm back.'

'Back from where? Are you're going to try Raúl again?' Carmina pulls away; her eyes instantly widen, anxious. She clears her throat. 'I'm sorry. It's none of my business, *cariño.*' She reaches for her cup on the other side of the table and takes a small sip. 'Please ignore me.'

'Don't worry,' Sarah says, 'I've got a plan.'

'A plan?' Carmina takes another sip.

'Yes. But not today. I've got other things to be doing.'

'I'm very glad to hear it! Now go and get yourself ready, Paco will be here by 2pm.' Carmina springs to her feet and turns up the volume on the radio again.

From the hallway, Sarah watches her dance, her reflection sketched in faded strokes across the kitchen window. She thinks how she'd like to be a reflection of this warm, kind, beautiful woman; a woman much loved, comfortable in her own solitude.

***

From the far side of the Roman bridge, Sarah takes in the sweep of the city she never thought she'd return to. The stretch of boxy white buildings with terracotta roofs skirt the old and new cathedrals and remind her of hollow cardboard cut-outs. It all feels a little unreal to her, the way the cathedrals' spires pierce the quilted sky and deep dive into the shallows of the Tormes River in blurred impressions. There's a floating city skimming the surface of the cold sapphire water into which Sarah might have chosen to submerge herself once before.

Not today. She makes her way across the bridge that suspends her above the city's mirror image and re-enters the streets that entice and elude her.

***

'Isn't this shaping up to be one beautiful day!' Charlie is kneeling in the yard outside the Archive building, grouting a few of the burnt orange tiles that chequer its entrance. 'Did you find us okay, love?' He gets to his feet and surveys his work, then doffs his cap at Sarah like she's someone important. The absence of tears bodes well, she thinks.

'Us? What do you mean? And I've been here before,' she says, taking the note from her pocket, unfolding it. 'But I've never been looking for anything. Just passing through, doing the touristy thing.'

'Well, there's a first for everything.' She feels his eyes on her as she rereads the note. 'It's personal,' she says, not wishing to share anything more for now.

'Of course. After you, love,' Charlie says, holding the door for her. 'There's someone waiting for you in there.'

Murmurings of visitors and a soft rumble of recorded footage playing in a nearby room filter into the entrance where Sarah skims the mahogany-framed information board.

'Wait here,' Charlie says, 'I'll go and get him.'

Anxiety prickles Sarah's neck, making the note quiver in her hands. She's meant to be here, but the sight of the posters on the wall beside her remind her of the reality of the war she's entering, the Spanish Civil War, of lives lost and hearts broken. She tries to imagine the crucifix throbbing at her chest, reminding her she's not alone.

Images of Franco and maps of Spain are plastered over the wall next to her; women and children, eyes wide with fright; armed soldiers, Republican and Nationalist slogans, and his name – FRANCO FRANCO FRANCO. Her head starts spinning, images colliding, collaging, guns and bombs and blood – so much blood – and rotting flesh.

'It's so nice to see you again, Sarah.'

'What? You!' His face is glacial, eyes absent, his coat lustreless in reverence to the dead souls screaming from the walls. Sarah instinctively retreats, then stops herself. 'They sent you here?'

'I've worked as an archivist before,' he says, his voice gentle, measured. 'And I've prepared what you need. Come with me.'

As she tries to block out the sound of death cries and images of shattered bodies, the man turns and heads towards a corridor up ahead. Sarah follows him closely, down the narrowing, darkening corridor despite the tremors that rack her body. From his sighs and occasional gasps, Sarah knows that the day's conversation will be reduced to a set of formalities, which is all she can manage herself. The man wears a plastic apron over his coat, badly tied at the back in a loose bow. The plastic claws at the walls which close in on the three of them as they proceed along the corridor. Charlie patters and puffs behind them, padding the space.

In the semi-darkness, a key scratches against a lock and a door opens into a dimly-lit library of sorts.

There are papers everywhere. Bundles of letters tinged yellow tied with string on the upper shelves; random piles of typed documents on the lower and middle ones; singed certificates curled at the edges, carelessly strewn across the desk in the centre.

'How can you make sense of all of these?' Sarah reaches for one of the certificates on the desk in the name of a Manolo García R – she can't quite make out the rest – but the man clears his throat and she thinks better of it. Charlie keeps his distance, lingering on the threshold of the room, his hands clasped firmly together.

'A slight hazard,' the man says, pointing at him, 'you know, all the tears, risk of flooding. We can't possibly take that risk. There's too much at stake in here.'

He sits down at the desk, his expression solemn, and puts on a pair of black rimmed glasses. 'For you,' he tells Sarah, indicating the chair opposite. The table lamp illuminates one side of his face and hair, transforming half of him into a man half his age.

'I'm sorry I yelled at you when I last saw you,' Sarah says quietly. 'If only I'd known.'

'No offence taken.' The man's tone is formal. 'Now, there are matters that are both important and difficult to comprehend. This is one of them.' He raises several documents to eye level, flicks through them and sets them carefully to one side. He then extracts a sheet of paper from a pile of certificates to his right and places it under the light of the lamp.

'Someone's been moving things around in here without permission.' The man glances across at Charlie, his brow furrowed; he waits. Charlie stabs a finger into his chest and shakes his head vigorously. 'But we got there in the end. Here.'

He holds out a page to Sarah. Hesitantly, she takes it from him and scans the rows and columns of names and places. Eventually, she lands on one she recognises. She pulls out the note to check she's not mistaken. 'José Luis Hernández López.'

'That's the one.' The man nods, a serious expression shadowing his face.

'But there's nothing here I don't know already,' Sarah replies, a little exasperated. 'This tells me he's from Madrid – I need more.'

'Yes,' the man says, opening the drawer of the desk, taking out the notebook Sarah first caught sight of in the bar in Belfast. She freezes, recalling her grandfather's signature written in real time as if he had been standing right next to her. 'And more you shall have.' He turns the notebook upside down; a small square of lined paper flutters into his open hand.

'Here you are,' he says politely, 'this is his address.'

Sarah feels a cold sweat nip her neck. 'Do you mean to tell me ... did you have this the whole time? Back then, when I last saw you. Is this a game to you?'

The man smiles and shakes his head. 'Of course not, you were always meant to come here. There are things here that belong nowhere else.' The formality of his voice has relaxed. 'Now then,' he adds, 'I have one more note to give you.' He indicates the page. 'Is there anyone else?'

Sarah checks again, wondering whether she's meant to look for 'Ana' perhaps, despite having nothing else to go on. It's then that she spots 'Doherty'.

'This is wrong,' she yells, turning the page to face him, jabbing at the relevant line. 'Tell him, Charlie!' She looks over at Charlie but he's staring at the ground, stepping from side to side. 'Charlie! Tell him, please!'

'We have a Thomas Doherty,' the man reads from the sheet. 'Place of residence logged is London.'

'No, that's not right,' Sarah says, fury pumping through her, conscious that her manners are slipping. *This man is trying to help. He is … he is.* She takes a deep breath. 'There must be a mistake.'

'No mistake,' the man says. 'I also have his address if you'd like to have it.' He picks up the notebook again, gently taps the spine and another square of paper floats into his hand.

'You're very welcome to have this.' He places it into Sarah's palm. 'I think you'll want it.'

'I think so too, Sarah,' Charlie says quietly.

Without saying a word, Sarah folds the addresses inside the letter, wondering what she's meant to do next.

***

'Here she is!'

'I'm so sorry I'm late!'

Paco stands in the hallway grinning, glancing at his watch. 'What time do you call this? Excited to see me, Carmina says. I don't think so!' He laughs and brushes his long chestnut-coloured fringe to one side, then steps forward with his arms open ready for her.

Sarah smiles and nudges him in his side, curls into him. She's missed this, the easy comfort of their friendship. She's missed him. There was so much she had to give up when she walked away that had nothing to do with Raúl. It has taken her until now to realise it, that her life in this city was more than just about him. A life she'd still be excluded from if it wasn't for her grandfather.

'How long are you here for?' She's already thinking she might delay her trip home if he's not staying long.

'Trying to get rid of him already, are you?' Carmina's voice trips from the kitchen in a soft tease.

122

'A few weeks,' he says, laughing. He turns towards the kitchen. 'If my beloved Aunt will let me stay!'

'For as long as you like, *hijo!*' Carmina shouts back. 'And you too, Sarah!'

'Can you stay a while?' Paco asks, doing his usual thing of not looking at her when he's nervous. He leans down to gather his bags and camera equipment from the floor of the hallway. Paco's never been one to push or interfere, just like Carmina. And with all the uncertainty and questions that the day has brought her, they are the people she needs right now.

'Let me help you,' Sarah says, crouching down beside him. 'And yes, of course I'll stay. A few days back home and I'll be straight back, I promise.' *I need you*, she wants to tell him, but thinks better of it.

Day 17: Old Haunts

It's one thing setting my Sarah on a journey of rediscovery and quite another not to be fully prepared for the consequences. Christ, am I really that naïve? Did I actually think I'd plant seeds to entice her back and she wouldn't go looking for answers? Did I think I'd come out of this unscathed, not having to confront my own past? Don't get me wrong, it does my heart so much good knowing that my loved ones are guiding Sarah, that they're stepping up for me – I'm not cursing helping hands – but exposing myself to what I buried long ago makes my heart hurt.

I suppose I wasn't prepared for making myself vulnerable. And vulnerability isn't something this oul' lad wears well.

I watch my Sarah hold her nerve, regardless of what's thrown at her and what's denied her. That's not down to the stubbornness I always teased her she got from me. She's packed solid with resilience, that girl, the sort my Annie has in bucketloads. And I watch her take on what's hers and all of mine, and Christ, I hadn't planned for this. I'm not sure how you plan for something like this.

There are faces of old friends and traces of others and nothing seems to add up. Charlie first, now José Luis. I wonder why he's sending my Sarah away, all the way to Madrid when he's right here in front of her. Nothing adds up.

Jesus, I can talk! The cheek of me to come out with something like that! Maybe the point is that you can't always force sense out of things. Maybe this dead man still has much to learn.

***

124

'I know, Mam, I know it's difficult to understand, but I just need a little bit more time.' Sarah holds the phone close to her ear and watches Paco study the camera, turn it over in his hands. 'Yes, Mam, Mrs McKee is fine with it and says not to worry at all ... Yes, I'm sure ... Yes, I'll get it booked today ... Yes. Bye, Mam.'

Sarah hangs up, sighs, and places the phone back on the oak dresser. She spins round to find Paco staring at her, a bemused look about him.

'Your mam is taking it well, then?'

Sarah smiles and flops down next to him. 'Well, she's very happy I'm going home a day early, not so happy about the coming back part.' She shrugs. 'She just worries, you know? About work, the flat, that kind of thing. I ... I hate lying to her. My time at the school is over, it was a fixed term thing. So no rush for me. I just don't want her to be concerned, that's why I haven't told her yet. And as for her, she just doesn't want me to mess up again.'

'Again?' Paco taunts her. 'You wouldn't do such a thing, would you?'

'Stop teasing me!' She laughs and points at the camera. 'Tell me more about this commission of yours.'

'Sure!' he says, leaning in close, placing his hand over her arm. His expression is unusually serious. 'Look, I obviously don't know the full story of what happened between the two of you ... you and Raúl, I mean, and I'm sure even someone like María wouldn't lie about a man not dying. But no one thinks you messed up. Things don't always last. Things sometimes break.'

'I know,' Sarah says, trying to compose herself, trying to repress the all too familiar feelings of guilt and shame. She doesn't like to consider how Paco and Carmina might react if they knew the truth: she's terrified she might lose them.

'I know,' she says again, 'now let's talk about something else. Your big commission – congratulations, *guapo*!' She forces herself to sound bright, excited, and prays he doesn't sense the worry that's threatening to ruin her.

'It's for the Tourist Board,' he says, smiling, holding the camera up to inspect the lens. 'New shots for a new publicity campaign. Makes sense to get a few here, such a beautiful city everyone deserves to see! I'm right, aren't I?'

'My God, yes!' Sarah's eyes widen as images of lectures and seminars and society meetings and pub crawls reel through her mind in quick succession. Untainted, pure memories of her younger self.

'I'm heading down to Plaza de Anaya soon,' Paco says, packing the camera away carefully. 'Fancy a trip down memory lane? And then you can tell me all about your plans.'

'I'd love to,' Sarah says, 'as soon as I get my flight booked. Meet you there in an hour.'

I don't remember where I was or what I was doing when the problems in Spain started being talked about. I suppose that's because the news of a military uprising, of a war between its own people, dominated papers and whispers and conversations very quickly. There was talk of a Crusade, of the fight for Catholicism over Communism, of Christ versus the anti-Christ, of the 'Reds' slaughtering the clergy. Tommy bought into it all very quickly; in fact, he told me that Father McMahon had a word with him at Confession about supporting the Irish Brigade. Our families bought into it too – the 'Holy War' part, the rhetoric being bandied about.

When Tommy sat his Ma and Da down to tell them he wanted to join up, to be part of O'Duffy's Brigade, it would be very wrong to say they were overjoyed at the prospect of their son going off to war. No parents would want that for their child. But they gave him their blessing and he filled in the application form and so began the waiting game to see if he'd be selected. I heard the parents whispering about it one night in the scullery, saying they and the neighbours were praying hard he'd be ruled if places were limited – maybe due to age, residence in the North, no military experience, anything at all. And all the while Tommy was being Tommy, overflowing with brute confidence, bragging to everyone and anyone who'd listen that he was already in, that he'd definitely be going.

If it hadn't been for Charlie, I'd never have ended up in Spain. That's not me blaming Charlie for us enlisting, absolutely not. What I mean is that, without having him to talk to as someone with similar views to mine, I'd never have been brave enough to go it alone. Perhaps he felt the same – perhaps he wouldn't have gone without me, perhaps we were each other's crutch. That side of things wasn't something we ever spoke about. We just ended up deciding – as young lads do, I suppose – that the threat of Fascism was one we had to stand up to. We were two young lads attracted to supporting something we believed in, no doubt about that. But we weren't fully aware of what it all really meant, where we'd end up, what it would do to us, to our families.

My conversation with my parents was very different to the one Tommy had with his. I knew it would be the case – Charlie knew it too – so we delayed it for as long as we could. There was no getting away from the mood in our district – though to be fair, it was a common one about our parts at the time – that joining the 'Reds' meant sacrificing your faith.

On 10th December 1936, the night before we were due to leave, Charlie and I made a pact to tell our parents. We'd thought about just running off, saying nothing, but we knew that would be wrong. We knew they would be worried sick.

Telling them was the hardest thing either of us ever had to do in our young lives up till then. Eighteen years of age, we both were, not even street wise but somehow thought we were brave enough to take on a foreign war. Charlie's luck fared a little better than mine, temporarily at least: there were tears and fists hammered against walls, but he departed with a reluctantly offered blessing.

I wasn't so easily forgiven – Da remained silent, not because he had nothing to say, but because Ma would do enough talking for them both. And talk she did – in between bursts of wailing – and she was very clear: she'd stay up all night and do a Novena, pray hard for me and Charlie to see the error of our ways. Walk over hot coals if she had to. She loved the two of us, always would, but she wouldn't tolerate such nonsense. And if I went without their blessing, I'd have no family to come back to.

On the morning of 11th December, Charlie and I set out from Belfast; Tommy headed to Dublin for his departure the following day with the O'Duffy lot. I'd have given anything for Charlie to come back with me on a pair of crutches.

***

The blue sky is slipping into red and copper tones behind the Philology building when Sarah reaches Anaya. She watches Paco tidy up his equipment by a small stone wall adjacent to one of the seating areas.

'Sorry that took so long,' she says. 'Have you got everything you need?'

'I do, thanks, but it will be nice to have your company for a few more shots when you get back. What do you say?'

'Sure,' Sarah says, 'I'm leaving tomorrow but I'll be back by Monday. 'And I wanted to ask you…' She stops, worrying it might be too much, too soon.

'What is it, *guapa*?' Paco says, putting his arm around her as they cross Anaya and head back up Rúa Mayor.

'Sorry if it's not appropriate, but …would you like to meet me in Madrid on Monday? Help me find an address?'

'Really? Of course, I'd love to.' He pulls her tight. 'Two birds with one stone, I could do with taking a few photos there, too. Okay?'

'Okay!' Sarah smiles, relieved that she doesn't have to search alone in a city she hardly knows. But more than that, much more than that, is how quickly he said 'yes'; how he won't have said it if he didn't mean it.

'Let's go and get a drink before we head back, shall we?' Paco scours a few of the bars on either side of the street for a free table. 'And before I forget, there's one thing you need to do before you go tomorrow.'

'Anything,' Sarah laughs.

'María called the *hostal*. She wants you to meet her for coffee in the morning.'

Day 18: *Woman in White*

'Are you sure about this, *hija*? I mean, you don't owe that *chica* anything.'

Carmina avoids eye contact and continues wrapping the food items on the board in front of her – slices of *chorizo*, wedges of *manchego*, a mix of *gordal* and *manzanilla* olives, bread sticks, pretzels. Sarah knows Carmina is preparing them for her, that they will be presented to her at the station just before she boards the train. There will be no discussion of whether she should or shouldn't take them, whether she has room for them, whether she can or cannot take them onto the flight. They are Carmina's silent gesture, a reminder that she's still looking out for her, that she's always there.

'Carmina is right,' Paco says, lumbering into the kitchen. His fringe spikes and juts, not yet settled after his night's sleep. 'What I said yesterday … you know, you don't need to do anything.' He yawns and pours himself a coffee, cups it with his large hands. 'You don't have to meet her.'

'Oh, I know,' Sarah says, shaking her head as he offers her more coffee. 'But what have I got to lose? Maybe I'll actually find something out for once.'

Carmina and Paco exchange an awkward glance that Sarah understands only too well. She knows that both of them will be hoping the other will take on the question neither wants to ask. The silence settles like a thick fog. She can put on a brave face and pretend there's no risk in turning up to meet the girl who has hated her from day one. The same girl who has been Raúl's eternal flatmate. The same girl who used to criticise her at every opportunity as soon as Raúl's back was turned.

The truth is, she has much to lose if she doesn't manage to

hold it together. She doesn't understand everything that's propping her up right now – the parts of her grandfather that linger, the strangers and even stranger occurrences – but somehow she must believe that it's enough to carry her through one conversation with María. That's all it is – one conversation which might provide something she needs to hear, even if it's something she doesn't necessarily want to hear. The truth.

'Listen,' she says, fixing her gaze first on Carmina, then Paco, wishing one of them would acknowledge her. 'I've got this. At least, I think I have.' She imagines the crucifix warming her chest, wills it to banish the gnawing self-doubt. 'I know what I need to do when I get back next week. Whatever she has to say won't change that. And besides, she can only have half an hour. I've a few things to get before I leave.'

'You make sure that's all she gets,' Carmina says, scratching some of the wrapped parcels in her rough grasp. She thinks better of it and lays them flat again, pats the foil. 'You're not missing your train because of one opinionated *chica.*'

***

María stands under the clock tower facing in the opposite direction. Her slender frame is a casual wisp of white fusing with bodies that crisscross behind and in front of her. Sarah calls her and she swings round on tiptoe in gleaming white trainers like an amateur ballet dancer. Her cropped white top and straight white trousers paint her tiny frame. She lowers her sunglasses just enough to let Sarah see her raven-black beaded eyes wide with enquiry, darting across her, scanning every visible inch of her.

'I thought we'd walk out towards the train station, get a coffee somewhere away from all of them.' She sneers and flicks her hand out towards the centre of the *plaza.* 'Too busy for my liking,' she says, turning her attention to her dark glossed locks that tip her waistband. 'What do you say?' She holds out a strand of hair like a peace offering, then tosses it over her shoulder.

'Sorry, but no,' Sarah says, 'I don't have time for that. Over there,' she says, indicating a free table just a few metres away. We'll sit there.'

'If you say so.' María tuts and struts over to the table, sits down and stands up again to interrupt the waiter who is busy serving customers at the next table. 'It's not very private here for a sensitive conversation, is it?' Sarah ignores her and orders a coffee with milk. 'And do you really want me to speak in public about all that you did?'

Sarah feels a knot form in the back of her throat and swallows hard.

'Look, I'm not here for an argument,' Sarah says, 'and you were the one who invited me. So just say whatever it is you have to say and be done with it.'

'Ha!' María snarls. She leans in and removes her glasses in a slow, ostentatious sweep, then fixes the black stones of her eyes upon Sarah. 'I'll never be done with you. At least, not until I take everything from you.'

She pushes back into the metal frame of the chair as if she owns the place and repositions her sunglasses, blocking out the world. Sarah regards her, almost feels sorry for her. But no, she won't do that, for this is a woman who finds pleasure in hurting others; who does so hiding behind her designer gear and shades.

Out of nowhere, María begins to laugh. There's a sinister, soft sweetness to it at first, as if she's just said something kind or complimentary. But then she starts rocking back and forth, flicking her dark hair this way and that. She could be beautiful, Sarah thinks, on the outside at least, if only she'd erase the scowl and upturn the corners of her mouth. Her heart needs a lot more work.

Whispers and mutterings fleck the warm air; Sarah presses her nails into the tops of her thighs by way of distraction from

María's laughter and poisoned talk. *Not until I take everything from you.* But Sarah has nothing left for the taking. Certainly nothing that's got anything to do with María.

It's nothing but an idle threat, she thinks. A callous remark to make María feel superior and cut Sarah to the bone. A pathetic attempt at a false sense of control over a future which she herself wiped out, thanks to her own stupidity.

'I don't have time for your games,' Sarah says, 'so either finish up or I'm leaving.' She opens her purse and places four euro coins on top of the bill receipt. 'Coffee's on me,' she says, pushing her chair back to make some room.

'A couple of minutes, then,' María chirps, clenching Sarah's wrist. 'You owe me that.' Sarah owes her nothing, knows that it will be an excuse for her to exercise more of her venomous tongue. But maybe, just maybe she'll have something useful to say about Raúl. So she nods and wrestles her hand out of her harsh grip.

'After all, you're the one who came back where you weren't invited, where you weren't wanted.'

Sarah waits for her to break the silence.

'I'm speaking for both of us,' she says. 'He told me to tell you to stay away.'

'Is that right?' Sarah says, her heart thumping. 'So it is true? He's alive?'

'Of course he's alive, you stupid girl. Didn't I already tell you that?'

Sarah seethes with rage. 'And was it too much for you to phone me? Put me out of my misery?'

'Ah, don't get angry now, *chica.*' María's mouth twitches as she tries and fails to offer something resembling a pitying smile. 'But I'd never put you out of your misery. Let me tell you something: a while ago now there was a desperate Irish girl who managed to string a few words together and a soft, kind-hearted Spanish boy who took an interest in her. After a lame excuse for a relationship, the pathetic Irish girl ruined it, and ruined him.' She stares at Sarah, tilts her head like an innocent lamb, waits. Sarah bites her tongue; she won't rise to it, she just won't.

María sighs. 'But he's better now, thanks to me. All me.' She crosses herself and nods in self-approval. 'And I love him. The end.'

Fury beats at Sarah's brow; she will not allow this woman to get back inside her head. 'That's nice for you,' Sarah says, her words knotted with a forced composure. 'I'm sure he appreciates all your help.' She wonders how much truth there is in any of it. *Christ, she despises her. Everything about her.*

'And about him telling me to stay away, I'm sure he can speak for himself. Now, I'd better let you get back.' Sarah stands up, trembling with rage and relief, and steps back in case María should attempt a staged embrace. She can't stand the sight or sound of her, needs to get far away from her. The girl doesn't love anyone but herself, she thinks, but the very fact of her saying it, that she loves Raúl, is too much. She knows it won't be reciprocal, it just won't be. He tolerated her as a flatmate all those years, but he would never choose to be with her.

'Don't be like that, *guapa*, people move on, people change. Let's talk some more.' The mix of pity and arrogance sickens Sarah to her core.

'All the very best to you both,' Sarah calls back, already making her way across the *plaza*. 'I've got to go, I've a train to catch.'

Paco is loitering under the sun-balmed arches at the back of the square as she approaches.

'My God, were you spying on me?' she asks, rolling her eyes.

'Not at all. I've only just ventured out. Are you okay?'

She wants to say she is, that she will be. 'No,' she says, and the tears come and she lets them. 'But Raúl is okay and ... and I hate that girl, God forgive me for saying it.'

'Come here,' Paco says, putting his arm around her. 'It's done now. Forget her. Let's go and get what you need before we go.'

Paco leads her away from the *plaza* and she tries to ignore the outline of María that burns her side vision. *The girl needs to take a hint and just leave her alone.* It is then she sees two men just outside the perimeter of the *plaza* with their backs to her, one capped with a shock of auburn hair brushing his white collar, the other draped in a coat too heavy for both the weather and his frame.

'Do you know what day it is today?' Sarah asks, holding herself tight against Paco. 'Friday 13th, maybe not the best day to meet up with María!'

'Don't give her another thought,' Paco says, not letting her go, 'at least you know now. One less worry. You can move on now.'

'Do you think she's okay, Da? I mean, it's tough when you can't understand what they're saying.'

'Look at her, Son. Look at how she's holding her own, despite the grief, the pain. I'm so proud of her. I can't understand every word, but I know she'll be okay.'

'Of course, Da, you can follow some of it, can't you? So much you kept from us.'

'I had my reasons, Son. And I know it's hard when you feel like you're on the outside looking in, not having a clue what's going on. Reminds me how I felt when I first arrived in Spain. Thank God we had Joe McNulty with us. Born in Ireland but Liverpool bred. First met him in London when we were getting vetted and ready to travel to Paris. No idea he spoke any Spanish until one night when one of the boys got himself into a bit of bother and Joe jumped in to help. Great lad, he was. Taught me bits and pieces too when I decided I was going to get my head down and learn the language.'

'And all this time, even our Sarah didn't know you spoke a bit? Jesus, Da.'

'Our Sarah didn't need any help from this oul' fool. Not for that, anyhow.'

'Are you sure she'll come back, Da? She won't be tempted to stay home?'

'None of us can be sure of anything, Son. Maybe some of us need to open the door to the truth just a touch, without stepping over the threshold. Maybe that's enough sometimes. But I don't think it's enough for Sarah. There's so much still here for her.'

**

It's half past one when the train pulls out of Salamanca station. The coach is quiet; there are only a few people in the odd window seat and a family spread out at the back next to the luggage rack. The mother's voice susurrates through the aisle as she coos her small baby to sleep. Sarah is glad of the peace and the chance to let the goings-on of the last few weeks descend like a fine sea mist. She may have company in the carriage, but she doesn't seek it.

She opens her bag and takes out a crinkled brown paper envelope with a variety of postcards inside. Books were always her grandfather's thing, but it was her grandmother Annie who collected postcards, still does. She keeps the most recent ones in a kitchen drawer and stores the rest in an expandable file in the cupboard under the stairs.

As someone who isn't fond of boats or flights, Annie's travels have been limited to a caravan break in Donegal, day trips to Portrush, a Butlins break just outside Dublin and a week in the Isle of Man worrying about having to fly home again. But postcards from her children and grandchildren allow her to dream, to imagine herself in exotic faraway places, swimming in crystal blue waters, basking in heat and light. It has always been about heat and light for her.

Her grandmother is very specific about her postcards: the picture must feature something special to the sender; the card should only ever be addressed to her; the text should tell her what they've been doing and never waste space on a weather update.

Sarah smiles, remembering how she instructed her in her plain, direct manner just before she headed off to Spain first time round. She would expect a postcard every week and under no circumstances was she to write about classes she was taking – that wouldn't be very interesting at all. She'd pulled out a sample of her grandfather's postcards from his time on the cruise ships to demonstrate how not to do a message home.

'Look at this claptrap,' she said, turning them this way and that, throwing them back onto the coffee table before Sarah could read anything. 'All the places Michael Doherty visited and just look at them! All the same, only ever pictures of boats! Why on God's earth would I want to see pictures of ships! Postmarks from all over the world and not one photo, not one!' Sarah said nothing, struggling to stop herself from laughing. 'And as for this,' she went on, jabbing the text on one of them with her index finger, 'what do I care about the weather and how many people are on board and what they're eating. How's that for boring!'

Sarah sets the pile of postcards on the small table in front of her. There are thirty of them in total and they're not for her grandmother. She's had her fair share of Salamanca postcards already. These ones are for the pupils she's leaving behind, eight for her A-level class and twenty-two for her GCSE group. She flicks through them, her city on speed, reduced to a set of flashing shots of the gilded arches of the *plaza*, a spike of Gallo Tower, sand shells and hints of golden cobbles and columns. She'll personalise them all, each and every one of them, with her pupils' favourite words and phrases. Just a little something so they know she's still thinking of them, even though she's gone. She'll give them to Amy to hand out.

But she'll not write them now. She'll write them when she's back home, after she's spoken to her grandmother and Amy. She'll write them before she returns to the city she's only just left, the city reduced to a series of images sweeping before her.

Day 19: Names and Crosses

During the first few months when I was in Spain, I used to write to Ma and Da as often as circumstances would allow. Little did I know then that they'd shipped out to England for my father's job. London bound, they were, and didn't leave a trace of themselves behind.

I never found out exactly when they left, or if they ever received a single letter from me. All I got was snippets of gossip when I eventually went looking for them. More fool me for going on the hunt for something long gone. They never wrote back, not even once to tell me they were leaving for good. It's one thing to know your mother and father have disowned you and quite another to discover they've abandoned you altogether with no forwarding address. I suppose as a young foolish lad, I reckoned that the disowning business wasn't real, or at most it was only temporary until I got back home again. There are plenty who might say I should have known better, that my mother had a reputation for taking no prisoners, that I made my own bed. She told me herself I wouldn't have their blessing. But Jesus, I never thought things would turn out the way they did. Ma loved me with every ragged bone in her body.

On that day in December 1936, she stood in the street in a navy buttoned-up coat and matching hat with rosary beads curled round her small, polite hands. Her face was phantom white. The McBrides stood behind her, Da to her right and Father McMahon to her left. The parish priest had been summoned to bless us; I could have his blessing alright, but not hers.

They made me and Tommy stand in front of the living room window and they all looked us up and down. Tommy was sorted first. A few prayers, a blessing and then his ma placed a silver crucifix in his hand and told him God would protect him at all times. Tommy scraped his bag off the pavement and squeezed my shoulder, didn't utter a word. His ma kissed him, his da shook his hand and Father McMahon nodded. And then he went, sauntered away down the street as if he didn't have a worry in the world.

All the worry parked in our street that day was caused by me and Charlie, they all said. They did a decade of the rosary before Father McMahon mumbled that he wouldn't bless any God forsaken 'Reds' and marched away.

When I look back on it now, that was the nail in the coffin, right there. Had Father McMahon blessed me, perhaps my mother would have felt that her place in the community was salvageable. Perhaps I'm just being gullible at this oul' age, trying to blame a priest for what my mother would have orchestrated anyway. It's one hell of a miracle I managed to hold onto any faith at all after that.

After Father McMahon disappeared down the street, my ma turned to me, eyes streaming with tears. She opened her purse, took out a crucifix identical to Tommy's and laid it in the centre of my palm. 'Carry this with you always, Son,' she said. 'This is my gift to you. As long as you have this, you'll always have me. I love you, Son, but you're not getting my blessing.'

I believed some of it for nine tough, life-changing months, even when I got no reply to my letters. I always wondered about Tommy, wondered if he finished with me and Charlie the day he left, the squeeze of my shoulder his parting shot. That didn't stop me worrying myself sick about what was happening to him when the three of us were out in Spain. Did he ever think about us? I worried myself stupid about whether the crucifix I found on the battlefield was dropped by a living or dead man.

For years afterwards, I held onto the two crucifixes and the ghosts of those long departed. The cards my mother sent for me, my children, my eldest grandchildren – none of it had any rhyme or reason. They were posted to an old neighbour in the west of the city who hand delivered them to us – God forbid we'd get our hands on my parents' London address. Birthdays and special occasion dates all channelled one way through the neighbour, none of it reciprocal. None of that was my fault. I tried to figure out a way to contact them, but in the end there were only best wishes and congratulations from a faceless mother who haunted a grown man throughout his life. And yet, all I could do was believe that the crucifix she gave me beat with a shred of love. That I could pour my heart into it and gift it to Sarah when my time was up. That Sarah too would gift it when the time was right.

***

It's 11:30am by the time Sarah lets herself in to her grandmother's house. Her delayed arrival in the early hours of the morning has played havoc with her schedule. Still, it could have been a lot worse if she'd been forced to hang around in the taxi rank in the pitch black until God knows what time. Tank was waiting for her at the pick-up point, his shadow looming over the half-deserted carpark. You couldn't mistake him for anyone else. It was no trouble, he said.

Now she has the best part of forty-eight hours and far too much to sort out. Her mother has taken to steaming the living room curtains and it scalds her already flustered cheeks. Her grandmother is laying out some cups next to the teapot with measured precision, as if preparing for a special guest or posh afternoon tea.

'Back again so soon? They must be paying you too much, all this toing and froing like some jet setter.'

'Hello to you too, Aunt Mary.' Sarah grimaces and wraps her arms around Annie. 'Good to see you, Nanny.'

'I've missed you, love. Now then, Mary, won't you leave us in peace? Sarah needs to talk to me.'

'Put out again to accommodate that one, for God's sake...'

'Shouldn't you be at work anyhow, Aunt Mary? You seem to have had an awful long time off. Mr O'Brien isn't so soft with Aunt Catherine.'

'That's because Mr O'Brien has a great big soft spot for your Aunt Mary, God help him,' her grandmother whispers, her eyes wide, bold. Sarah allows herself a much-needed laugh after months of upset.

'Jesus, Sarah, you can talk! And what's that you're saying, Mammy? Hope you're not spreading rumours about me, now!' Mary lights up a cigarette and clops her way to the back door, her feet slipping and snagging in a pair of stilettos far too big for her.

'She's gonna break her neck in those,' Chrissie says, 'and the last thing any of us need is another hospital visit.'

'Let her run on,' Annie says, pouring the tea. 'Now, love,' she says, handing a cup to Sarah, 'tell me what this is all about, why you've come rushing back here.'

Sarah looks at her for a moment, at the weight of tiredness curtaining her dulled eyes, at the sweep of rouge highlighting her dented cheekbones. She can't imagine what grief must feel like at her age, how you keep going without the man you'd devoted your whole adult life to, what you do with banks of memories formed over decades. And in the midst of all this, here Sarah is, about to quiz her on a name and address that can't mitigate the pain, that can potentially do more harm than good. This woman doesn't need more questions than answers about the man she loved all those years.

'Come on, love. It must be important if you couldn't stay put and pick up the phone.'

Sarah backtracks. She tells her grandmother that she's home to prepare some things for her pupils, that they're time sensitive and can't wait, that she's got to collect some important things to take back with her. She tells them both, mother and grandmother, that she's taken some unpaid leave for a few weeks

141

and they're not to worry because the Head has signed it off and the supply teacher is excellent and a good friend. *A few white lies on top of a few more won't do any harm.* She promises Annie she'll send her a postcard from Madrid when she arrives back on Monday and she'll make sure it isn't one featuring a landmark she's already seen. She asks if she can have a quick look again at her grandfather's postcards in the file under the stairs because she wants to remind herself how not to write hers.

She excuses herself and hurries out to the hallway. She knows exactly where his birth certificate and address book will be. She's only got a few minutes: as soon as her grandmother finishes washing the dishes, she'll come looking for her.

Sarah casts an eye over the stairs and listens for the tread of unwanted footsteps. Her grandfather always said their house – her grandmother's house now – was teeming with waifs and strays. There would be someone doing an odd job, fixing this or that inside or out; Mam or Aunt Catherine doing some housework; great grandchildren running about the path; the odd neighbour popping in with a plate of dinner, especially when her grandfather took sick. It's a house brimming with love and life of all kinds. Sarah checks again, contents herself that she won't have any immediate visitors, and opens the latch to the cupboard.

His birth certificate is right at the front of the indexed file where they keep all their personal documents and latest utility bills. *Michael Joseph Doherty*, she reads, then checks his father's name. Not a 'Thomas' in sight, so she quickly slips the certificate back into place and fishes out his address book.

She knows it's there, not filed under any particular letter but hidden away at the back. She was the one who had to go searching for it when they were making the funeral preparations for the extended family – not all of the 'English visitors' came, but some showed their faces.

It was the only contribution Sarah made, retrieving the address book; the rest of the time, she drowned in self-pity in the upstairs box room. She wishes now that she had done more.

She sifts the pages of the address book, starting with the people she knows are arranged in alphabetical order by first name. 'Elizabeth', 'Gracie', 'Mavis': all related to Annie and all in London for years. None of their addresses match the one she has committed to memory.

She tries 'Ma', 'Da', 'Doherty', 'London': no matches. She remembers at some point – she doesn't recall exactly when – thinking how strange it was that she'd never met her great-grandparents on her grandfather's side. But it was nothing more than a fleeting thought, never a concern that plagued her. Somehow she must have rationalised it all, accepted it in the same way as everyone else did. They were afraid of flying, her grandfather often said, and not very comfortable on the phone. Didn't that make them just like Annie?

She hears the soft hush of her grandmother's voice behind the living room door and buries the book in her coat pocket. She'll check it again later before she heads back to the flat. No one will notice it's missing, not for a couple of hours, and she hasn't yet had a chance to check the 'Ts'. She'll make sure there's no 'Thomas' or 'Tommy' or 'Tom'. If there are any ghosts hidden between the pages, she'll find them.

Day 20: Reflections

The more I think about it, the more I understand how much I took faith for granted. I don't mean faith in a religious sense, the kind that got me through some terrible times, especially those months on the battlefield. I took none of that for granted. I held onto it for dear life, fought so hard against the voice in my head that told me I was doomed, that I had been abandoned, that I would never be saved. I closed my eyes and heart to the talk and sightings of ruined churches and murdered nuns and priests and focused on what I'd gone there to fight for. On the love I'd found there... No, the faith I took for granted was my Annie's faith in me.

I put that woman through the mill at times, up and went and left her with four children. The neighbours were great, God bless them, all pulling together. Just as well because Annie's sisters were away by then and her parents weren't too well. Even when I got back from the ships, when I decided to build that café at the top of the road, she worried and fussed but never doubted I'd pull through when she couldn't change my mind. She welcomed Tank like one of her own, always scraped together a dinner for him if he wanted it, made sure the lad never went without.

Our Mary was our biggest test. Once Cormac and Chrissie were married and away out of the house, we had some tough years with that one. And she was a grown woman by then. Got herself into all sorts of whatnot and insulted too many good people for my liking. The best thing I ever did was put her out of the house for a few weeks. My Annie stood by me, as awful as the situation was, holding back her tears until the windows and blinds were shut. Then it was just me and her, cradling each other in desperation, praying Mary would see sense. I'm still hoping she'll see sense. Christ, nearly fifty years of age and still a nuisance! If she's not letting her mouth run away with her, she's traipsing about with boyfriends half her age and wearing clothes our Sarah wouldn't be seen dead in. The wee grandchildren have more sense than that one!

I digress from my dear Annie: I don't know where her sort of faith comes from. Where did she find the strength to believe in me, to not ask questions about my past, to willingly sacrifice half a family I denied her? And now my Sarah, questioning but not judging, not giving up on me.

***

Amy is sitting next to the window overlooking the street with a pile of exercise books in front of her. Her blonde bob is pulled back into a stub of a ponytail and half of her face is hidden inside a thick dark scarf. The half that's left carries enough tiredness for two people. She sighs and waves her biro over a page of text, not quite knowing what to do with it.

'Lucky you!' Sarah says, checking the street. It's mid Sunday afternoon and a few students are walking past with wrinkled carrier bags from the local supermarket. Apart from them, the street is empty of life and rammed with cars parked up for the weekend.

'I bloody hate this time of year!' Amy says, unwrapping her scarf, throwing it onto the sofa. 'You've had a lucky escape! Don't suppose there's room for one more at the Spanish inn?'

Sarah laughs. 'Ah, Carmina would love you, I just know she would. Maybe you'll come over in the summer, once school finishes?'

'And how long have you been promising me a trip? I'm just teasing you,' Amy says, nudging her, slamming the book shut. 'That lot can wait until tomorrow, it's not every day your best friend shows up for twenty-four hours.'

'It's a bit rubbish, I know. Sorry about that.' Sarah follows her into the kitchen. 'I'd stuff to sort over in Nanny's and Mam's.'

'So how long are you away for this time?' Amy takes a bottle of white wine from the fridge, unscrews the cap. '*Vino*, right? You won't say no, will you?'

'Definitely not, no.' Sarah smiles and pulls up one of the dining chairs. 'It's been an interesting few weeks. And it's hard to tell ... I mean, how long I'll be out there. Thank God for Carmina, she's a walking saint, that woman.' She takes the glass from Amy, raises it into the air. 'To friends and strangers and all the other madness going on in my life right now!'

'I'll drink to that!' Amy smiles and takes a long sip from her glass.

It's hard for Sarah to imagine what it was like before Amy. What it was like not having someone she could confide in. And yet, when it came to Raúl and what happened between them, there was no way she could share the truth, because she detested every disgusting inch of herself.

But she's here now, ready to tell her. She's done with guilt and self-loathing.

She tells her how they didn't have an argument and didn't agree to separate; she tells her how it was all her fault. She tells her how his cousin Felipe came for the weekend, how Raúl was at a society do and asked her to take care of him. She tells her how she and Felipe went out and partied and drank too much and enjoyed themselves too much. She tells her how he kissed her – one long, soft kiss in the street outside *Camelot* – and she didn't stop him. How she didn't want to stop him because in that drunken moment, it felt good. How it was nothing more than a kiss, and once the drunken fog had lifted, she knew she'd made a terrible mistake. How she despised herself. How she went to tell Raúl and he already knew. How María got to him first. How she didn't try to explain. How she was too afraid and let María's version, whatever it was, sit there. How he told her he never wanted to see her again. How he drove his car off the road and smashed headlong into a wall.

Amy doesn't say anything and continues to sip her wine. Silence hangs low like a shroud. Sarah has no idea if she's said too much or not enough.

Amy gets up and walks to the other side of the table, crouches down next to her. She stares at her as she has done many times before: her face not hardened in judgment, but stilled with compassion and love and all that Sarah needs to see.

'Jesus Christ, Sarah, you're only human after all. It was one kiss.' They clink glasses and let all that's been said linger there for a while until it dispels into the air. Rising, falling, rising, until it begins to drift away.

***

The faint light from the bedside lamp fractures the long shadows that crimp the walls of her bedroom. It's almost midnight and Sarah is gathering up the last of her things for her return journey. Her head and heart buzz from the few drinks she's had with the girls, the sharing of stories, the freeing of herself from a long-guarded secret. She might just be on the cusp of a reacquaintance with herself, a rediscovery of what she'd like to be, to feel.

She packs the Márquez novel into the top of her hand luggage and removes the second crucifix from the box Michael left her. She wraps it carefully in tissue paper, raises it to feel it pulse in time with the cross at her chest and slips it into the zipped part of her wallet.

Next, she tiptoes into the lounge and slides behind the sofa where Amy sleeps in a grey curl under a dark fleece blanket. She finds the Salamanca album, takes out a photo of her and Raúl in front of the lake at Retiro and returns to her room. She holds the image out into the darkness, perhaps so the shadows can protect her from any pain that might resurface. But there is no pain, no hurt; only a memory of a love story they never got to finish.

It takes her a few minutes to find the set of keys she hasn't used in six months. She's forgotten how well she's hidden them, a self-imposed deterrent in case she was ever tempted to go back to the flat. As if that would ever have happened. None of this would be happening now without her grandfather.

She slots the keys into her wallet next to the crucifix and surveys the room for any last-minute items. Satisfied, she crawls into bed and pulls the duvet close to her face. Shadows scamper across the walls, moulding themselves into figures she knows only too well. Tomorrow she'll look for a stranger in Madrid. Later, she'll make peace with her ex-lover in Salamanca. And later still, she'll seek out someone else in London.

Day 21: Offerings

Tank pulls up outside the flat right on time. That's according to his own clock, for he's always a few minutes early.

Sarah scans her bedroom one last time and checks the lounge. The only thing she's forgotten to do is give Amy the postcards for her pupils. But that's alright, she'll leave them there on the worktop in two neat piles with a thank you card for Amy for giving them out.

Tank hurries up the steps awkwardly, half-running to try to take her bag as she locks the front door. There's a gentlemanly air about him that doesn't sit quite right; he's always tried too hard. Sarah thinks it's because he's in a perpetual state of gratitude to her dead grandfather. *Dead grandfather.* Dead and buried, but not gone. Not yet anyway, not for her.

'Ready?' Tank says, pulling out of the parking bay. 'Definitely a wee flying visit, wasn't it?'

'I'm sure I'm putting you out,' Sarah says, 'Monday's always been the busiest day for deliveries.'

'I spend enough of my day hauled up in there! And anyhow, it will do the lads and Bernie no harm to have to fend for themselves for a few hours.' Tank laughs and glances at Sarah, shakes his head. 'You know, love, I don't know how you do it.'

'Do what?' Sarah asks, watching the sweep of dark terrace houses and yellow Harland and Wolf cranes slot together like jigsaw pieces as they climb the mountain road.

'All the travelling and running around, all that on your own, out there where you've nobody belonging to you.'

'But I'm not on my own,' Sarah says. She tries to imagine what it must be like for Tank, a lone soul who's never left Ireland, a man who isn't even aware he's on his own because he's always working or fixing something or taxiing people around. 'It might seem strange when you're used to the Estate, but you find people who care about you in other places. Do you know what I mean?'

'No!' Tank chuckles and indicates left to follow the sign for the airport. 'I've enough going on trying to work out the neighbours and so-called friends, never mind having to start from scratch somewhere else. And anyway … Jesus!' He bangs the steering wheel and sounds the horn at the white Seat trying to overtake the single lane traffic. 'I've enough problems speaking my own language, never mind taking on somebody else's!'

'You only think that,' Sarah says, wishing there was one of those Jesus handles to hang onto in case the man in the white Seat tries his luck again. 'It might do you good to get away.'

Tank says nothing and concentrates on the road ahead. Sarah wonders if trying too hard is the reason why he doesn't have a partner. In all the time she's known him, she's never heard as much as a whisper about him being with someone. Or perhaps he's just not interested, perhaps the single lifestyle suits him; after all, he spends almost every hour God sends in the café. She'd never ask him – that would be like asking her uncle, or her dad, God rest their souls, about their love lives.

Tank drives into the airport, bypasses the drop off area where he let Sarah out last time and indicates right to go into the short stay car park.

'What are you doing?' Sarah asks. 'There's no need to come in with me. Honestly, Tank, I'll have to go straight through to departures anyhow.' She checks her watch. 'My flight leaves in fifty minutes so I better get going. Thanks, though.'

He says nothing and takes a ticket from the machine, waits for the barrier and pulls into the empty space in front of them.

'I won't keep you,' he says, reaching inside his jacket. He pulls out a small brown envelope with her name on it and puts it in her hand.

'You've enough going on with all the running around without having to worry about money as well,' he says quietly.

'No way,' Sarah says, tossing the envelope onto his lap. 'I can't take your money. I won't.'

'But you will, love,' he replies, putting the envelope back into her hand. 'This isn't my money. I only have a job, a life, because of your grandfather.' He turns away for a moment and wipes something from his eye. 'I don't know what you need to do out there, but I won't see you stuck. If you don't need it, fine, you can always bring it back.' His voice has broken and he fidgets in his seat to compose himself. 'Go and do what you need to do, for you and your grandfather.' Sarah nods, unable to speak, not wanting him to see her upset. 'And I'm only ever at the end of the phone if you need anything else. We'll sort something out. Okay?'

Sarah smiles and nods a second time. She notices how the colour has drained from Tank's face; she knows he's not used to baring his soul.

'Cheerio, Tank,' she murmurs, stepping out of the car. She throws her overnight bag over her shoulder, mouths a 'thank you' through the side window and walks briskly towards departures.

***

'Did you put him up to all that, Da?'

'What's that, Son? That there? Not at all. Never said a word to Tank about my Sarah.'

'So how does he know, then?'

'Know what?'

'You know what, Da ... that she needs looking after.'

'He doesn't.'

'What's he at, then?'

'Listen, Son. That's the way Tank is. Don't you remember?'

'Aye, I remember him working with you all those years, head

down, always polite enough in his quiet way. Not one for a pint with the lads. An awkward big giant, he was.'

'Well, now I think about it ... I suppose you never really got to see him stepping up for our lot. It mainly came after you.'

'What do you mean?'

'Look, Son. The day we lost you, I collapsed into a heap. Couldn't talk ... Christ, couldn't walk for weeks. God knows how I managed the funeral – I don't remember anything about it except my Chrissie and Catherine holding me up somehow. And then, when I got a bit of strength back, I couldn't leave the house because I couldn't deal with the stares or the pity raging through the Estate. Jesus, there's nothing worse than pity, people not able to look you in the eye, all the desperate small talk or no talk at all. Devastated, I was. So Tank took over. Ran the business, brought down meals for us – not that we went anywhere near them for weeks. Kept everything ticking over for months. I lost you, Son, my only beloved son, but thank God for Tank.'

'I'd no idea, Da. Jesus! Well, they're in safe hands now, aren't they?'

'Now wouldn't you think they'd all be grateful? There's always one.'

'Our Mary?'

'Who else? That Mary one kicked up such a fuss years ago when I tried to get Tank to buy the place and let me retire. Over her dead body, she said. Tank was having none of it anyway, and rest assured Mary didn't influence his decision. He wanted none of the responsibility, just wanted a job and a wage.'

'That's good of him.'

'The lad knows what side his bread's buttered on. I knew he'd want things to carry on as they were, even if I wasn't about, so I signed the business over to your mother not so long ago. Our Chrissie helped me sort it out when I was in the hospital. I knew the vultures would be circling.'

'And were they?'

'God, aye. Mary is raging. Can't you see her face? The girl can't stand the sight of Tank. But that's alright, Son. He'll see my Annie right and my Chrissie will keep on doing the books, and as for Sarah ... sure he's right there for her, like a strange big guardian angel, hovering in the wings. Christ, he'd probably run a mile if he heard me talking about him like that!'

'You better believe it, Da.'

***

The cool air of the arrivals hall makes Sarah's skin tingle as she navigates bodies and trollies. She's trying to push her way through, away from flapping arms and extended name placards, away from chattering couples to get to the Metro that will transport her across the city to *Nuevos Ministerios* where Paco will be waiting.

She winces at the unwanted tapping on her shoulder and swings round, ready to confront whoever it is. Paco is standing there, his smile broad, his eyes glistening. There's an impish quality about him. His shoulders lift in expectation.

'Imagine finding you here!' He grabs her arm and pulls her against him, tousling her ponytail.

'Hey!' Sarah says, tapping his chest with her free hand. 'Why didn't you say you'd be here? I could've missed you.'

'I'd never have missed you,' he laughs. 'I've been standing here watching that door like a hawk! Anyhow,' he says, 'last minute decision, I brought the car ... easier to manage the camera equipment ... so I thought I'd meet you here.'

Sarah takes him in: his skin-tight black jeans, dark fitted t-shirt, fringe held back in a side quiff by a thin headband. She likes this look on him. It's a bit of a departure from his usual style, though he looks more like a boy band member than a photographer.

'Let's go,' he says, taking her hand. 'We're going out tonight and we'll look for the house tomorrow. Okay?'

The outfit now makes sense. Sarah considers how they've never been for a proper night out. 'But I thought we were going to check out the address and head straight back,' she says. 'No?'

Paco puts his arm lightly across her shoulders and takes her bag. 'Carmina thought you could do with a break and I agree with her. It's all sorted. Trust me, you'll have fun. Are you up for it?'

'Yes!' she says. As they stroll to the exit, she pushes ghosts and addresses from her mind and considers whether she has a decent outfit for a night out packed inside her bag. At her back, the ghosts follow quietly, biding their time.

Day 22: Tetuán

Sarah can't be certain how long she's slept for when she opens her eyes. There's no sign of light or life in their hotel room. She knows Paco is there, somewhere, and that's enough to relax her.

They didn't overdo it the previous evening; it was just a few *tapas* and drinks in a couple of bars in Cava Baja near the *Plaza Mayor*. A few hours to catch up on six months apart was never going to be enough; it didn't have to be. So much uncertainty tears at her right now, but there is one thing she knows for sure – some part of her belongs here, with Carmina, with Paco. They have taken root deep within her soul and whatever happens, she will not neglect them again. She cannot. She knows who to thank for that.

Paco had ordered the food and steered the conversation away from talk of regrets or absences. He was the same as always – his manner casual and easy, protective without overstepping the mark. They talked about places they'd been, swapped stories about when they first met at *El Pintor* five years before, laughed at mistakes they'd made. A few people Paco knew said hello and joined them for a while. Afterwards, they found a small bar just off the *Plaza Mayor* and took their *cañas* out into the street. They joined the crowd surrounding a flamenco guitarist and threw a few euro coins on top of his guitar case laid out on the pavement. They stayed there a while, with the soft notes of the song, cold beers, the warmth of each other.

Sarah hadn't planned on telling Paco about Raúl, about what she'd done, but something in that moment – their closeness, perhaps – gave her a sudden compulsion to do so. She pulled him away from the crowd and the music to a quiet, dark corner at the side of the bar. She explained it as she had done for Amy

– a series of facts with no emotional attachment. She waited for any judgment that might come her way.

She hears Paco slide open the shower screen door before the shower begins to hiccup and splurge. A low hissing sound fills the room.

They'd gone for a walk after she told him, through the semi-darkness of the busy *plaza*, up onto Gran Vía past the women framed in gloomy shop doorways waiting for potential customers. He seemed to hold her a little tighter than usual; perhaps it was just the fused heat of the alcohol and night air that made her imagine so. She pressed her side against his and tightened her grip around his waist.

When they reached the hotel, they fell into the twin beds that Paco had separated before they went out. She heard a soft scratching sound coming from the back of his throat as he slipped into sleep. She imagined herself watching them from above – resting like two siblings, two friends, uncomplicated. She drifted into sleep, imagining more.

'Good morning. Did you sleep? Are you feeling okay about today?' Paco is standing in last night's clothes, towelling the dripping lengths of his hair.

'All fine, thanks. I'm just going to get a quick shower myself, then I'll be ready to go.' Sarah gets out of the steel mesh chair next to the window.

'It's a bit strange, isn't it?' Paco throws the towel onto the empty chair. 'This art deco, sort of sixties vibe and then there's that.' He points through the window at the convent dominating the small square. 'Still, so good of Carmina to book this place for us. A hidden treasure, she said it was, and really close to where I need to take photographs today.'

'Are we doing that first?' Sarah calls from the bathroom. 'The photos, I mean?'

'We'll have breakfast first, then photos, if that sounds okay? Then let's see if we can find this acquaintance of your grandfather's.'

***

They sit at a table close to the edge of the street where the Opera House is in full view. Rows of pastel pink flower beds sit in perfect symmetry in front of it, perfuming the air, reminding Sarah of the pretty rose gardens at Botanic Gardens. She wonders if Botanic will be busy today, if she herself would be there if she were back home. She thinks of the man there, wrapped in his coat and considers how far away all of that seems, as if all of it happened to someone else. Much of what she's experienced in recent weeks makes her feel like she's caught in a dream. Not today – today she's stepped out into the real world, with Paco.

She shivers under the large cream parasol sheltering them from the globe of morning sun and asks Paco for his jacket.

'Would you prefer to go inside?' Paco puts the jacket across her shoulders.

'No, I'm fine here. It's so beautiful, isn't it?' Sarah indicates the Opera House. 'Have you been there before?'

The waiter appears with two *cortados* and two croissants, sets them down with the bill without saying a word.

'Quite a few times, yes,' Paco says, 'classical concerts mainly, just one opera with my mother.' He takes a bite of the croissant. 'Don't ask me what it was, I can't remember. Opera isn't really my thing.'

'Nor mine,' Sarah laughs, 'though I'd love to see what the place is like inside.'

'One day, I'll take you. A pity we don't have more time today. But we will come back, I promise.'

Sarah knows he means every word of it.

'Listen … about last night.' He moves his fringe to one side and fixes his eyes on her, his gaze bright with kindness. 'I know how it can't have been easy for you to tell me about Raúl, but I'm glad you did.' He takes her hand and holds it in the heat of his. 'I don't know what you want to do when you get back, but whatever it is, I'm here, okay? I don't want you getting hurt again.'

Sarah takes it all in, repeats it to herself, doesn't say anything because she knows she doesn't have to. They sit like that for a while, her hand resting in his, her body no longer shivering, her heart not hurting.

***

It's half past three when they find the street in Tetuán in the north of the city. It's not an area Sarah knows well, though she's passed through it many times on the Metro. The leaning Kio Towers blink in the distance as they search for a parking space.

They walk along the empty street, through the blast of tropical oranges, yellows and greens that pop on the pavement, the walls and window grilles. There are terracotta pots, an orange gas cylinder and a yellow bath towel hanging on a washing line that adjoins houses on opposite sides of the street. Sarah smiles, feeling as if she has stepped onto the set of a Pedro Almodóvar film. Competing lunch menus stifle the air. It's the sort of street where houses will be full at this time of day, families crowded around kitchen tables.

'This is it,' Sarah says. They are halfway down the street where a long narrow table covered in plastic and plant pots sits under the front window. 'Listen … can you do me a favour, please? I need to do this part by myself.' She shifts nervously. 'Sorry, I'll explain. It's just … I don't know what I'll find on the other side of the door.'

'Of course, no problem. I'll wait in the car.' He squeezes her arm. 'If you need me, just come and get me.' He heads back down the street as Sarah moves a purple-checked shopping trolley away from the door of the house. She knocks lightly.

A murmur of adult and children's voices echo inside and Sarah hears the clop of footsteps on tiles. A woman who appears to be in her mid-forties swings open the door. She is agitated, not in the mood for visitors. She wipes her brow and dabs at small beads of sweat just above her mouth.

'I'm so sorry,' Sarah says, 'did I interrupt you?'

'Who are you?' The woman taps her fingers on the door impatiently. 'We are trying to eat. What do you want?'

'I'm sorry to disturb you,' Sarah says, 'but I'm looking for someone. It's important. This is the address I was given. Does a Mr José Luis Hernández López live here?'

'I don't have time for this,' the woman says, making to close the door. Sarah puts her hand up.

'Please, *Señora*, I need your help.' She swallows hard. 'Does he live here?'

'You've got the wrong address,' the woman snaps. Now if you'll excuse me, I have to go.'

'But –'

'But nothing. Bye,' she says, slamming the door. Sarah waits a moment, unsure what to do next, when she hears the slide of a lock and the gentle creak of a door just past the table and pots.

A young woman looks out and beckons Sarah to come closer, her hand fluttering, feather-light. At first Sarah thinks the glare of the sun has settled on her, her presence caught in a haze, growing fainter the closer Sarah gets to her. But then she sees her, flicking in, out, like an image caught in an old movie reel. The woman from the photograph. Ana. *It can't be. Can it be her?*

'I'm Sarah. May I talk with you, please?'

'I know who you are.' Ana's voice is a whispered rustle, half caught as she fades in and out.

'Why … why are you like this? Can it stop? It's difficult to see and hear you.'

'It's because I never felt my company was wanted. I've been waiting for you a long time.'

'For me? How long?' Sarah gasps. 'Please, I want to see you.'

'Let me try. Is that better?' Ana stands in the doorway, a perfect copy of herself.

'Much better,' Sarah says, trying to settle her nerves. 'I came looking for José Luis, but I've found you. Are you his…'

'Sister, yes. I was there, too, in Salamanca, waiting. But five years is a long time to wait and I thought that maybe you weren't interested…'

'Five years? When I first went there?'

'Yes, Sarah. It's not possible for me to know when your grandfather told you things … *if* he told you things. I was there, just in case. There's much for you to see there. I … I loved him.'

'You loved my grandfather?'

'Yes. And I can come back to show you his diary, his notes, if you'd like me to. Is that what you want?'

'I don't know. Yes, I think so … yes. Did you really love him?'

'I have something of his I can show you now, to prove our love was real. Would you like to read it?'

'Yes, please.' Sarah takes it, her heart pounding.

'Will you read it out loud for me, please?'

My Dearest Ana,

I leave with my heart full of love for you, and I trust it will not break under the weight of time and distance that will keep us apart until this war is over. Who can tell when our paths will cross again, but I'm certain they will when the time is right. Our story might not have reached its conclusion, but that doesn't mean it was never real.

Your Michael.

'I must go. I'm sorry,' Sarah stammers, hastily backing up the street to where Paco waits. 'Please come, I want you to come. It's just … it's just a lot. Please come to Salamanca. I have so many questions.'

'We all have so many questions, Da. You have your own too, I know you do.'

'Ana. She is just as she was. Please God, don't tell me she didn't get the life she deserved. Not another one.'

'I don't think her story reached its conclusion, Da.'

'My heart breaks for her, Cormac. I don't want my heart to break for my Sarah, too.'

***

'Are you alright? Ready to go?' Paco says, switching on the engine. 'Do you want to talk about it?'

'More than ready,' Sarah says. 'I'll tell you all about it, just not now. I'm exhausted, I don't think I can take much more today.'

'You sure you're okay?'

She squeezes his hand. 'Yes, I will be. Just so much to take in. Thanks for all of this.'

'What else would I be doing?'

As they drive away, Sarah watches the streets of Madrid slip past in broken fragments blurred by sunlight. That's what her grandfather and Ana had, broken fragments of a love against the backdrop of war and conflict, of death and loss. A love obscured by the passing of seventy years. She thinks of her love for Raúl – a love of its moment, too. One that, for different reasons, may no longer belong in the present.

She closes her eyes and concentrates on the city that awaits her. Just a few hours and she'll be back amongst the ghosts and all that she knows and that which she is yet to discover. She wonders what Charlie will show her next, what the man might be saving for her in the Archives. The same man she now knows to be José Luis. She'll wait for Ana, for what she'll bring. She won't be scared.

It's time for her to see all that her grandfather has left of himself, of his life here. She wonders about Paco, about how she'll feel when it's time for him to leave the city, or when it's time for her to go. Because it will come, someone's turn to leave. And the story will still be real.

Day 23: Sightings

I first encountered José Luis in January 1937 when he returned to the village of Madrigueras. It was the middle of the month, just a few days after the terrible meeting that took us all by surprise. All of us Irish lads were summoned and asked out of the blue whether we wanted to remain with the British or join the Lincolns some twelve kilometres down the road. It was put to a vote and quite a few of our boys opted to leave. Not me, not Charlie.

On the day José Luis limped through the village, tensions were running high. The lads who were due to go to the Americans in Villanueva de la Jara hadn't left yet, but had no interest in continuing their so-called training. Some of the villagers were complaining about them getting drunk on cheap wine and anis. As for the British, they couldn't wait to see the back of them. Christ, it was a terrible mess. Charlie and I kept our heads down and ploughed on.

I saw José Luis staggering in the distance without knowing who he was. How could I know he was the son of the kind people who were putting me up? I watched him through the window – a sad, bedraggled state of a man. His clothes were filthy and worn and his rope-sandalled feet were caked in mud. His face was a mess, eyes absent under hardened blood. The rain lashed at him, assaulted him like it was working for the other side. He'd already taken more than enough.

We were just about to sit down to a modest meal of lentils and sweet potatoes when he fell through the door. His poor mother collapsed into a weeping heap, while his father tapped the floor with his stick and muttered something I didn't understand. I still can't begin to imagine how they felt, how the sight of him shook them to the core. God almighty, he was a stranger to me and my own heart leapt in distress.

Ana took charge and I followed her lead. I hadn't even been there three weeks by that stage and all I had was a smattering of Spanish words. But there was no need or time for conversation then. Everything I needed to know, everything I needed to do, came from Ana: in the way she moved, how she furrowed her brow in concentration, how she snapped single syllables at me. That was enough.

Although I suspected it, I wouldn't discover until later on that day when the man was cleaned up and sound asleep that he and Ana were brother and sister. Until then, I fetched towels and water and watched Ana tend to his wounds. José Luis never told us how he was injured, or where and when it happened, not that day, not any day. You can't knock a man for his pride, or his embarrassment.

His arrival brought with it several changes: a renewed stubbornness in Ana to return to the front, the thought of which was enough to scare me half to death; an unexpected friendship with José Luis; and, above all, the realisation that I had fallen in love with the woman I had known for just a few short weeks.

***

Charlie is mopping the tiles outside the Archive in slow swirling motions when Sarah arrives. The more he mops, the more water appears, puddling by his feet, flowing steadily towards where Sarah is standing. The sight of him there, sleeves rolled up and feet damp before the sun has yawned its way over the horizon, makes Sarah shudder.

'Oh, am I glad to see you, love,' he says, leaning the mop against the façade of the building. 'Maybe I'll stop worrying so much now you've come back. I wasn't sure that you would.'

'Why's that, Charlie?' Sarah asks, sidestepping the stream

now flowing towards the main entrance. 'I'm a bit like my granda, I'll keep at something if I have to.'

'I should have known.' Charlie smiles and gives her his hand. She takes it and jumps across the small pool of water separating them both. When she looks down, the stream has already evaporated, leaving behind only the curved streak of itself in a chalky outline.

'He's waiting for you in his office,' Charlie calls after her. 'His sister, too. I'll stay here; they're showing you something today which I don't need reminding of.'

'Sounds ominous, Charlie. I'm not sure I want to see it either.'

The library is in as much disarray as it was on Sarah's first visit. The light in the room has been diminished to the wink of a dimmed torch beam positioned on the desk opposite José Luis and Ana. It flashes on, off, every few seconds.

'Welcome back,' the man says, without getting up. 'Tell me, are you happy with what you found?'

Sarah tries to distinguish him between the flashes of light, to reconstruct the man who is faceless, formless. Sensing her disquiet, the man hits the table lamp with an aggressive knock and the room and papers turn a flaming orange shade, as if they've been set ablaze by a careless match. Ana remains the same, a flickering half-presence.

'Why didn't you tell me you were José Luis?' Sarah asks, shielding her eyes. 'Why leave it to your sister?'

'Come and sit down,' he says. 'It's not always possible to explain why things happen the way they do. But you're ready now, I'm certain of it.'

'Ready for what?' Sarah hopes she doesn't sound too impertinent. She won't allow herself to be distracted from remembering this is how it's meant to be, however much she doesn't understand it.

'Please check this over one last time.' José Luis holds out the sheet of paper Sarah recognises from her last visit. Her eyes have adjusted to the light now and she notices that the man seems younger than before, perhaps not much older than Charlie. The folds in his neck and deep lines around his eyes have vanished and his hair is set in thicker, darker layers. Ana sits next to him, a quiet, beautiful observer.

Sarah reads through the paper again. She'll take her time; process every first and second name, every surname, every place of origin, just to make sure she doesn't miss anything.

Her eyes skip to where she knows José Luis' details are logged, then on to where she found 'Doherty' before. She rubs her eyes hard to make sure she's not caught in some dreamlike state. She looks again.

There is no 'Thomas' this time. Instead, printed in capital letters, bold black as if only recently inked on the page, is MICHAEL JOSEPH DOHERTY. Sarah gasps and drops the paper. *Is this you, Granda? Are you doing this?*

'How did you do that?' she asks, struggling to catch her breath. 'He wasn't there last time, I know he wasn't.'

'Perhaps he was,' José Luis says taking the paper, pulling it close to his face as if examining it for the first time. 'Or indeed perhaps he wasn't.' He nods his head, sage-like, and gets out of the chair. He starts pacing up and down behind the desk, holding his chin in a thoughtful pose.

'We only ever see what we want to see,' he states finally, resuming a more formal tone. 'Perhaps you didn't want to see your grandfather's name there when you first came.' He clears his throat. 'Because seeing makes it real.'

'I see,' Sarah says, though she doesn't because she is still processing the man's words. 'So does this mean that there is no 'Thomas'? Because I couldn't find him. There was no trace of him in my grandfather's address book.' She is aware she's rambling now.

'That you will figure out for yourself, young lady,' José Luis replies in a soft, kind voice. 'The same way you'll know where to go next in this city. My sister will be waiting for you. Won't you, Ana?'

'Of course I will,' Ana whispers. 'This is why I'm here. Together, we will uncover your grandfather's papers. I have much to show you.'

'Trust your instincts and above all, trust your heart, young lady. And now, we have something for you, before you continue your journey. An extract from your grandfather's diary. Pass it to her Ana, please.'

'Another one? I don't know what to say.'

'Here you are,' Ana says. 'Won't you read it for us? And be warned, Sarah, there is much grief in this one.'

'Do I have to read it, then?' she asks, reluctantly accepting the paper. José Luis and Ana bow their heads. 'Then only if my grandfather reads with me. Granda, read with me, please.'

I curse the day I ever decided to come to fight this war. I curse myself for not checking the road. I curse those responsible for not giving us what we needed to fight against the rebels.

'Ach, listen to me, Son. Curse this, curse that. Droning on as though I'm penning the next Book of Exodus.'

~~*We were never going to be a match for them*~~. 'Forget that! What I should have said was there was no way on this earth we were all getting out alive. As for Charlie!'

How can I ~~return home~~ **survive** *without Charlie? My heart is sore.* **No pain like it**. *Day one of combat with God knows how many more to come. How can I survive this ~~valley of demons?~~* **hell hole**.

'Can someone please tell me what's going on?' Sarah drops the page in fright, her trembling hands unable to keep hold of the document which is changing before her eyes. Who's doing this? What happened to Charlie?' she cries out. 'Do you mean that same Charlie who's standing out there? Please, someone tell me!'

'Please calm yourself, young lady,' José Luis says in a hushed voice. 'You'll know everything your grandfather wants you to discover. And war is never kind. Here,' he says, lifting the note from the floor and offering it to her, 'something from your grandfather can't hurt you, now, can it? Isn't it why you came, to uncover the man he'd tried to erase?'

'Yes.'

Yes. To find the man my grandfather tried to erase. To make certain I'm not losing myself.

'Can you please just set it there on the desk, for now? I understand, at least I think I do, but it's difficult.'

'Of course, there's no rush. But you no longer require my help for the time being.' José Luis nods in Ana's direction. 'My sister will guide you; and Charlie, dear Charlie is here if you need him. Trust the pull of your heart and you'll find what you're looking for. I'll see you again when this part of the story ends.'

'What do you mean?'

José Luis continues to regard her as he lifts his coat from the back of the chair and drapes it over his shoulders like a mantle. 'Your name will be etched here, in place of your grandfather's.' He pats the left side of the coat.

'Wait!' Sarah calls after him again, but he has already turned and is retreating slowly into the fiery depths of the room, the flames like tiny angels of light settling along the hem of his coat.

'My heart still aches, Son, even now. All of this: for me, for my Sarah. And as for Charlie ... I'll always taste his death on my lips, smell the stench of his rotting flesh. Left like some rabid dog, like he was no one. But he was always someone to me. I lost him on day one of that damn war, but he never left me. Carried me through, still carrying me now. Salt of the earth.'

'And what now, Da?'

'Now we wait for Sarah to confront her own ghosts ... and for me to confront the rest of mine.'

Day 24: Uninvited Guest

The flat looks much the same as it did when Sarah was last there, though a little more rough around the edges. There's nothing welcoming about it; there never was. It always felt like a stopover kind of place, never a home.

The grey leather sofa opposite the balcony looks a little more stretched and swollen; the peacock blue cushions overlaid with silvery feathers are new and can't disguise its years of wear and tear. *María's wonderful interior design choice*, Sarah thinks unkindly. *Definitely not Raúl's choice.*

Apart from the cushions, the rest hasn't changed – the same thin Aztec-patterned rug wraps itself under the sofa and the walls still cry out for a paint job. Sarah was never comfortable here, avoided it as much as possible. She'd invite Raúl round to hers or meet up with him in the centre. Avoiding the flat also meant one less dose of María.

It isn't really trespassing if she has a set of keys. Raúl would have got in touch if he'd wanted them back. She's doing him a favour, returning them of her own accord, cutting the final ties between them.

She knows the risk she's taking, turning up in the first place, letting herself in. Any of the neighbours could have seen her and she has no guarantee that Raúl and María will be out.

She had listened carefully outside the door of the flat, pressing her ear against the paper-thin outer wall for any sign of life. She won't entertain the nonsense María spurted about 'love', but she'll have one last go at trying to speak with Raúl. One last chance to talk things through, to apologise to him properly, to give him the opportunity to apologise for not contacting her; one last chance for him to explain why he let her think he might be dead.

This is what Sarah tries to convince herself is the right thing to do as she tiptoes across the lounge to Raúl's bedroom. She tries to focus on the copy of Márquez, the photo inside it and the bunch of keys jangling in her pocket. She'll do anything to steer clear of self-criticism. She opens the bedroom door and hesitates, only then considers she might not want to go in. What if it contains traces of the woman she can't abide and who hates her in return? What if the sickly peach-infused perfume María has always worn penetrates the room? What if there is evidence of her tiny clothing, her large hoop earrings, her very breath? Because if she's been in there, if the room is now one Raúl shares with her, even only occasionally, Sarah will know.

She senses nothing but him in there. The fusty smell of damp clothes in need of washing in a pile next to the wardrobe; the faint hint of his cloying aftershave she never told him she didn't like; the badly-made bed; the pile of novels on the bedside cabinet which he won't have started reading yet.

The slam of a neighbouring door makes her jump and reminds her that she's on borrowed time. She quickly removes the books and places them on the floor next to the bed to make room. She looks for the silver framed photo of them taken at their first picnic by the river. Although she doesn't expect to find it, she can't control the twinge of sadness that spasms through her.

She carefully sets the copy of Márquez on the bedside table, bookmarked at chapter eleven, as far as he read to her. Then she lays the photo of them in Retiro on top of it, the one in front of the artificial lake, his head leaning against hers, blue rowboats bobbing in the background. She won't study the photo; she can't. There's no room for sentimentality today.

She takes the keys out of her pocket and reaches into her bag for the white envelope in which she's already placed the note. Her words are sparse, just enough to let him know she's glad he's alive and hopes for forgiveness. Maybe she already has it; maybe he hasn't been in touch because he doesn't know she's back in Salamanca as the uninvited guest.

She slides the keys inside the envelope, seals it and lays it next to the book and photo. Conscious that she has already outstayed her welcome, she slips away, down the corridor towards the lift, past the sweet doughy aroma of fried *churros* wafting from one of the nearby flats. As she waits for the lift to arrive, she wonders whether she should have checked María's room for signs of Raúl, whether she was right to relinquish her final remnants of him.

The first time I ever heard about Salamanca was when Ryan uttered the city's name. How strange it is that the sound of a placename, the repetitive click clack of its broad 'a', can intrigue you. That's how it was for me, when Ryan began telling us about the Irish Brigade here in the north-west of the country. Feet only just treading Spanish soil and them enjoying special blessings and special dinners and even their very own interpreter. Us lot, we just had to make do. I swore then that I'd have to learn more about it.

The next time I heard mention of the city, it came from Ana and I didn't understand what she was trying to say. Her face saddened when its name passed her lips. It wasn't until a few weeks later that I worked it out: a combination of my Spanish patter and José Luis' smattering of English helped me discover that he and Ana were born here. They vowed to return when it was safe to do so.

And then along came Sarah, her eyes glinting with excitement at the thought of the adventures she'd have here. She'd turn up with guide books and pictures and lists of subjects for me to look at and Christ, I didn't know how to digest it all. So I'd just sit silently in the scullery, trying to focus on what she had to show and tell, trying to stop an assault on my thoughts of all that I'd pushed away long ago.

I never would have imagined that I'd end up here, in death, alongside friends and loved ones. Perhaps fate really does exist.

I wonder if this city is capable of love. Or only hurt.

Day 25: Guest List

The tourists who move around the courtyard in small packs are oblivious to the man levitating above them in dripping wet clothes. Charlie doesn't notice Sarah observing him from the edge of the yard. He continues buffing one of the marble columns of the upper balcony with his back to her, erasing the ghostly reflection of his own face before it reappears again.

'I'd like to return this to you,' Sarah calls. The shell he gave her when they first met balances in her outstretched hands. People close by regard her with puzzled expressions; she doesn't care.

'I'll be right with you, love.' Charlie hangs the cloth over the balcony rail and descends like a graceful bird, landing right in front of her. He removes his cap and scratches his head.

'There's no need to return it just yet,' he says, pointing at the shell. 'You can be sure I've got plenty to do in here and the exterior can wait for another while. There's no rush.'

'But I've got no use for it,' Sarah says, 'what could I possibly want with this?' She turns it over in her hands and sighs impatiently. 'I don't mean to appear ungrateful, but what happens if it goes missing? Or if I break it by accident?'

'That's not really why you're here.' Charlie frowns and takes the shell, tucks it into the chest pocket of his overalls where it flattens smooth as putty against his body. 'It'll be safe there for a while. Now,' he says, indicating where the banner had been on display on Sarah's last visit, 'are you looking for anyone or anything in particular?'

'Alright,' Sarah says, regretting her raised tone. She is sorry about the fate of this man who's been dead seventy years and yet continues to help her.

'Can you tell me where I can find Ana? Please, Charlie.'

Charlie smiles at her, his green eyes filled with kindness. 'You know where she is, love. If you think about it, you'll know. And you have to do this part yourself.'

Tiny shells rain into the fountain in the centre of the courtyard and Sarah imagines them pelting at her heart. 'Jesus, Charlie. Come on, now.'

'You'll find her, love, but not here,' Charlie says again, donning his cap as he ascends to the balcony. 'It's how your grandfather would've wanted it.'

***

'Great timing!' Paco beckons Sarah into the private lounge at the back of *El Pintor* while he

checks to make sure Carmina has definitely gone. There is a small pile of cookery magazines

on the glass-topped coffee table and one of the regular news readers murmurs through the

television screen in the corner. 'My Aunt's got a sixth sense,' he calls from the hallway,

'always knows when something is brewing. Nothing gets past her!' He rushes back into the room and halts at the sight of Sarah. 'My God, what happened to you?' His face pales with concern. 'Are you alright? You look like you've seen a ghost!'

'Funny you should say that! It's fine, really, I've just got a lot to think about.'

'I wonder whether too much thinking is the problem right now.' Paco shrugs and sits down on the sofa next to her. He inches a little closer and Sarah senses his nervousness. 'Look, I'm not judging or preaching, you know me better than that, but you've been through so much and maybe you just need to stop and breathe.'

'Actually, I think you're probably right,' Sarah says, overwhelmed suddenly by the enormity of it all. 'I sometimes

172

think I've got this under control, and then I end up having something else to figure out ... and then it becomes a bit much ... I'm sorry,' she says, wiping her eyes with her sleeve. 'It really will all be okay. It's ... it's the ghosts, Paco, they're killing me.' She gives a little smile.

Paco tilts her face upwards and gently wipes away her tears with the back of his hand. 'You've said so little about your grandfather ... about what happened ... I know we all have to deal with grief in our own way. And as for ghosts,' he says, taking her hand, 'maybe they're just angels watching over you? Us?'

'I know,' Sarah says, remembering the phone call he'd made to tell her about his mother's passing, three or four years ago now.

She knew his mother had been ill for a very long time, before she even met him, and they'd already told him by then that she wouldn't ever get better. He'd called Sarah after the funeral to say it was the send-off he hoped she would have wanted. Family flowers only, donations to the local hospice.

'God, I'm so sorry I wasn't there for you then, and here you are fussing over me. Jesus, I don't deserve any of it.'

'You deserve every bit of it. And I never would have expected you to come all the way from Ireland for the funeral. Neither would my mother. Look, the pain won't ever go away ... but you'll learn to deal with it.' He hesitates a moment; tears fill his eyes.

'Is that how you feel, about your mother. Is the pain always there?'

'Yes, it is ... but without pain, I don't have her. She's always here.' He touches his head first, then crosses his heart. 'And that's enough to sustain me. Plus, I've got Carmina, of course.' He lets go of her gently as if she might break and leaps up to check the hallway again.

'You're so nervous. What's up with you?'

Paco smiles. 'It's her birthday in three days ... Carmina's ...

on Castile and León Day. Imagine Carmina having a birthday holiday every year! What do you say we do something special for her, since the two of us are here?'

'I think it's a great idea. I'd love to!'

Sarah leans back and relaxes into the sofa, giving Paco her full attention. He flicks through one of the cookery magazines with total disinterest and tells her he wants to prepare a special meal.

'But I can't cook. Can you?'

'Not really,' she says. They scan a few of the recipes in the magazine on top of the pile and dismiss them all as too advanced. When they land on the chicken and chorizo *paella*, they pledge to make it together.

He tells her he wants the meal to be for just the three of them, but he'd like to invite some of her friends for drinks afterwards. He asks her if they should have a guest list.

'Absolutely! Only the best for Carmina!'

And they remain like that, planning a party of sorts. They know that when night falls on Carmina's birthday, they'll take to the streets amidst performances and dances and join the rest of the city commemorating the public holiday. Sarah says how right it is for Carmina to have a special day to share with the whole community. 'Just what she deserves. She's so loved, isn't she?'

'Yes, she is. Listen, do you mind if I say something else?' Paco's face flushes pink and he shakes his fringe over his eyes.

'What's got into you?' Sarah teases him. 'You're full of talk today!'

Paco looks down at the floor. 'It's just that you've been so distracted and you've been spending a lot of time by yourself.'

'I'm just figuring things out. That's what I came for. And I'm not by myself. What about those ghosts I mentioned?'

'I know.' He clears his throat. 'You don't have to be frightened of telling me anything. I'm staying a few more weeks. Is that okay with you? It means you need to share with Carmina a while longer.'

'Won't you have to get back for work? Santiago is a long way away.'

'I'm freelance now,' Paco says shyly, 'I didn't know if I should tell you beforehand as I didn't want to complicate things. I can stay as long as you want me here.'

Sarah doesn't understand how Paco staying might complicate things; it's him leaving too soon that worries her.

'That's nice,' is all she says. 'Now, let's sort the birthday food and I'll arrange the present.'

A twenty-minute conversation with her mother is all Sarah will allow herself. Chrissie has to bear the cost and her budget is tight.

Sarah doesn't tell her about her discovery in Madrid, about those looking out for her, about the absence of Raúl. She doesn't tell her that she's on the cusp of uncovering something and might never be able to share it with her family. She tells her mother that everything's fine, that she misses them all, and she'll be home soon. A litany of half-truths, because she doesn't yet know the full truth.

Her mother tells her that she and Annie are fine and resting, that the days are getting brighter and easier. Her own version of half-truths.

Sarah doesn't tell her that she might be falling for the man she always regarded as a brother, a best friend.

***

Outside, the street is filling with tourists and students and vendors waking from afternoon *siestas*. Carmina is back, merry after a few drinks with friends in a pre-birthday celebration. She hums to herself in a far corner of her bedroom she shares with Sarah for the time being; she touches up her red lipstick in the wardrobe mirror. It's as if she has somewhere to be, a soul departing rather than returned.

The ringing of the phone shuffles its way through the walls. Sarah knows it can't be her mother again, not so soon. It will be a booking, a friend of Carmina's checking on birthday plans, or perhaps the Tourist Board seeking an update on Paco's progress. She wonders what the Board will do with the photos Paco has taken, how they'll ever be able to select from the many beautiful, intimate shots all taken in natural light.

She thinks of Ana captured on camera inside her pocket, now roaming the corners of this city. She wonders if Raúl ever thinks of her anymore; if he ever will again.

There's a knock at the door – once, twice, three times by an intolerant messenger on the other side. Carmina is quick to invite him in.

'What is it, Paco?' Sarah says.

'Yes, what is it, *hijo*. Tell us.'

'It's for you, Sarah,' he says, agitated. 'It's the one you've been looking for.'

Day 26: *All that she does not see*

All of this feels too much. Sarah loiters in the street, an unusual chill in the wind nipping at her bare arms and legs. Doubt eats away at her – at what her love for Raúl was, is, when she thought she had it all worked out.

It's not that she regrets agreeing to see Raúl – and none of this would be happening if it hadn't been for her uninvited visit to his apartment. It's being here, in Avenida de Portugal, the lack of neutral territory. It's the place she used to avoid at all costs and yet is now about to step back inside.

It's much more than that, too. He's inside her head again, taking control, deciding on the time and location without her even questioning it.

Perhaps she should have listened to Carmina and Paco. Perhaps she should have called him straight back and put things right. She doesn't know if she has the strength to confront him. She didn't even mention María during the call; neither did he. For all Sarah knows, she'll be in there somewhere, fluttering like a trapped bird, nesting where she isn't wanted. Not by her, anyhow. It's Saturday and María wouldn't dream of working weekends, not even for an attractive overtime package. She was never one to put herself out, the same María.

The buzzer sounds; Sarah attempts and fails to push the door open. It is pulled away from her too quickly by a thin, rod-like hand. She's not expecting to see Raúl just yet; there should be several flights of stairs between them and several minutes for her to straighten herself out. She's not ready.

'Hello,' Raúl says meekly, looking past her. His face has always been gaunt, but now appears even more skeletal, crowned by a mop of dark hair that drapes like thick curtains down over his ears. His body is emaciated, broken, not that he had any weight to shed in the first place. Sarah wonders if it's the aftermath of surgery or drugs or a broken heart. That's how she feels – heartbroken at the sight of this man, embodying the mess they made of everything.

Raúl holds out his hand as if trying for the sort of handshake they'd never shared before. He used to laugh at the formality of the gesture, how anyone could ever choose an exchange of hands over two kisses, *dos besos*, one on each cheek. It didn't take Sarah long to get used to the culture of *dos besos*: it just clicked. Like many things in this city, the perfect fit. Or so it seemed. Strange, she thinks, what you get used to, what you mould into.

'Hello,' Raúl says again, slipping one hand into his pocket, closing the door with the other. 'Not here,' he whispers. 'Walls have ears.' Sarah nods, relieved. In the street, she feels María's taunts close but distant enough not to touch her.

All the while Sarah says nothing; for now, all she can do is follow him to the other side of the street, consumed by her sadness for him, for them.

There is a café on the corner with three metal tables and some chairs splayed here and there. Raúl takes hold of two of them and slowly moves them to the nearest table. He waits for Sarah to sit down before he lowers himself into the chair, carefully, as if his bones are too brittle for normal speed.

Sarah sips at the glass of water he has poured for her and turns down his offer of a coffee. She feels the distance between them, like an ice wall lodged deep through the centre of the table. Perhaps it's his frozen stare that is causing it, his eyes trapped somewhere between despair and incredulity. Those are the eyes she couldn't stop seeing, for months, every time she closed her own.

'I'm glad you came,' Raúl says, tapping his fingers against his water glass.

Sarah ignores the pleasantry. 'Is it true María didn't tell you I called to see you?'

'Don't you want to talk about us first, how we've been? But yes, it's true.' He pauses. 'I know she had her reasons.'

Sarah bangs her fist against the table. 'Christ, Raúl, I don't have time for this. Do you know how difficult it was for me to come here? Six months, nothing from you for six months. You knew I'd be sick with worry. I didn't know if you were alive or dead. And I certainly didn't come to talk about *her* reasons, or for you to explain *her*.'

'Listen, I'm sorry. Please, just hear me out. I wanted to tell you, many times, but María said it was best not to call...'

'And you listened to her? You let her dictate all of this?'

'She said you wouldn't speak to me. I wanted to tell you, and time just passed and ... I never meant it to take this long. And I was ill, Sarah. I'm sorry.'

'Would you ever have told me if I'd never turned up here? Would you have continued to punish me, make me feel guilty? You've no idea what it's been like.'

'Nor you for me, Sarah. Please let me explain.'

'If you must.' Battling her tears, she turns her chair away and concentrates hard on the cracks zigzagging the orange terrace tiles. If only she could step outside herself, imagine he were speaking to someone else, she might be able to dull the pain. *Did she ever know this man?*

He tells her. He tells her about the day she has spent six long months regretting and trying to forget. The day she couldn't forget. He tells her things she already knows and things she doesn't want to ever hear again.

'But I didn't mean it,' he keeps on saying. 'You must believe me. I didn't mean for it to turn out like this.'

'Didn't mean what?' Sarah's patience is wilting, like this relationship she's been clinging onto. She turns to face him. 'My God, Raúl, won't you just tell me!'

'Okay.' He sighs deeply. 'When Felipe came, you'll remember we were just about to close the sale on the flat. We'd all the paperwork ready to go.'

'I know that.'

'Sorry. So ... I suppose I was beginning to question things a little.'

'What?' Sarah bangs the table again, harder this time. 'You were beginning to question me? What about me exactly? Are you serious, because clearly —'

'Let me finish. I don't mean questioning you. I think my nerves were getting the better of me. You know? If I was questioning anyone, it was myself.'

'No, I don't know,' Sarah says, her words choked. 'I never doubted you.'

'It all began as just a bit of fun.'

'I was 'fun' to you?'

Raúl shakes his head. 'It all began as something not serious at all. Felipe said I was lucky to have you, that you were too good for me.'

'And?'

'And that you deserved someone more like him. A bit more handsome, a bit more extrovert; someone who wasn't so serious.'

'This isn't getting us anywhere. What did you do? Just tell me!'

He coughs into his hand. 'So, he challenged me ... that he could take you. And I thought ... I thought that was maybe how I'd know if you really wanted to be with me. If we should take the next step with the flat and all that.'

'Take me?' Sarah stares at him, incredulous. She breathes hard; she won't speak, not yet. This broken man, this man who broke her. For what? Because of some fucking dare? Her body begins to shake. Sadness and fury ooze from her every pore. She looks him over and she feels nothing but pity. Pity deep in the pit of her stomach for him; regret that a man she'd given every piece of herself to, the man she'd loved with an intensity so strong it frightened her to death, could have so little faith in her.

'You did all of that to me?' she says finally. 'You doubted me that much?'

'No,' he says, his voice breaking. 'No! It was a moment of weakness. Don't we all have those? And that's why I took the car, that's why I tried to hurt myself.'

'But you made me believe that was all my fault!' There's a profound ache in her heart and the tears rise from the depths of her, up, up, up. 'How could you hurt me like that?' she sobs. 'All this time...'

'Please, Sarah,' he says, grasping at her arm in desperation. 'I wanted to tell you ... and I tried...'

Sarah looks him straight in the eye. 'You didn't try hard enough.'

She stands up, turns away from him, ignores his protests. She starts down Avenida de Portugal, breaks into a run – a futile, haphazard run that cannot fix the pain or give her back all the love she poured into him. She wants to tear into every part of herself, to truly make herself hurt until all that's left is nothing. Nothing, that's all she wants: of him, of herself.

Thunder rumbles in the distance and the sky drops into momentary darkness. It's as if time is standing still, giving her a chance to run and run and break out of her head, her body, this damn city.

'What did I say, Son, about a city full of hurt? My Sarah's taken her fair share. Please, Cormac, get Ana. It's time.'

Sarah runs and runs, through the rain that pummels her face and legs, through the beat of the crucifix. The pulse at her neck is relentless, like the rain and hurt and images of her and Raúl on fast forward in her mind: crashing, warping, disintegrating into nothing.

She stops dead outside the Church of St Mary Magdalene and enters without hesitation this time. The air is still and warm as she walks up the aisle towards the altar alight with candles. Her clothes dry gently against her skin as she genuflects and moves into the first pew on the right.

She watches the candles pattern the altar and speckle the golden columns on each side. She wonders how many special intentions they represent and offers up her own. For her soul; for Raúl's. She kneels down and looks through the flames in search of those she loves, those who love her. Faint swirls of gold twist and mould into the thin, bearded face of her grandfather, then fade away. She wraps her arms around herself to trap the heat and looks again. The flames dance and curl into the face of a young woman she recognises with dark glossed hair curving above her shoulders.

She sits there for some time, continuing to offer up her special intention, afraid to take her eyes off the candles in case she loses everything and the pain stops subsiding.

Sarah doesn't see the young woman standing at the back of the church, regarding her. The same woman she met in Madrid, who now wears the dark shirt and trousers of a *miliciana*, the ill-fitting uniform of her war days. The woman's black hair gleams in the candlelight and her eyes burn bright with youth.

Sarah doesn't yet know this woman only got to live a fraction of the life she had mapped out for herself. Ana has been waiting for Sarah for the longest time.

'Here she is again, Son. All those years when I tried not to remember, but I always wondered what became of her.'

'She's here now, Da. For Sarah. For you.'

'And I must prepare myself. Look at them: Ana and Sarah together. The things I buried are about to resurface.'

Day 27: Sketches

When Charlie and I and the rest of the boys first settled in Madrigueras, Ana was nowhere to be found. It wasn't until a few days later that she arrived, stomping into the village in a white blouse and wide-leg slacks, full of attitude. The woman mesmerised the drip of a lad that I was back then, moving around with an arrogance I could only dream of. Turned out we were the same age, but Christ I felt so naïve next to her.

'Do you want me to come with you?'

'Not at all. I'll be back before you know it. You concentrate on getting the last of the things for Carmina's party tomorrow.'

Sarah knows Paco has questions he won't ask but she can't pretend she doesn't see the worry line threading his forehead.

'Please don't worry. We'll talk later.'

'Okay. I'll see you in a few hours. We've lots to do, and the cooking is just one of them!'

'I'll be back before you know it.' Sarah hugs him and rushes out onto the street, walks briskly across the *plaza* and straight up Calle Zamora to the church. She crosses herself with a dab of water from the font at the entrance and makes her way up the aisle.

Ana is waiting for her in front of the twinkling bed of candles.

'I'm very glad we're together, Ana. Thank you for all you're about to do.'

'I can see you're nervous. Please don't be.' She lays a shawl like a holy relic at the foot of the altar. 'This is what you came for, isn't it?' Ana looks at her with a kind, delicate smile and moves slowly towards the back of the altar with a lit matchstick in her hand. Another row of tealight candles appears and she walks from one candle to the other, bringing them to life.

'I wish I'd known you, sooner, Ana. I wish I'd met you back then, when I first came here.'

'No, no,' Ana says. 'We hope and we wait for the right time.' She holds out the burning matchstick to Sarah. 'Here, for the one in the centre, offer up a special intention. Now's the time.'

Sarah takes the match and lights the pillar candle in the middle of the altar. Then, she closes her eyes and visualises her mother and grandmother standing side by side against a blank white background, arms wrapped around each other. All she wants is for them not to hurt, for them to be at peace.

'Ready?' Sarah opens her eyes again as Ana shakes out the shawl and wraps it tight across her chest. Small beads of dust pierce the tips of the candle flames. 'We have somewhere we must be.'

'I'm ready.'

Sarah follows Ana back down the aisle and out into Calle Zamora. They cross the cobbles to the opposite side of the street where Sarah observed the bell tower for the first time. Ana points at her neck. 'Your grandfather was a very good man,' she says, her eyes moist with tears. 'And he never took that off. Not even when he was in action.' She opens a large grilled door and waits for Sarah to step inside. 'It meant everything to him.'

'Really? Do you know who gave it to him?' Sarah climbs the stairs, her head spinning with all she wants to ask.

'I do, but it's not my place to say.'

At the top of the landing, Sarah watches Ana remove a large iron key from her coat pocket and dust it lightly with a handkerchief. 'Just in case,' she nods at Sarah, 'this hasn't been used for quite some time.'

The walls of the apartment are laced with cobwebs and light creaks through a small gap in the curtains. 'Not too bad, considering,' Ana says, pushing the curtains back to flood the room with light. She fluffs cushions and wipes away cobwebs as if she's just settling in, not long departed. As if nothing matters but the present moment when Sarah is aching for what remains of the past.

'What is this place?' Sarah asks politely. 'Does anyone still live here?'

'Not at the moment, but soon.'

Sarah nods, watches her lift the lids off a line of boxes by the main window and put them back again.

'We had to wait for you.' Ana smiles at her warmly. 'To remove the past, so it's ready for someone else.'

Sarah shivers, remembering the apartment she and Raúl viewed just a stone's throw away.

'Here we are.' Ana beckons Sarah to join her at the window and brushes down a small table next to her. She takes a framed picture from one of the boxes and lays it on the table. 'I have two to show you,' she says. 'This is the first one.'

A young man in uniform, sketched in pencil, stands next to a dark-haired girl on what looks like a mud-clad country road. White single storey cottages modestly populate the background.

Sarah feels her face burn with anticipation. 'Is this you?' she asks, shaking. She removes the photo from her pocket and lays it next to the picture. 'It is you, isn't it? Did you sketch this?'

'I did,' Ana says, 'though it was a very long time ago. In Madrigueras, where I met your grandfather.'

'Madrigueras?' Sarah is only half listening now because she's studying the young man next to Ana.

Ana watches her intently. 'Do you recognise him?' she asks, finally.

She can't see anything of the Michael she knew in the figure; and yet, the crucifix at his neck. It must be. 'My grandfather.'

'Yes,' Ana says, lifting the picture. 'Michael Doherty. My love, back then. We only managed a matter of months together.'

'You and my grandfather.' *Of course it's him. It really was him, he really wrote those words.*

'It was a long time ago.' Ana sighs. 'But that doesn't mean it didn't mean anything to me ... to us.'

'No,' Sarah says. She imagines her grandfather arriving for the first time and all the fear and uncertainty he must have felt. *How much younger he looks than she did when she first arrived here, in Salamanca.*

'Tell me more about this place – Madrigueras.'

'It's a small village, not far from Albacete. You'll learn much more about it another day. I have another picture you must see first. Here.'

Ana lifts a second framed pencil sketch from the box and sets it at the front of the table. 'I'm sure your grandfather would want you to have this.'

Two young men stare back at Sarah, each of them in different uniforms. One wears a flat cap; the other, a type of garrison hat. One is slightly broader across the shoulders; one is slightly taller than the other. Their faces are identical.

'I don't understand,' Sarah says, 'It can't be my grandfather and José Luis – these two look like...'

'Brothers?'

'Yes, brothers. So this is Thomas? Tommy? But it doesn't make sense ... my grandfather never talked about a brother.'

'That doesn't mean he didn't have one. They were very hard times, Sarah, and not everything turned out how we would have liked. Now, take another look.' Sarah kneels down next to the picture and bends over the men's chests to observe their faces. Only then does she see the tiny crucifixes at each of their necks. She reels backwards, not knowing what to say.

'It's okay,' Ana says, holding onto her, 'it's a lot for one day. A whole family, different lives to process. How about you come back tomorrow?'

'But I can't tomorrow, it's Carmina's birthday.'

Ana nods her head knowingly. 'I see. Well, the day after, then. I've got lots more to show you and we can talk some more.'

Ana's mind turns to the small crucifix wrapped in crumpled

tissue paper inside her wallet back at the *hostal*. She wishes she had it with her, that she could reunite it with its owner. Her grandfather had a brother. *Jesus, Granda, why didn't you tell us?* She'll look over the other crucifix when she gets back to see if there's any trace of him, of 'Thomas' or 'Tommy'. She's already checked it again and again, trying to figure out who it belongs to, asking herself why it's the same as the one she wears. *Why didn't you tell me, Granda?*

'Can I take this with me?' Sarah brushes her palm across the glass of the framed sketch of the two brothers. 'Please, I'll look after it. I just need some time to look at it.'

'I'm sure your grandfather would like that.'

'Thank you.' Sarah holds it close to her chest. 'Thank you for showing me, for telling me. I really need to go now.'

'As do I.' Ana draws the curtains and is about to put the first picture back into the box when she changes her mind. 'I think I'll let this rest, just here.' She laughs softly and her eyes glisten. 'Your grandfather never made it to this city.'

They descend the stairs to street level. Sarah leads this time, her heart full of fear and love.

'I have one more question, if I may?' she says.

'Of course, Sarah.'

'What was Thomas like? Was he like my grandfather?'

'I'm afraid I never met your great-uncle. He was never with us.'

Day 28: Birthday

The table is laid with the finest crockery that only comes out for special occasions. With the three of them together for the first time on Carmina's birthday, it seemed right to bring out the best dishes stippled in strokes of mauve and silver.

Paco has done a fine job, making sure everything is colour coordinated, just as Sarah requested. Silver balloons tied with purple ribbon sway against the centrepiece bouquet of lavender gilly flower, purple Peruvian lilies and white roses. Carmina's present from them both sits in a silk lilac pouch at the far end of the table.

It hasn't been easy getting Carmina away from the *hostal* while they prepare everything, not without raising her suspicions. On an ordinary day, they could have sent her off for some special pampering, but a public holiday brings its own challenges. In the end, Paco secretly called her good friend Elisa and asked her to take her out for coffee.

The garlicky aroma of the *paella* spills into the dining room as Paco sets down the pan between the three table settings. Sarah lays out the side dishes of warm crusty bread, tomato salad and roasted red peppers.

'Have we forgotten anything?'

'Just the guest of honour.' Paco laughs. 'I'm only teasing; she'll be here any minute. Elisa is under strict orders, though they're not as bad as mine from you!'

'Hey!' Sarah throws a napkin at him. He catches it and throws it back at her.

'What's all this, *hijos?*'

Carmina stands in the doorway, beaming, a vision in a fitted red dress in a ruche fabric and pretty snakeskin effect court shoes.

'Look at you, Aunt! You're so beautiful today!'

'Thank you, *hijo*.' Carmina gives Paco a knowing wink, kisses him on both cheeks, then does the same to Sarah. She steps back to take them in, her eyes darting from one to the other, mischievous, shining with excitement.

'I can't believe you did all this for me! I'm meant to treat you on my birthday, not the other way round!'

'Not this year, Carmina. This year, we do it the Irish way!'

Carmina looks at Sarah. 'Was this your idea?'

'No, it was all his,' Sarah says, nudging Paco in the ribs. 'Honestly.'

'She's too modest, Aunt. None of it would have happened without her.' Paco steals a glance at Sarah. 'Have you seen her in action? My God, she turns into something else!'

Sarah shakes her head and pulls a face at him. 'Don't listen to him, Carmina. You come and sit down here. This is the seat of honour for the birthday girl.'

'¡Feliz cumple, Tía!'

'Yes, a very happy birthday!' Sarah kisses her on the cheek.

Paco makes a point of looking after them both, passing dishes around and refilling their glasses as Carmina talks animatedly. Sarah can tell she's nervous, unaccustomed to the attention she's receiving; she's much more used to lavishing it on others.

Carmina regales them with stories of past birthdays gone wrong – there's the one when she went out for Castile and León day with her girlfriends and had so much wine by early evening that she had to miss the live performances in the *plaza*. Then there's the one when her blind date insisted on pulling her ear for good luck. He'd ended up tugging so hard that he ripped out her earring and proceeded to drop it. 'It was one of the diamond studs you bought me, Paco,' she laughs, 'and you can be sure I never saw that man again!'

Sarah falls back in her chair, her sides hurting from a combination of laughter and too much good food. It's been a long time since she really let herself go. She sees Paco looking at her out of the corner of her eye. 'What?' she says.

'Nothing at all.' He smiles at her and she keeps looking at him for a moment or two. His cheeks flash red with embarrassment and he begins fussing with plates and cutlery. 'Let me clear this away, then we'll do presents.'

'I've been spoilt rotten! Thank you!' Carmina hums softly and runs her fingers over the lily petals of the bouquet. 'But this evening is on me. We'll go out to the *plaza* and I'll treat you, as the birthday girl should!'

'You're not quite done here yet,' Paco says, starting to relax again. 'We've got a few more surprises for you first.'

'Oh?' Carmina is by the fireplace now, taking in the several bouquets in bold and pastel shades lining the hearth. 'Are all these for me?'

'Aren't they pretty? You have a look at all those and Sarah and I will be straight back.'

Sarah takes his cue and follows him into the kitchen with the empty glasses.

'What was all that? I'm sorry, did I embarrass you?'

'Oh, don't mind me,' Paco says, letting the sink fill with soapy water as he scrapes the plates. 'I just forgot myself for a moment. More to the point, I forgot for a split second all you've been through, including that business with Raúl the other day. I was just sitting there and thought ... you look really lovely today.'

'Stop it!' Sarah laughs, flicking the tea towel against his arm. 'Listen, normal has been a long way away from me recently. But that felt pretty normal in there.'

'Didn't it?' Paco dries his hands and puts his arms around her. 'Is this okay?'

'It's more than okay. Look, once we've done presents and Carmina's friends arrive, can I show you something? It'll only take a few minutes.'

'Anything.'

'Okay, great.' She pushes him away gently. 'Let's get back in there, before she starts wondering where we've got to!'

***

'Did you see the look on her face? She really loved it, didn't she?'

'She really did. She's in there showing it off already, I guarantee you. Thanks for picking it out for her.'

'No problem. Hopefully she'll be able to build it up, add more charms linked to special moments. Come here.' Sarah unwraps the brown paper from the framed pencil drawing. 'Look at these two. I don't have any memories of that man.' She taps the glass at the taller man in the garrison hat and sits down on the bed next to Paco.

'Where did you get this? Who is he?'

'You know I'm here trying to find out some things about my grandfather … well, it's a long story, but someone said I could borrow this.'

'So who is he?'

'See this?' She holds out the crucifix. 'Do you remember I told you my grandfather gave it to me not so long ago? Now, look at the picture again.'

'Oh, I see,' Paco says, continuing to stare at the photo. 'But there are two of them.'

'Exactly. Two men, two crosses.' Sarah takes her wallet out of her bag and carefully removes the second crucifix. 'And here's the other one.'

She gives him a moment to turn it over in his hands, to survey the picture again.

'I think he's my great-uncle, Paco. And I can't tell you why I think so right now, but I think he's in London.'

'And you never knew him?'

'My grandfather never uttered a single word about him.'

Paco gets up and walks over to the window. Carmina and her

girlfriends sing softly through the half-open door; Sarah gets up and closes it.

She isn't asking anyone's permission to go to London. If it's true, if the man in the picture is her grandfather's brother, then there's a strong possibility that, like her poor grandfather, he's already passed. There doesn't seem to be too much of an age gap between them, not from Ana's drawing anyhow.

But she doesn't know this. She doesn't know if he's older or younger, alive or dead. She has no expectations about finding the man, or indeed about finding anything at all to do with him if she decides to go. And in the end, she's come to realise that finding those things isn't always the point. The more she travels this path in her grandfather's name, the more she understands it's about the journey for them both.

'I'm sorry, should I not have told you?' Sarah gathers the cross and picture and puts them back where they were.

'I'm so glad you did,' Paco says, turning to face her. 'I'm just trying to imagine how all of this must make you feel. But it's a good thing, isn't it? Getting closer to the answers you've been looking for?'

'Yes. But please don't tell Carmina, not until I know a bit more.'

'I won't tell a soul. It's your business. But I'll be here, whatever happens. Not like some people.'

'I don't want to talk about him today, Paco, please!' As much as she distracts herself with pictures and crosses and celebrations and whatever else, Sarah hasn't yet come to terms with what Raúl has done to her. All that needs to simmer, to balance in the furthest recesses of her mind while she focuses on the rest.

They sit down again, two souls threatening to steer off course. She won't stand for it. 'Look, I'm not letting him get between us,' she says quietly, 'why would I, when we never let him before?'

Paco's eyes meet hers. He won't have it either. She sees it all there – how he won't break her or be the broken man that the other one has become. He's like something injected into her, all the best parts of him, drip feeding her even after five years. They're both still going, sometimes adrift, sometimes temporarily drowning, always resurfacing.

'Let me come to London with you.'

'What? No! I can't ask that of you!'

'But you didn't ask. I offered.'

'This is madness!' Sarah laughs, trying to shrug off her embarrassment. 'If this is because you're afraid I won't come back, trust me, I will! I'm not done here yet.'

'I'm not afraid,' he says, taking her hand. 'I mean it. Let me come with you. How do you know I'm not meant to anyhow?'

'You are mad!' Her mind drifts back to Tank, sitting there in the airport carpark, handing her the envelope.

'I need to go soon,' she says. 'Very soon, in fact. In a few days' time.'

'That's no problem.'

'And I promise it will only be a few days, no more.'

'I can do that.'

'And…' she places her hand over his, 'on two conditions.'

'Whatever you say.'

'We have two days and one of those days we do things together. You know, fun stuff.'

'Okay.' He smiles at her. 'Who would have thought that my first trip to the UK would be connected with an unknown man at an unknown address for an unknown reason?'

Sarah laughs. 'When you put it like that!'

'Tell me, what's the second condition?'

'I'm sorting it – the flights, the hotel. Take it as a thank you.'

'If you stop shutting me out.'

'I can't promise that. Not yet. But maybe soon.'

Day 29: Remembrances

I'd have given anything to stand shoulder to shoulder with my brother like that. The two of us united by blood, the notion of blood ties being enough to keep us together.

I don't know if it was the same for him, but I used to wonder where he was, what he was up to. It's hard to admit it, but there were many occasions when I couldn't think of him in a kind way. Christ, no. I lost count of how many times his name triggered anger, and God almighty, I had a lot of that to burn off. I couldn't help it, even though I knew, deep down, that a combination of things broke us. But there were other times, when I was at my lowest, when I wept like a baby for him: worried myself sick about him being injured or riddled with regret.

I wrote of him in August 1937 when I requested to be sent home. Still remember what I wrote, word for word: *I don't know where our Thomas is. The reports say that O'Duffy and his Brigade have been sent home, but I'm never sure whether what we hear is true. Is it wrong of me to pray it's true? I'm only interested in the welfare of my brother, not the vainglory of men. Will he judge me if I leave too soon?*

I used to wonder how things would've turned out if I'd just sat at home like a good lad, done what I was told and not got involved in anyone else's conflict. Or if Tommy hadn't been swayed by the other side and had come with me and Charlie. Would my mother have disowned us then? Would she have given up on two sons?

And none of that even matters now. All that matters is what I'm allowed to have of him now, whatever that might be.

***

Sarah isn't expecting to see Charlie at the church. 'For you, love,' he says, holding out a shell filled with water. 'It's of the holy kind, a special delivery.'

'Good morning, Charlie. What brings you here?' Sarah dips her hand in the water and crosses herself. 'I didn't know you were joining me and Ana today.' She sees Ana waiting for her in the front row, her head bowed. 'You're very welcome, of course.'

'Oh, I'm just checking in, love,' Charlie says, 'as your grandfather would've wanted. If you ladies are fine, I'll be gone now.'

Sarah treads softly up the aisle and slides into the pew next to Ana. 'I'm glad to see you again,' Ana says, patting her hand, spreading her shawl across both of their laps.

'As I am you.' Sarah smiles at her, grateful for the peacefulness that seems to flow from this woman and saturate the church.

'Tell me,' Ana says, 'what do you see up there?'

Sarah observes the altar. 'Just candles. Lots of them.'

'I know you see more than that. You did before.'

Sarah nods and focuses on the glint of the flames.

'Tell me,' Ana says, sitting up straight. 'What would you like to know?'

'I'd like to hear all about the version of my grandfather I never met.'

'Very well.'

Ana goes back to the very beginning, to her first encounter with him. She admits that when she stormed into Madrigueras in late December 1936, she had no regard for anyone except her parents. 'They were the pretext upon which José Luis sent me back to that hellish place. He said they needed looking after, but there was more to it than that.'

She tells Sarah how her brother was never in favour of her adopting a militant stance, how at most he only wanted her at the front-line distributing food and supplies. 'The protective big brother,' she says, 'when I didn't need protecting.' José Luis feared deeply for her life and wanted her away from it all, even the shelling in the streets of Madrid. 'But I was part of the direct defence,' she says with pride, 'and I was fully committed to the resistance.'

It was an injury on the Madrid front that became the last straw for José Luis. Ana had promised him that if she ever got hurt, she would retreat to their God forsaken village. She never meant it, never thought anything would happen to her. And so it was that a blow to the arm forced her back to the remote village she despised.

'Perhaps 'despise' is too strong a word,' she says, 'but I had no love for it. I'd already been a few months away from it, trying to find my feet in Madrid, and there was nothing back there for me. Then the war broke out and all my plans were turned on their head. The war gave me purpose,' she says thoughtfully, 'something to believe in.'

'So that's how you met my grandfather?'

'That's right, I'd never have met him otherwise. And when I began to sense something between us, I stopped being so bitter. I never lost my militant streak, though. We can't change who we are, can we? I got my way and eventually returned to the front, but it cost me a dear piece of your grandfather – something we'd made together. They say things happen in strange ways.'

'What was my grandfather like, back then?'

'The truth? He was a timid young man, didn't adapt naturally. To be fair to him, he wasn't alone. The olive oil and cheap alcohol were the bane of the lives of all the foreigners in the village!' She reaches into her coat pocket and produces two small candles. 'Let's light a few more of these while we talk. For your grandfather and his friend Charlie.'

Sarah's heart leaps at the mention of Charlie's name.

'He's still watching out for you, Charlie, he won't leave your side. You know that, don't you?'

'I know.'

'As for your grandfather, it was his timidness and his care for me and his soldier friends that began to dawn on me as my temper calmed. He was a polite man, mastered pleasantries and greetings in Spanish before most of the others even attempted a few words. Did he stay like that?'

'What do you mean?'

'Polite, shy. Was that the man you knew as your grandfather?'

Sarah takes a moment to think. 'Well, yes. He always encouraged good manners, said we'd get far enough if we had those sorted, along with keeping our wits about us.' She smiles, remembering him sitting in his chair next to the hearth giving one of his lectures on kindness and respect.

'And as for shy, no, I wouldn't call him shy. People knew him as the quiet man, but he'd never hold back if he'd something worth saying.'

'Ah, the shyness of youth!' Ana taps the altar where she'd like Sarah to place the recently-lit candle. 'Please, you offer that one up for Charlie, God rest his soul; I'd like this one to be for your grandfather.' She holds her candle aloft, then sets it next to Sarah's.

'I noticed later that he was handsome. A pale man, fine-featured. If I'd known we'd only have a few months together when we first met, I wouldn't have taken so long to notice.'

Ana stares into the middle distance and Sarah wonders what image of her grandfather she holds, tries to re-create. 'My love for him wasn't instantaneous; it came after a few weeks, like a sea washing over us both. Does it make sense to you?'

'I think so,' Sarah says. But all she can think about is her grandmother, about the love she and her grandfather had for each other.

'Your turn,' Ana says, beckoning her down the steps of the altar. 'Come and sit back down here and tell me about the man you knew.'

Sarah won't mention Annie's name; she won't hurt this

woman with another woman's love for her grandfather. She focuses on herself, her cousins, her mother and aunts – the Michael Doherty who had four children and five grandchildren, the storyteller she knew and loved, the well-travelled man. She tells her about the café and surprises herself by mentioning Tank. She won't tell Ana that her father or Uncle Cormac died.

'Do you have any children, Ana?'

Ana stares at her with intent; Sarah cannot read her thoughts, though she sees hurt, emptiness.

'I'm so glad Michael got to have the life I hoped he would,' she says finally. She sighs softly and kneels down next to Sarah. 'I don't have any children, no. I suppose they weren't meant for me.'

She crosses herself and stands up. 'Come on, let's go outside.'

'Can we light a candle for you and José Luis first?'

'We'll do that next time.'

Ana processes down the aisle like the bride she never got to be. There's a whole lifetime within her that Sarah still has no sense of.

'Do you see down there?' Ana points at a gap between the shops on the opposite side of the street. 'Next time you come, go down there and you'll find the door that leads to the apartment. Just follow the steps we took last time. I've got something else for you.'

'Can't we go now?' Sarah is aware of the soft plea in her voice. She doesn't want to have to wait for another visit in a few days' time. She's lived enough dragging hours and days.

'I know you're going to London tomorrow,' Ana says, nodding wisely. 'When that's done, come and find me again.'

'But I still have so many questions. What happened to my grandfather? To you?'

'As do I, dear. There are so many questions.' Ana glides backwards slowly, her features beginning to blur again, flickering as they had done when she and Sarah first met in Madrid.

'No!' Sarah cries out, 'you can't go yet!'

'Everything is merely fleeting.' Ana's voice is barely audible, a whisper on the warm breeze. 'I'll come back soon.'

***

Paco joins her where she asked him to, at the far end of the bridge from where they can contemplate the sweep of the city. The sun has faded to a pale haze of gold trapped behind the spires of the cathedrals.

'It's a strange place, isn't it? Does it make you feel like that?'

'I guess it didn't until you came along. I mean that as a compliment.' He laughs, holds her close. 'Though I'd probably describe it as changeable rather than strange. Right, then. Do you want a photo here? Is that why you wanted me to bring the camera?'

Sarah looks down into the River Tormes in search of the city's reflection, but it no longer ripples there.

'Not today,' she says, wondering when the reflection will return, when her own will reappear. When she'll see Ana again.

Day 30: London Town

They arrive in central London just before 2:30pm after a smooth flight and not so smooth road trip to Barajas airport, which had involved an accident on the A-50, a tailback of several miles, and a delay of almost an hour. Still, they are here now, Sarah thinks, as they stand in the short queue at reception to check in to their budget hotel near King's Cross.

She turns to Paco, but he's no longer by her side. She spots him at the entrance to the hotel, snapping photos of what Sarah supposes can only be the street and pedestrians, the odd black taxi and double decker bus. It's her first proper trip to London – catching flight connections at Heathrow don't count as visiting – but she's seen enough of her grandmother's postcards from family members to at least feel like she's been here before.

She'd thought about letting her mother know she was coming, but in the end she'd decided against it. It wasn't to keep anything hidden from her – it was only to avoid any potential questions about why she couldn't take an additional one-hour flight home to see them all, or at least call to see to see the English side of the family, as Annie calls them, in Greenwich.

As she stands there waiting, she wonders why adding anything additional onto their two-day schedule would have been so terrible. She's never had a chance to see her grandmother's relatives in their London home. And at any other time, she'd have jumped at the chance to see her mother and grandmother, even if it was only for a few hours. But the last few weeks have taught her that she's still got some way to go, that slow and steady is the way forward. For now, potentially meeting up with a new family member – one she isn't even sure is aware of her existence – is more than enough to deal with. She'll head to East Croydon tomorrow by herself, in search of Great-Uncle Thomas.

'Come on, Paco, let's go.' Paco comes bounding towards her, all smiles, swinging his small suitcase in one hand, holding onto the camera strap around his neck with the other. 'It looks wonderful out there,' he says, taking in the other guests who are also waiting for the lift. 'Freezing cold, but wonderful.'

Within half an hour, they're outside King's Cross, wondering what to do first.

'Do you have a preference?'

'Not at all,' Paco says. 'I'll be led by the expert.'

'I keep telling you, I'm no expert. This is my first time, too. Exciting, isn't it?' She rubs her hands and pushes them deep into her pockets. 'My God, you're right, it is cold. I know, let's head to the tube and start with some of the main sights.'

They embark on a whistle stop tour of London, in and out of dark, packed tube stations, through crowded streets of vendors, tourists and Londoners going about their everyday business. They start with Buckingham Palace and make their way to Westminster. Their conversation is sporadic, their attention focused on taking in as much as possible of what's going on around them. They buy pretzels from a street cart and snack on them as they cross the Thames at Westminster Bridge. Paco clicks his camera incessantly and only stops to catch his breath once they're on the opposite bank.

'Thank you for all of this,' he says, fishing out a few more pretzels from the cone. 'I don't know if I'd ever have got here if it wasn't for you.'

'Don't be silly, of course you would have!'

'I'm not so sure,' Paco says, sizing up Big Ben on the north bank and the London Eye on the south through the lens of his camera. 'It's easy to talk about doing these sorts of things, much harder to do them on your own. Especially if you don't really speak the language.'

He puts the camera down for a moment and points to the bridge. 'Go and stand there. Let me get you in at least one of the photos.'

'If you insist.' Sarah smiles at him and positions herself a few metres ahead. 'Is here okay?'

'Perfect,' he says. 'Now give me your best pose!'

Sarah laughs and swings around like a small bird released from its cage. 'Like this?' she says, fake pouting, touching her chin, leaning towards the camera.

'Just like that!' Paco says, laughing hard.

***

Early evening is bedding down beneath a brisk nip of wind when they reach Covent Garden. A couple of street performers are gathering their boxes of coins and instruments outside St Paul's Church. Sarah wonders who they might be; if they're a duo or strangers to one another. There's the odd human statue as they stroll towards the market – a man chalked white with angel wings and a Charlie Chaplin lookalike. The warm aroma of roasted chestnuts hugs the air.

They pretend to consider al fresco dining under the fairy lights of the piazza and instead turn back into one of the roads running off it. A waiter waves at them from the doorway of what looks like a decent grill house and they rush inside without checking its name. He leads them to a small wooden table in a nook by the window.

'This is great,' Paco says, blowing his hands. 'We'll be warmed up in no time, what with the heat of this place and a few nice drinks. What do you say?'

'Sounds good to me!' Sarah takes the menu from the waiter and scans the starters and appetisers.

'I don't know about you, but I'm starving,' she says. 'Do you fancy something for starters?'

'You choose anything you want. This is on me.'

'Okay,' Sarah says, knowing this battle isn't one worth fighting.

She orders for them both and moves her chair a little closer to the radiator. The velvety Rioja warms her throat and she begins to relax a little.

'So tell me,' she says, 'what do you really make of old London town?'

'Let's just say it hasn't disappointed so far, although I don't think I could do the one hundred miles an hour thing every day.' He smiles, pulls his shoulders back and stretches. 'Honestly, how do people do that?'

'I don't know. I suppose it's just like everything. You get used to it.'

'I suppose you do.'

'Listen, what you said earlier, about it being harder doing things by yourself ... we could start doing more together.'

Paco leans forward, brushes her hair from her face. 'Do you really mean it?' He takes a drink and nurses the wine glass between his hands.

'Yes, I do,' Sarah says. 'Too much time has been wasted. We need to get out and about more.'

'I'd like that,' he says, looking pensive. 'Though it might be a bit trickier if you're back home and I'm in Spain.' Sarah can't work out if it's a statement or a question.

'Belfast is next on your list,' she says. 'You'll have to come and meet the family, see the flat, get a chance to look around the city. There's plenty to photograph there.'

He asks her to tell him more and settles back in his chair while they wait for food. They're both aware it's just an easy conversation filler to prevent them from talking about what's really going on between them.

'Your Aunt Mary sounds like fun. Is she anything like Carmina?'

'I can promise you they're like night and day. My God, you wouldn't wish Mary on anyone!'

They both laugh and thank the waiter who's arrived with two medium steaks and a range of sides.

'We could feed an army here!' Paco says. 'Carmina would love this.'

'Do you think she bought it, our story about coming here?'

'If anything, I don't think we'll ever hear the end of it!' Paco laughs. 'Not that it bothers me. We didn't really tell her a story, did we? We just conveniently forgot to mention the part about you looking for your great-uncle. She'll be reading all sorts into this, you know.'

'I know.'

'And I don't mind at all,' Paco says.

Day 31: Reproductions

'I can't believe this is happening, Son. God knows who or what's behind that door. Seventy years is far more than some people even get – look at you, for Christ's sake – and here we are dealing with seventy years wasted.'

'It may be something or nothing, Da. One step at a time.'

The house in East Croydon is a modest end terrace in need of some loving restoration to its exterior. Scalloped black railings sit atop a dirty white wall spewing moss and grass, while the ornate cream period pillars of the bay window don't match the white PVC door. There are no curtain or blinds on the front window; from where Sarah stands at the gate, the naked window offers nothing except the reflection of half a grey terrace and a slice of a red house on the other side of the road.

She's aware that too much time loitering, her gaze fixed on the house beyond the gate, is likely to attract the attention of neighbours. She looks from the bay to the two slim upper windows and wonders which one Great-Uncle Thomas is behind, if he's there at all.

She waits impatiently for the door to open, even though she's certain it takes no time at all. Time is meaningless when competing against an assault of anticipation and anxiety. Sarah shields the side of her face from the glare of the front window. She knows that it's irrational, that seeing anything inside before she's invited in won't determine whether she's welcome or not. But she'll continue to stand like that anyway, just in case.

When the door opens, there's a brightly-lit hallway and a woman in a crouched position, gathering up a few letters scattered across a grey 'Welcome' mat. 'Sorry, just give me a second please,' she says, not looking up.

As soon as her eyes meet Sarah's, there's a mutual gasp and both women step back. Sarah scans the woman, who must be in her mid to late fifties; she looks just like her mother, only with dark hair and a few additional crease lines next to her eyes and above her mouth.

'May I help you?' the woman stammers. 'Who are you?'

Sarah hesitates and for a moment wonders at the absurdity of the situation. Here she is, a total stranger on someone's doorstep, seeking an invitation into their home without being able to clarify exactly why. She thinks she should have brought some ID, like a desperate cold caller, and immediately dismisses the ridiculous idea.

'Hello, sorry to bother you. I'm looking for ... Does a Mr Doherty live here? A Mr Thomas Doherty?'

'Who's asking?' The woman turns round, sets down the letters on the hall table and picks up a pair of glasses. Her brow furrows when she puts them on, her expression studious. Sarah feels her eyes track up and down the length of her.

'Look, please let me try to explain. I know all of this is going to sound a bit weird. But I'm here about Michael Doherty. A Belfast man, he is ... was.' Sarah takes a few seconds to control the tears collecting in her throat that threaten to drown her voice. She coughs lightly.

'Michael Doherty, you say?' Eimear steps forward and touches Sarah's hand. Well, aren't you a sight for sore eyes! You'd better come in. I'm Eimear by the way.'

'Nice to meet you, Eimear,' Sarah says on a sort of autopilot, wiping her feet on the mat, watching the woman who is making her way down the hall in front of her. She's already forgotten her name and will ask her to repeat it when she gets to the lounge.

'It's no problem,' the woman says kindly, 'it happens to the best of us. I'm not very good with names either. It's Eimear.'

'Thank you. Sorry again.' Sarah waits for Eimear to indicate where she should sit. 'I'll just go and put the kettle on and then you can tell me which one owns you.'

The lounge is nothing like the tatty exterior. Everything is immaculate in shades of cream and gold, the furniture and floor coordinated in varying tones of oak. The walls, fireplace and display cabinet are sparsely decorated and there's nothing on the coffee table except four pretty coasters with images of flowers and the names of the seasons. It's a room created with love, the few decorations selected with obvious care. The carriage clock on the fireplace, similar to her grandmother's, is the only impersonal item. The pictures on the walls and cabinet ornaments are photos or reproductions of photos in the form of paper weights and glass cubes.

'I can't believe how like the Dohertys you are.' Eimear moves the coasters and sets down two cups of tea. 'Won't you have a biscuit with that? You can't have a cup of tea without a wee something to go along with it.'

'I'm fine, thanks.' Sarah smiles, wondering about Eimear's hint of an Irish accent.

'I just need to know, before we get into anything else, is there a Thomas Doherty and does he live here?'

'He does indeed,' Eimear says, walking over to the door, listening out into the hallway. 'He's just having his mid-morning lie down. The tablets take their toll on my poor father, God love him.'

'You're Thomas' daughter? Is he okay? What's wrong with him?'

'I certainly am.' Eimear leaves the door ajar and sits down opposite Sarah. 'And there's nothing wrong with Da, don't you worry, just a few bits that start creaking and grinding to a halt. Know what I mean? He turned ninety last week, God bless him. So tell me, who owns you?'

'I'm Chrissie's daughter,' Sarah says, 'and you're the image of my mam.'

Eimear goes on to ask her how old she is now, if she has any siblings, if her grandfather's café is still going strong. And the whole time, as she responds with the bare bones of answers, Sarah's trying to understand how this woman knows something of her, of her family. How she can know and never have made contact. How Sarah can have a whole family she never knew existed.

'The entire situation is a bit of a nightmare, to be honest with you.' Eimear sets the cup down a little abruptly. 'I knew nothing about any of you until about twenty years ago now, when my grandmother – your grandfather's mother – passed away, God bless her.' Eimear sighs. 'I tried to get that oul' fool up those stairs to make contact with your grandfather then, but he was having none of it. Said you can't just waltz into a man's life after fifty years and upset the apple cart.' She taps her fingers nervously on the edge of the table. 'I'm so glad to see you, love. But I'm not sure if Da will be able to handle this.'

'I don't want to cause any trouble; that's not what I'm here for.'

'Oh, I know, love. Don't you worry at all about that.' She moves across to the sofa next to her. 'Is this alright, me sitting here?' Sarah nods. 'Jesus, I tried, but that one' – she points to the ceiling – 'that one told me if I dared to try to go over to you lot, he'd never speak a word to me again. And he's your great-grandmother's double. Look what she did to this family! No way I could risk losing my oul' father, even though he drives me round the bend most days.'

Sarah gets up and moves across to the window. It has started to rain now, tiny droplets staining the exterior of the red house in front. Some of it is starting to make sense: the cards from her great-grandparents never posted directly to her grandparents, them never showing up in person, the few cards stopping altogether when Sarah was only a child.

'You've gone very quiet, love. You sure you're alright?'

'What did my great-grandmother do to them? Did she stop

Michael and Thomas seeing each other, is that it? Is that why I don't know him?'

The ceiling creaks under the tread of feet crossing the bedroom. 'I'm sorry, love,' Eimear says, getting up. 'I don't know the ins and outs of it, but this family was broken. I better go and see to my father. He's not too great on the stairs anymore, though he insists he's in fine shape. Stubborn as a mule, he is.' She goes to leave the room and stops, turns round to face Sarah. 'If you're not in too much of a rush, do you mind giving us a bit of time? I can have a word with him, get the lay of the land. If you call back in, say, half an hour or so, we can take it from there.'

'That sounds fine,' Sarah says. 'I'll see myself out. And Eimear, thanks for this.'

'I'll see what I can do.' Eimear pats her on the shoulder and nods reassuringly. 'He'll be delighted to hear about your grandfather, I'm sure. Talks about him all the time now – I don't know, I think it's an age thing. How's he doing anyhow?'

Sarah's face falls. The rain is heavier now and Sarah feels as though it is trickling through her. She wishes it could dampen the grief that has been lying dormant and is stirring once more.

'Michael – my grandfather – passed away exactly a month ago. You might want to tell Thomas.'

***

Forty minutes later following a soggy stroll through Park Hill, Sarah is back outside the house. She worries if she's given them enough time to themselves, if Thomas is ready to meet his great-niece so soon after learning he's lost a brother. She wonders how this loss compares with losing him all those years ago and if he's already grieved for him.

Eimear waves to her from the front door and beckons her in. Sarah goes inside quickly, dropping her umbrella roughly into the stand in the hall and throwing her coat over the bottom of the banister. Although she knows her grandfather traces every step with her, that he's right there with her, she would give anything for him to reappear in the flesh right now.

Thomas is sitting in the chair next to the fireplace in a white shirt and navy wool cardigan buttoned up to the chest. His hands are joined together on his lap and he stares into the distance; there's a solemn, thoughtful demeanour about him. Sarah's heart is sore at the sight of him – he might as well be her grandfather sitting there, a little older, a little more dilapidated, a little greyer. His silver hair has been combed back carefully and tiny prickles of white facial hair suggest he hasn't shaved for a day or two.

Eimear nods and Sarah knocks the lounge door with a light brush of her knuckles. 'Ah, you're here, love,' Thomas says, swapping his more serious expression for a kind look. He raises his hand and shows her the sofa. 'Please come and sit down. I'm delighted that you're here.'

'I'll go and make a pot of tea and leave you to it. If you need anything in the meantime, just give me a shout.'

'Thanks, love.' Thomas' voice grates like old trodden floorboards as he wipes a handkerchief across his mouth. 'My poor brother,' he continues. 'Tell me, love, did he have a peaceful death?' He coughs and puts the hankie across his mouth again, then slides it into his trouser pocket. 'At this rate, I'll be no distance behind him!'

'Yes, Mr Doherty. It wasn't too bad, considering.'

'Considering? Considering what?'

'Ah, it was a bit drawn out, you know, but thank God they managed the pain for him.' Sarah's mind slips back to night after night by his bedside, watching his body thin out and words fail him. It seems like no time at all has passed and yet, it sometimes feels like a whole lifetime ago.

'I bet he had you all spoiled rotten as children, always was a bit soft round the edges. Not like me.' He lets out a small laugh. 'I was the tough nut.'

'I'm sure you weren't,' Sarah smiles, 'and you look just like him. Do you mind if I ask whether he knew you were in London? Why would he never mention you?'

'There's a lot in those questions of yours, love.' He shifts in the chair and a sweep of pain flashes across his face. 'Bloody oul' bones. Be grateful for your youth while you have it! Come over here a second, let me get a good look at you.'

Sarah crouches next to him and he squints to see better. 'You're definitely a Doherty, aren't you? Thank God and his Holy Mother for that.' He pats her hand gently. 'Apart from the hair.'

'Oh, I'm red like my nanny, and my mam,' Sarah says, pushing her hair back over her shoulders.

'And I take it my brother gave you that?' He points at the crucifix at her neck.

'Ah, yes. He did.' Sarah feels her face flush with the comfort of him recognising it, of what the sight of it must mean to him.

'I had one just like it. Anyhow, where's our Eimear with that drop of tea? Jesus, I'm gasping here.'

'You're just like my grandfather,' Sarah says, trying to take everything in. 'He'd have done without many things, apart from a bit of heat and a cup of tea.'

'Good man!' Thomas straightens his cardigan and runs his fingers through his hair, as if preparing himself for an important encounter. 'I don't know if he knew where I was, love, but it wasn't my place to let him know. No, not place … it wasn't my right to let him know. Ma wouldn't have tolerated any of it.'

'I don't understand. What did he do that was so awful?'

'He was a young man with a big heart and an even bigger stubborn streak. I can talk, it ran all the way through the two of us.' He takes a moment to catch his breath. 'Do you know about the war, love?'

'I didn't, but I know now you were both out in Spain. My grandfather didn't tell me anything before.'

'Right you are.'

'You feeling okay, Da?' Eimear puts the mug between his hands and puts her own hand underneath to steady it. 'Have a drink, then I'll set it down for you.' Thomas does as he's told and then pushes himself up in the chair.

'Eimear, could you do me a favour? I need to have another yarn here with Sarah and there's some stuff in the attic I'd like her to see. Would you mind taking a race up later and getting it down? So I can show her tomorrow?'

'No problem, Da. But I'm not sure if Sarah's able to come back tomorrow. Are you, Sarah?'

'I could do early morning if it suits,' Sarah says, hoping not to sound too desperate. 'I've got a flight to catch at midday, but I can come back over before I leave.'

'I'd like that,' Thomas says. 'I'd like you to tell me a bit more about our Michael and what you're doing with yourself.'

'I'd like that, too,' Sarah says, 'and to know what you and my grandfather got up to.'

Thomas' face darkens. 'I'm not proud of everything I did. Oh, the moment it hit me, when I realised I'd made a grave mistake. How can it have been seventy years ago...'

Day 32: Confessions

'When I went off to Spain, I was certain I was doing the right thing. All the talk that was going on, and the talking to I got from Father McMahon, reinforced it. He told me to treat it as a form of penance for my sins, a true standing up for my faith.

'I can't deny that I wasn't also lured by the sense of adventure. I was a twenty-year-old working with my father and our Michael in Belfast and I needed to get away. There was only so much more of Belfast I could tolerate.

'I worked on Michael, tried to cajole him into filling in one of O'Duffy's forms, too. He was having none of it. I earned my place. And Michael earned his place, too, though he kept his plans hidden until the very last minute. That was another thing my mother couldn't bear, him not being straight about things. I wasn't the one off doing what I shouldn't have been at. I mean, we'd reports of burning churches, broken statues of saints and nuns' corpses flung into the streets. How is a young man meant to deal with that? They don't tell you that now, do they, when they're teaching you the history? Making us out to be the awful ones.'

'You're right,' Sarah says. 'There's so much I don't know.'

'And all the while, I thought Michael was burying his head in the sand. I'd no idea he was thinking of fighting for the other side. He was far too quiet for such things. And even on the day we were leaving, I still tried to work on him.' Thomas takes out what looks like an old letter from the pocket of his cardigan, unfolds it and scans it, then puts it back.

'I don't mean to be unkind,' Sarah says in a low voice, 'but history has certainly revised itself, hasn't it? That's not your fault, of course it isn't. How could you have known?'

213

Thomas takes out his handkerchief, this time to dry his eyes. 'They can re-write history all they like, but they can't rewrite a man's experience. Why do you think I feel so much shame?' He looks around the lounge for any sign of Eimear or anyone else. 'Years of it, on top of losing a brother. I'd never tell my daughter; God knows what she'd think of me.'

Sarah regards him, aching now at the mere thought of his pain. She can see he's nothing but a shell of the man she never even knew. 'So you gave up on my grandfather, is that it?'

'Not at all,' he whispers, his voice hoarse. 'It was Ma, our whole community who gave up on him. Abandoning his religion, they said, not taking a stand against communism, all of it just wasn't acceptable. As for me, I was told I was doing the right thing. Michael had so much to give,' Thomas continues. 'And I swear to you, that day we said goodbye, without actually saying it, I didn't know I'd never see my brother again. I headed off to Dublin while he and Charlie were picked up in the city centre.'

'Charlie?' Sarah's heart thumps hard. 'You knew Charlie?'

'What do you mean?' Thomas turns to look at her. Up until now, he's been staring ahead at the bay window. Sarah knows that Doherty trait very well – speak but don't look to retain any guard you have left. Her grandfather was a master at it.

'You said Charlie.'

'Yes, of course I knew him. He was your grandfather's best friend. Probably meant more to him than I ever did, and that's not me being a sentimental oul' fool. Your grandfather and I were very close as youngsters, but I always wanted to be a big lad and left him in my shadow. Who's the big lad now?'

'So Charlie went with him.' Sarah already knows it; Charlie told her as much himself, all those days ago when he first mentioned Ana. And then there was the candle offered up for him. And her grandfather's diary entry. But that's not the same as him being transformed now into a living, breathing young man through her great-uncle's words. She slots together the wafer-thin figure who's been following her around Salamanca and the fresh-faced soldier in Ana's drawing. *Neither of you will be alone.* It's an affirmation for herself, for them.

'We went our separate ways,' Thomas says, looking away from her again. 'I got my checks done in Dublin and then they took us to Galway. I'll never forget it, sitting in traffic in a packed Eyre Square in the early hours of the morning and then the whole palaver of boarding the Urundi in the teeming rain. We were shattered by the time we got to El Ferrol, but thank God I wasn't ill like a lot of the other lads. I managed the twenty-four hour journey alright to Salamanca.'

'Salamanca?' Sarah gets to her feet. 'I lived there, you know, I ... I've just come from there.'

Thomas doesn't comment for a while. 'Can it really be true that you ended up there?' he says eventually. 'What must Michael have thought?'

'He never talked to me about the place.'

Thomas' face pales and he begins to tremble slightly. 'I knew a few months in that I'd made a mistake. I could accept the shell fire and filth and bombing and boredom if only my brother would remain safe. Jarama was the worst: friends, siblings, spread out on opposite sides of the plain. I swear I saw Michael there.'

Sarah notices him struggling to get comfortable in the chair and goes over to help him. She hands him a clean handkerchief from the small pile on the table next to him. 'I was glad to get out,' he says, wiping his eyes. 'Four months was more than enough.' He takes the letter out of his pocket again. 'This was the only letter Ma and Da ever sent me, took months to get through. Thank God it got to me in the end; that's how I knew where to go.' He holds the letter out to Sarah. 'Would you like to see it? They sorted me out.'

'It's okay, thanks,' Sarah says. Somehow touching the letter of those who abandoned her grandfather would seem like an injustice, a tarnishing of his memory. 'But I don't blame you for any of this. I don't want you to think that.' She takes his hand and is struck by the cold weightlessness of it. 'I know it can't have been easy, but thank you for telling me all of this. I just needed to know.'

Thomas asks her to help him out of the chair. She hoists him up as gently as she can, afraid she'll hurt his empty frame. He holds onto her arm and shuffles out to the hallway.

'There,' he says, pointing at a box on the stairs. 'That's what I was talking about yesterday. All my letters to Ma and Da are in there. I don't know why, but they kept them for some reason. I've no need for them. By God, if anything, they continue to torment me, even stuck up there in the attic.'

Eimear comes out of the kitchen, her eyes bright. 'Are you two alright? What are you up to, Da, you shouldn't be up on your feet for no reason.' She turns to Sarah and indicates the box. 'I brought that down to content him, no idea what's in there.'

'Thanks,' Sarah says. 'I don't think there's anything in there I need to see. But I have something for you, Great-Uncle Thomas, which I know my grandfather would like you to have.'

Between them, Sarah and Eimear help Thomas back to his chair. 'You've gone cold, Da,' Eimear says, tucking a heavy blanket around his legs. 'Wait there and I'll go and put the heating on.'

Sarah reaches into her wallet and takes out the crucifix. She unwraps it carefully from the tissue paper and places it in the curve of Thomas' palm.

His face lights up at the sight of it. He clenches his fist around it with all the strength he can manage and opens his hand again to check it's still there.

'A present from your brother,' Sarah says.

My poor brother, God bless him. My poor, poor brother. I pray he finds peace now. No greater gift could be given to him at this point in his late life. I want to wrap my arms around him and tell him I'm here. I'm sure he'll understand in time; Sarah will make sure of it.

'Are we done now, Da? Your time is almost up.'

'Not quite, Son. There's something I need to share with Sarah, and something she needs to do for herself.'

Day 33: Madrigueras 1

'How are you, Mam? How's Nanny?'

'We're both fine, love, thanks. Things seem to be easing a little.' Mam's voice crackles down the line and Sarah instinctively starts uncoiling the phone lead. It's during those calls, when the connection is less than perfect, that she misses them most of all.

'Does that sound selfish? I mean, your nanny says things are getting better, but you know how she's got a tendency to conceal the truth to protect everyone else. She's receiving some visitors now, not just Tank, and she's back at her weekly bingo.'

'That all sounds positive, thank God. And what about everybody else?'

'Tank is flat out at the café, which is great as it means more work for me. I'm much better when I'm occupied, love. As for Mary, God bless her, she's back at work at long last and your nanny's getting a bit of peace. I'm sure that's it,' she laughs, 'the main reason why she's feeling better.'

Sarah laughs, too. 'Her head must have been away, stuck in the house with Mary day and night.'

'You better believe it. So, any news on when you're coming home?'

Her pause is too long. 'Not yet, but if you ring me at the same time next week, I can let you know then.'

'That's an awful long time, love. Don't you be forgetting about us.'

Sarah hangs up after a few more minutes, checks her bag for her keys and purse and heads for the front door.

'Have you rung him back yet?' Carmina makes her way down the stairs, a wicker laundry basket balanced between her hands.

She looks like she's ready for a lunch out with the ladies, rather than a cleaning day. Her hair is freshly curled, her lips glossed a deep ruby red after several applications. She's wearing the new cork sandals Elisa bought her for her birthday and her charm bracelet glints against her cream lace sleeve. 'That's the third time he's rung now in so many days.'

'I know. Not yet,' Sarah says. 'I'll do it when I'm ready. I won't have him calling the shots. If he phones again, you can tell him that.'

'I'm very glad to hear it.' Without further comment, Carmina glides towards the kitchen, the soles of her new footwear skimming the hall floor.

The street is busier than usual with Saturday shoppers and people enjoying a relaxed coffee morning or brunch date. Paco has already left for a commission in the nearby pretty walled city of Ávila and it'll be a few hours before he gets back.

As she retraces her steps under the clock tower back onto Calle Zamora, Sarah knows there's the slimmest chance that she might cross paths with Raúl or María. She won't be caught off guard again; she'll remain fully protected behind her own wall. She imagines it trekking along the cobbles in a row of low turrets, veering right to fortify the entrance to Ana's apartment.

Sarah climbs the stairs and hears a shush of female voices tumbling onto the landing through the half-open door. It sounds like a small community gathering, an invitation-only event.

'Come straight through,' Ana calls, her voice drowning out any others Sarah thinks she might have heard.

'Good morning.' Sarah lets herself in without hesitation. The room looks the same as before, except for the thick blanket of cobwebs trailing the width of the window and cascading down to the skirting board. It filters the natural light from the street, transforming the space into a protected private retreat. There is no one there apart from Ana. She waits by the window in the same *miliciana* clothes as before and holds a bundle of worn, frayed papers between her hands.

'Sit here next to me.' Ana's voice seems a little sharper and more authoritative than Sarah remembers it. 'I hope you had a good trip to London.' She's laying out the pages like she's handling treasured objects. Her hands are protected with the nitrile gloves of a conservator.

'I did, thanks,' Sarah says, 'but what is all this?'

Ana's face has blanked, stripped bare of any trace of sentiment. It unsettles Sarah and she wonders if Ana's soul has abandoned her fragile body; if her desire for another time, for another state of being, has been granted for a precious moment.

'These are your grandfather's diary notes, the last things I have for you,' she says finally, colour rising in her cheeks again. She sets the rest of the papers on her lap. 'Would you like me to share them with you?'

Sarah fights against the convulsion of emotions pumping through her; she's frightened of what the pages might already contain, what might still be written on them. And yet, this is her grandfather, waiting to share his voice. 'Yes, please. Tell me what's in them.'

Ana lifts the first page and hands it to Sarah. 'This is all your grandfather left behind with me in Spain. You've seen something of them already, but the rest of his account is here.' Her voice has faded to a whisper. 'This is the man you've been searching for, the man who belonged here.' She continues looking at Ana, her eyes crystalled in tears. 'Please read his words.'

The paper quivers within the gentle clasp of Sarah's hand.

'Please, Da, read with her. Read with Sarah.'

'Okay, Son, but only if I can do it my way. It needs to come from this man, the man I am now.'

Madrigueras, January 1937
I've never been one for many words and I've certainly never written

any down. Back in Belfast, I was always doing something or other and the thought would never have crossed my mind. I wonder, now, if the urge takes me because I'm away from everything I know. Thank God for Charlie. Someone ~~familiar,~~ **constant,** *at least.*

I wonder, too, if it's because ~~I've time on my hands while we're waiting for our involvement to start.~~ **I'm bored out of my mind and we've no idea what's expected of us.** *Every day throws something different at us,* **though very little of it is to do with war or training.** *Charlie and I both said it, we've been through so much in a month.*

~~Home feels like a whole other life.~~ **Does home still exist for me?** *Waiting for letters is hard and I wonder what Ma makes of it all now.*

We caught a boat-train from Victoria to Paris, a lorry to the Spanish border and walked the stretch across the Pyrenees in darkness. Everything is strange – the mix of languages as we crossed the border with fellow travellers, the landscape, the food. But the strangest thing is what this experience is doing to us and I'm still trying to figure that out.

When we arrived in Figueras, our first stop in Spain, we were given decent underground billets in a fortress with plenty of room to accommodate us all. From there, we caught the train to the Brigade headquarters in Albacete. None of us thought much of the place, though the Gothic cathedral in the main square was something to look at. Overall, it was a bit dismal and isolated, and probably seemed worse because it was the week before Christmas. **I've never been away at Christmastime before.** *Charlie said he'd never seen such forlorn streets.*

I keep reminding ~~myself~~ **me** *and Charlie why we're here. For the democracies of Ireland and Spain. ~~To fight for the Spanish people.~~* **To fight for what is right.** *And though ~~they~~* **the community, priests and bishops** *tried to tell us back home we were abandoning our faith, I've held on tight to the crucifix Ma gave me and I won't part with it.*

They moved us here to this small village of Madrigueras a week or so after we got to Albacete. A tiny place, nothing at all like what we expected when we set out for Spain. We weren't expecting much; we were coming to war after all, but none of us were prepared for the freezing temperatures and hardships. The British volunteers said the same. All of it set Charlie off with his oul' worry, before we even got stuck into anything. **And Charlie's worry set me off**.

Food is in short supply. Coffee is more bitter than I ever remember and we complain about it constantly. Coffee and dry bread for breakfast, a bit of butter if you're prepared to have the awful stuff. ~~I'd rather scratch the throat off myself~~.

We're up at the crack of dawn for training but ~~the guns are ancient and ammunition is in such short supply~~. **we've no decent weaponry and there's no sign of things improving. The whole situation is farcical**. *We're struggling to make decent soldiers of ourselves through no fault of our own.*

What happened earlier today is a concern. Some of our boys have voted to go over to the Americans. The move away from the British is what's driving them, but they forget these men here are like us: working-class fighters against fascism. I'm trying to reassure **me and** *Charlie everything will be alright. Him worrying makes me worry.*

There's something else — someone else. There's a woman and she's the daughter of the kind people putting me up. She doesn't want to be here but I'm very glad she is. We don't speak because we can't, but I'm working on that. It will take some time.

~~She's different compared to the rest of the villagers, even ones her age~~. **She's exquisite**. *She doesn't notice me, other than seeing me as just another foreigner here to help.* ~~She's generous but serious with all of us~~. **She's one of the most kind-hearted, earnest people I've ever encountered.** *She spends her days tending to her parents and at night treads the muddy streets. She doesn't go to the cinema, or the café.*

I didn't come here other than to fight for ~~the Spanish people~~. **what's right**. *Now I wonder what it is I'm beginning to feel for this woman who fills my thoughts. I've never been in love before. Can you be in love with someone who doesn't see you? I'll keep wondering for now.*

I'll smoke the foul Spanish cigarettes and drink the rancid coffee to distract me. I'll keep ~~trying to be~~ **pretending to want to be** *the soldier I came here to be.*

Sarah hesitantly hands the paper back to Ana, not knowing if she'll accept it. She can't know if the straight-talking grandfather she recognises, the man whose spirit has seeped into this moment, is the same man Ana remembers.

'Are you alright, Ana? Can we continue tomorrow?'

Ana takes the page from her and nods in approval. 'I take back what I said,' she says quietly. 'This isn't the man you've been searching for; this is the man we've both been looking for, who belonged here and elsewhere.'

Day 34: Madrigueras 2

'Come on in, I'd like your expert advice!'

Sarah and Carmina look at each other; one shrugs, the other smiles. 'We are experts in many things, but photography isn't one of them!' Carmina flops onto the end of the sofa and Sarah sits on the arm of the chair where Paco is working. On his lap is what looks like an oversized photo album; he tells them it's his portfolio for the Tourist Board.

'I've got to send off a sample,' he says, studying the contents of one of the pages for a few seconds before flipping it over. From the angle at which Sarah is perched, the pages strut in a V-shape and she can't see the photos properly.

'Let's have a look, then!' Carmina scuttles across and kneels down, resting her hand on Sarah's leg to balance herself.

The photos flit past a few pages at a time before Paco pauses and points at one. 'Do you remember missing this, Sarah?' He runs his finger over the plastic film coating the Philology building. 'The day you went to book your flight. The conditions were perfect that afternoon; that's exactly how it was: no filters, pure beauty.'

'I don't recall it ever looking so bronzed and beautiful,' Sarah says, 'and the façade looks like it's been restored. Isn't it strange the things we don't notice? Day after day I set foot in that building, up and down the steps, and I always thought it was special without really noticing it. Does that make sense?'

'It's a little too much for me.' Carmina pats her leg and laughs softly. 'It looks great, though, *hijo*. What other ones did you take here?'

Paco turns the page and the *Plaza Mayor* appears in all its splendour; there are day and night shots when the arches fizz with gold dust, a close-up shot of the clock tower, and a group of *Tuna* musicians in dark robes serenading onlookers at the Duero café.

'That's the pièce de resistance. I'll never tire of it.'

'Me neither,' Sarah says. Despite some unfortunate happenings she'd rather forget, none of them tarnish her love for the *plaza*.

'What about down by the bridge?' Carmina asks.

'Ah, now, I'm waiting for Sarah for that one. I don't quite know what it will be like, but I know it will be special.' He flicks to the next set of pages. 'Here's where it will go,' he adds, indicating the blank space on the right. 'Sarah has something very particular in her head that she'd like me to capture. Don't you, Sarah? I'm trusting her instincts on this one. She'll be looking for a credit next!'

Sarah doesn't catch everything he's saying; her attention is focused on the shadow brushing the façade of the House of Shells in the photo on the left.

'Do you both see that?' she says, interrupting their conversation. 'There, that shadow, do you see it?'

Paco and Carmina follow the trace of her finger along the front of the building.

'I don't see anything.'

'Neither do I.'

'Then I must be mistaken,' she says, staring at the outline of Charlie. It's a moment captured in mid-flight.

'Perhaps we can use this one of the bridge while we wait for Sarah's?' Paco is laughing, holding out the photo of a windswept Sarah on Westminster bridge.

'Let me see that!' Carmina shrieks, snatching it from his hand before Sarah gets a chance to look. 'Congratulations, *hija*, I love your pout. You just need a little gloss to make it really stand out!'

Sarah takes the photo and smiles, the memory of it warm, soothing. 'So embarrassing,' she says, laughing along with them, wishing she could recreate the image with Paco alongside her, wondering if he's thinking the same.

'I'll leave you to it.' Carmina springs to her feet and heads for the door, sensing she's imposing on an intimate moment. 'I'll go and start preparing some food,' she says, 'and maybe you two can hang out and take that last photo after all.'

Sarah waits for her to leave before returning the London photo to Paco. 'Forever the matchmaker, isn't she?'

Paco slots it behind the cushion and brushes the back of his hand across Sarah's shoulder. 'Is it really such a bad thing?' He looks around the room as if checking for eavesdroppers and fixes his eyes on her. She moves his fringe to one side and sees the reflection of herself within them. The image is unfamiliar at first; a veil of sadness no longer hangs over her and her eyes are brighter. Her cheeks are different too: not full, but not gaunt either.

'Isn't it incredible how a photo captures a fleeting moment in time?' Sarah says.

Paco places his hand over hers. 'That's why I love taking pictures. But there are important things that last longer than a moment, too.'

'True. Do you think they can, even if two people are far apart?'

Paco laces his fingers through hers and continues staring at her. 'I think it's worth taking a chance if you believe in something. But you have to be sure.'

'I know.'

But there is so much Sarah still doesn't know. She doesn't know whether she'll ever forgive Raúl for what he did. She doesn't know how much longer she'll feel her grandfather's spirit guiding her. And she doesn't know that just then, an elderly gentleman in East Croydon is experiencing a thudding in his chest and struggling to breathe through it. He has no fear.

Madrigueras, January 1937

I don't know what José Luis is thinking right now, if anything at all. ~~He's looking a little better than he was, his face and clothing no longer clogged with blood. The swelling around his eyes is going down~~. **He's looking so much worse and the swelling around his eyes is forcing them shut.** *~~But he's still~~* **He's** *a shell of a man, his right leg trailing behind him on the very rare occasion when he stands up. It looks like his leg is playing catch up. I can't imagine the damage on the inside. It always hurts worse on the inside.*

Is it wrong of me to be content he's here? He's only here because of his injury. But him being here has made her — Ana — see me.

I can tell José Luis is asking Ana about me in the way he looks at me when he's saying a few words. I'm not sure if he's quiet by nature or if his voice is one of those things war has kicked out of him. I pass him drinks and straighten his coverings and he nods in appreciation. It's very little, but I ~~feel more useful in a very small way~~. **I feel closer to Ana that way.** *Charlie could do with someone to distract him too.*

We're both feeling the weight of the departure of some of the boys. Now that they're out of the way, some of the British are calling them troublemakers and are ~~very pleased~~ **delighted** *to see the back of them. We've befriended a Welsh man, Morris Williams, from the Rhondda, who looks like he's more cut out for this than us. Must be all that graft in the mines.* **Morris is a true gent, no question about it.** *He smokes too much and eats even less than I do, but he seems a mild-mannered, robust lad. Charlie is especially glad of his company when I'm not around.*

New recruits are coming in too and we're building ourselves up again. We didn't just lose to the Americans, but to the enemy ~~at Lopera~~. Too many heavy casualties, and so many bullets, they say, that they made up their own song. **We have our own traditional songs to keep our spirits up. Charlie always loves the chance to belt out a few tunes.**

We still don't know when it will be our turn to join the fight, but with every day that passes, the day gets closer. I'm learning more

Spanish and José Luis is helping me from his sick bed, as if he has the strength for that. I'm finding it easy enough to remember the names of things he points out. He has a little English too which helps.

Ana has started to sit down next to me at the table and she repeats some of the words José Luis tells me. She teaches me how to say the food items that are put out for us, but there's so little, there's not much to learn. Today I told her my name, where I was from and that I had one brother. **Christ, I've fallen for the girl.**

Day 35: Departures

The crucifix continues to tick against Sarah's chest, though with less speed and frequency. When it first started to do so the previous afternoon, Sarah had dismissed it as an irregular beat of the pulse she'd become accustomed to. But on her way back from Ana's flat, as the intensity increased, she'd considered how her grandfather might be attempting to send her a different kind of message.

Her immediate reaction was to call her mother to check that everyone was fine, especially Annie. She often worries how long her grandmother's stoicism can last before the weight of grief immobilises her. Her mother confirmed they were all well and Sarah had no reason not to believe her. Although she had a tendency, like Annie, to shield her from what she deemed to be unnecessary concerns, Sarah knew she wouldn't withhold anything serious.

She'd been struck, then, by the urge to telephone Eimear to ask after Thomas' health, undeterred by how strange such an enquiry might seem. As far as she was concerned, she'd found a long-lost family member and it was natural to care about his welfare. Not everyone would get it, and perhaps the likeness for her grandfather and proximity in age was causing a misconception about a premature bond. But she'd dialled Eimear's number, regardless.

'Hello.'

'Hi, Eimear. It's Sarah. I'm sorry to bother you.'

'Ah, Sarah, I'm so glad you called. I was just thinking that, in the rush the other day, I gave you my number but you didn't give me yours. Listen, I wanted to let you know ... my father has taken a turn for the worse.'

'What?' Sarah said. 'When did it happen?'

'Just this afternoon. It's his heart. He's stable and peaceful, for now at least, and the doctors are monitoring him closely. Isn't it such a coincidence you called?'

'Yes, so coincidental.' Sarah took the crucifix between her fingers and blew on it as if trying to extinguish a candle. 'I'm so sorry,' she said. 'Can you please keep me updated?'

'Of course, love,' Eimear said. 'You know, when you left, he seemed more settled and tranquil in a way I hadn't seen him for a long time. He hasn't let that cross you gave him out of his hands.' The tremor in her voice crumpled her soft laugh. 'The nurse says he can't wear it round his neck for now, so I've put it on the edge of the bedside cabinet. He'll see it as soon as he wakes up.'

'It's nice to hear it's brought him some comfort. Isn't it strange how things pan out sometimes?'

'Please say a prayer for him.'

***

There are a few people filtering out of the Church of St Mary Magdalene when Sarah arrives. Four elderly women remain inside in separate pews. Sarah is unsure whether she's intruding on the final prayers or reflections at the end of daily mass and tiptoes silently to the front, hoping to go unnoticed.

There's a small marble table directly in front of the altar where rows of half-lit tea light candles cast flickering shadows. Above it, a crowned Virgin cloaked in a bronze mantle stands guard with child in an arched window.

Sarah places a few coins into the red velvet collection plate, takes a candle in each hand and holds them into the lapping flames. She can't remember the first time she offered up an intention with her grandfather, but she can't have been more than five or six years old. Her grandmother complained that she was too young and might scald her hand or burn the ends of her ringlets; her grandfather simply shook his head and told her she was worrying about nothing.

They'd often offer up intentions after Sunday mass. Her grandfather would tell her to think about someone who had just died or someone who was sick, even if they weren't very sick, and ask for their protection. Half the time, Sarah couldn't come up with anyone, so she'd light the candle for her grandfather instead. She never told him, but she reckoned there was no harm in building up her intentions to stop him getting unwell.

'For you, Thomas,' she whispers softly, laying a candle on each side of the table; one from her and one from her grandfather.

Chinchón, February 1937

The rebels aren't too far away and we're preparing for the battlefield. I don't know what awaits us at the front; I don't even know if our action will be offensive or defensive.

~~*I'm not ready for war.*~~ **I'm nowhere near ready for war: not physically, not psychologically**.

It's been a matter of weeks of basic training and I haven't even fired a shot. There are men here much more able for action than I am. ~~*But I didn't come here to complain or retreat from the enemy. I'll put up a fight; Charlie will too. We're*~~ **Me and Charlie are** *in the same Company and we'll look out for each other. I pray Charlie gets some sleep tonight, so he's got the strength for* ~~*it.*~~ **the fight**.

I wasn't prepared for leaving Ana. ~~*It's easy to pretend sometimes that she's*~~ **She's** *the* **main** *reason I'm meant to be here, not the fight for democracy.*

We caught a train to Albacete and then a lorry here. I don't think the distance is too great. But Ana already seems so far away from my heart. I love her and **I know for sure** *she loves me.*

José Luis gave us his blessing and I don't think Ana's parents know. I'm certain José Luis wants love to be a distraction for his sister, something that will take her mind off notions of returning to the front. He doesn't want her there; we hear more and more reports every day of people being evacuated from Madrid. I know José Luis prays that Ana won't try to follow me.

Not everyone here knows about my love for Ana and I prefer it that way. Charlie does, and so does Morris. We wait until the streets are sheltered with darkness and then we walk through the village, share a cigarette, hold hands. **There's so much else shared between us.** *Her touch is as gentle as a feather and her raven hair shines silky smooth under cover of night.*

I don't know how long it will be before I see her again. She tells me I'll see her face at the front, something which makes me happy and ~~frightened~~ **scared** *out of my wits at the same time.* **I'm sure I saw her, one day, with a Machine Gun Company, but war plays cruel tricks on your mind.**

I don't want to see her face and not be able to touch it – that would cause me more pain than not seeing her. How can I protect her?

Charlie says there's no room for love in war and perhaps he's right. The war will end eventually and we'll go back home. What will become of our love? We can't choose who we fall in love with. I must try not to think about all that too much. I must concentrate on what lies ahead tomorrow and look forward to seeing Ana again.

The food is no better, probably worse in fact, but my love for Ana sustains me.

What will become of José Luis? He continues to say very little and his leg doesn't seem to be healing. **At least his eyesight is improving.** *I think he's a scholarly type of man, although he wants to be a soldier first and foremost. From what I can understand, he's writing about his experience of the war so far – I often see him with his notebook while he convalesces. Perhaps knowing something about his experiences so far might help me.*

I ~~wonder~~ **obsess** *about our Tommy and where he is right now. Please God, don't bring me face to face with our Tommy. Will he be feeling unprepared like I am and afraid of encountering me? I wonder if he ever thinks about me these days.*

What will Ana be doing now? Will she be thinking about me? I hope her heart doesn't feel like mine.

I have to keep reminding myself that I ~~came here to be part of the fight~~ **still have to fight, even if I'm far more interested in love**.

Day 36: Jarama 1

'You're doing that thing again, you know.'

'What thing?'

'Where you look as if you're miles away, locked in your own world.'

'There's just lots going on right now.'

'Anything I can help with?' Paco runs his hand over Sarah's as she zips up her bag.

'You're doing more than enough.' Sarah smiles at him and the silt of worry lifts from his face. 'You don't think I should try Eimear again, do you? She said she'd call if there was any change.'

'She'll be true to her word.' Paco takes Sarah's coat off the back of his chair and hands it to her. 'So after today, you'll have a bit more time, yes?'

'Yes. Apart from Thursday afternoon. I'm speaking to Raúl then.'

'Raúl?'

'It's nothing for you to be concerned about. Just sorting myself out. Shall we do something tomorrow, just the two of us?'

'How about we go down to the river?' Paco says quietly.

'That sounds great,' Sarah says, threading her arms through the sleeves of the jacket. 'And maybe we can take the photo then, so you can get that sent off?' She points at the portfolio that lies open at the page filled with shots of the *plaza*. 'You're so talented,' she says, studying the night shot of the square where three familiar shadows now skim the golden clock tower.

***

Sarah lets herself into the apartment without waiting for Ana to invite her in this time. Ana is nowhere to be seen, but Sarah senses she's not too far away. The cobwebs have been tidied away from the main window and a globe of Salamanca sun rebounds coquettishly off the individual sheets of paper drenched with her grandfather's words.

'I didn't hear you come in. Sorry.' Ana enters with a tray of coffee and water from a side room. 'I wonder where my manners have been these last days,' she says, balancing the tray on the edge of the table while she shuffles the papers together. 'Would you like to read some more? It's not too much, is it?'

Sarah wonders if she could do the same as Ana and Michael are doing for her, if she could hand over a love story to others. All of those obstacles in their way, and yet they only found themselves through war, the most tragic of circumstances. She contemplates the many hurdles she's had to cross and the ones she's still facing. Those that she is now responsible for placing in her own way.

'It's not too much for me, if it's not too much for you.'

'I no longer matter,' Ana says, sheathed in a veneer of gold from the midday sun. 'Just remember, things don't always turn out as you expect.'

Jarama, February 1937

I've experienced the worst days of my life. ~~I feel dead inside. Perhaps I am dead and all of this is a mere illusion.~~ **I am dead inside. Dear God, have mercy, for this is my reality from now on**.

A few days ago, in the very early morning, we arrived a short distance from the Jarama river. We were instructed to climb a plateau overlooking the river at Arganda. Charlie went in front where I could keep an eye on him.

We had breakfast at the cookhouse and took up our positions. ~~I'm not sure what time it was then, but the~~ **The** *morning sun was already warm. We were all in decent spirits, though nervous about what the day might bring. No one more than Charlie.*

They told us to cross the narrow road, move over the ridge and make our way down into the Jarama valley. We passed small olive groves in the rising heat but there was little else. I was conscious that we had very little natural cover. We didn't know where we were going; we didn't even have maps to guide us.

And then they came. Bullets whistling through the air, followed by utter chaos and confusion. It took me a moment to realise what was happening, that we were under fire. How are you meant to understand something you've never experienced before? Charlie cried out in fright; I tried not to, in order to reassure him we'd be okay. I pulled him back to the top of the ridge where our Company was put into a reserve position.

After that, much of the rest is a blur. Constant machine gun fire, artillery barrage, shells exploding, bodies falling down around us. Our machine-gun Company were given the wrong ammunition and our other Companies suffered awful casualties. Man after man was being gunned down by Moroccan troops.

When they told us we had to come out of our reserve position to stave off the threat, I saw the look on Charlie's face. He didn't say a word, just traipsed up like the rest of us to the top of a small bare hill away from the other men.

The Moroccan troops appeared and began firing at us, over and over and over. Charlie still didn't utter a word, but he was ghost white. We retreated, but the bullets kept coming. And then it happened – Charlie collapsed in front of me, his blood splaying us both. I signalled to one of the runners that we needed a stretcher and they came quickly, bundled him on. The blood continued to pour from him, his right leg hanging on by a sinew. But he was breathing, thank God he was breathing. Then they took him away. **And I just let them. I didn't even know if I could go with him; I didn't ask.**

Men continued to fall around me as the bullets hailed down. I don't know why or how I was spared. I prayed to sweet Jesus **and his Holy Mother** *that Charlie would make a full recovery.*

He was all I could think about as we held our position and later dragged wounded comrades back to headquarters. I asked if anyone could tell me how Charlie was, but no one seemed to know anything. I kept asking. It was just his leg, ~~I told myself, it would be fine, they would fix him.~~ **I told myself there was no damn way it would be fine; they wouldn't save him.**

We lost so many that day, and still no news of Charlie came. Morris asked too, but nothing. **I knew, deep down, that he was gone.**

It wasn't until after dark that ~~we learned of Charlie's fate.~~ **Charlie's fate was confirmed.** *We found him lying on a stretcher in the narrow road along with about fifty other men. They'd never come close to any medical help.*

~~It wasn't anyone's fault, they still say.~~ **It was somebody's fault.** *It was a desperate day, they say, and these men had been forgotten about.*

How could this happen to Charlie? How could he be left like that? Alone, so desperately alone. And petrified. I know he'll have been petrified. **Fear will have driven him into an early grave. I'll always be plagued by the sight of poor Charlie's corpse.**

When they gave us the news, I walked down to the sunken road with Morris to find him. I'll never forget that day – standing in a wasteland of death, of the dead, and the stench, the flies, swarms of them. And me, dead inside. I prayed then that the Moroccan soldier who killed my best friend would show his face ~~and kill me too~~ **so I could kill him stone dead**.

When I found Charlie, I closed his eyes with trembling hands and Morris and I both held onto him and prayed a decade of the rosary. He was stone cold by then. I rocked him to sleep, though I knew he had long slipped into his nightmare. The prayers were all we could give him as a goodbye.

Day 37: Jarama 2

Jarama, February 1937

We've been in this hell **hole** *for six days now. Several of the men who are left don't understand why I've removed myself to the cookhouse. They say it's too quiet now that the drum of machine-gun fire, the crack of tank shells and explosions have eased for the time being. Not for me.* **Christ,** *I can still hear the machine-gun round that killed Charlie, the screams which I think were mine, not his.* **I'll never stop hearing it.**

I'm holed up here wondering if the stench of rotting flesh and gunpowder will ever go away. The decaying corpses are the worst; there are bodies that still haven't been found, neglected out on the vast plain. We'll continue searching for missing comrades.

By day two, we were already a hell of a sight, filthy and blood-stained. But it was the hardened faces I won't forget. Every man was grieving for someone, but there was no ~~time~~ **place** *for pity or respite.*

That second day, they put our machine-gun Company in a forward position because the bullets they needed had arrived. The promise of tanks and decent air support never materialised. We continued to be no match for the rebels. I did as I was told and tried to stand firm, but we were surrounded again as the day wore on. Some of our men panicked and several comrades from our machine-gun Company were captured.

When you think the horror can't get any worse, it always does. I watched more men being mowed down; later they told me that the rebels killed them with the machine-guns taken from our own Company.

The remaining men say that day three was a victory of sorts. Can you call a stroke of luck a success? **There was no damn victory.**

Our comrades continued to be shot down while dust and stones rained upon us. Eventually, the line broke and we had no choice but to retreat. I could barely put one foot in front of the other by that stage. And I wasn't the only one. Those of us who were left staggered down the slope towards Chinchón Road, wrecked inside and out.

But it wasn't the end. We were the only ones left between the rebels and the Valencia Road and we had a duty to make one last attempt to hold back the enemy. That's how I understood it.

Courage and strength sometimes come in the darkest of hours. We picked ourselves up, we rallied our comrades and we prepared for what some of us thought was our final fight.

A good number of the men sang the Internationale; all I could do was listen. As we marched back up the hill, I'm sure I saw Ana watching me, nodding in approval. ~~Her clothes were spattered with dust and mud but her face was a picture, her glossed hair gleaming under a tilted cloth cap.~~ **Jesus, she was immaculate; pretty as a picture. A vision to behold amongst the chaos, so I knew rightly well she wasn't real.** *I turned back to look at her again, but she was gone.*

We fooled the rebels and forced them to retreat. A bedraggled group of us united in song and spirit was enough to make them think we had brought reinforcements.

I hope I see Ana soon. The memory of her on the road lingers, but it won't last forever.

I must write to Charlie's parents when I can. They deserve something from me. They'll want to know their son is resting in peace.

***

The riverbank ripples with memories of Raúl, like brittle leaves shed from trees. The skinny, dark-haired, bright-eyed student he once was, propped up by his rucksack and dreams and his own version of love.

Sarah knows what she must do. She will extract all that is good from these memories – the sustenance that fuels her spirit and self-worth – and let go of the rest.

'I wanted to tell you something,' Paco says. Sarah rests her head in the warm curve of his neck and watches the reflection of the city flutter in the gentle flow of the Tormes.

'Sure, go ahead.'

'These friends of mine are getting married this weekend – Sunday – and they've asked me to take some photos for them.'

'That's great news!' Sarah runs her fingertips down his side in approval, feels the quiver of his body next to hers. 'Can you do it? At such short notice?'

'You can probably guess, I wasn't their first choice.' Sarah feels the soft heave of laughter across his chest. 'Their official photographer let them down last night. I was going to tell you then, but I could see you were occupied with other things.'

Sarah hadn't expected the details of Charlie's death to hit her as hard as they did. She'd gone looking for him afterwards in the places he normally frequented, but she hadn't been able to find any trace of him. Sometimes, she thinks, people don't wish to be found.

'Sorry about that. Did you tell them yes?'

'I did. And I thought … as I'm sending off the portfolio soon, I'd have a bit of free time anyway, and the break in Mallorca would be nice.'

'Mallorca?' Sarah sits up and looks at him. 'I didn't realise. How long will you be gone for?'

'Only a few days. But I wanted to ask if you'd come with me, maybe?'

Sarah wants to say yes, of course she'll go with him, she'd love to go with him. Instead, she says, 'Are you sure that's a good idea? I mean, you'll be working and I'm not on the guest list. They might think it's odd you asking them if I can come when we're not a couple.'

'I think you're reading too much into it.' Paco pulls her close and she lets him, wondering if he can feel all the love for him coursing through her. She'll not tell him; not yet; not until her path is clear.

'I don't care what people think anymore, do you? And Manolo is a great friend, Sofía is too, and they'd love to have you.' Paco doesn't say anything for a few seconds. 'You'll get on really well with them. And wouldn't it be fun to have some time on the coast, away from everything? When else will we get the chance?'

There are so many chances we don't take, Sarah thinks. And Ana and her grandfather had so few. She's sitting here with a good man who wants to spend time with her and that's what she wants, too. The rest – his job, her job, where they'll be, what might work – none of it matters, here and now.

'I'd love to go.'

'You would?' Paco grabs her face and kisses her hard on both cheeks. 'That's settled, then. I'll let Manolo know and we'll sort the tickets today. They're getting married on the beach. It'll be very special.'

'Yes, it will be!' Sarah jumps up and starts putting away the glasses and leftover scraps of *tapas*. She hopes Paco doesn't notice her face flushed with embarrassment, her cheeks still warm from each kiss laden with much more than friendship.

'And by the way,' Sarah says, 'in other good news, my best friend Amy – you know, Amy – is finally coming to visit. Next month, a long weekend with her new boyfriend Nick. Apparently, he's a Maths teacher. Don't hold that against him!'

Paco laughs. 'Alright, I won't. And is that your way of telling me you'll be staying for a while?'

'Maybe!'

'Great! Now, how about we take that photo? Seems like a perfect day for it.' Paco rummages in the camera case, taking out the equipment and laying it on the blanket. 'Can you keep an eye on all that for a moment while I go over there and set up the tripod?'

Sarah nods and watches him make his way to the edge of the bridge. His fringe flaps about his eyes in the gentle breeze; he pushes it back and moves the tripod over to the left. 'You can tell me if the angle is okay once I get the camera into position.'

Sarah stands next to him while the city glints gold and spills into the Tormes. 'Now,' she says.

Day 38: Lost and Found

Raúl arrives promptly at *El Pintor* at 4:30pm; he hesitates to accept Sarah's invitation to go inside. 'I'd rather not,' he says, a little flustered. 'I'd rather wait here if you're not going to be too long.'

'If that's what you prefer.' Sarah gives a nonchalant shrug and leaves the door ajar while she fetches her bag. She isn't sure whether it's memories of the place or the possibility of small talk with Carmina or Paco that's keeping him out.

They walk silently towards the Cathedral Quarter, Raúl leading the way. He doesn't cast a single glance at her in the few minutes it takes to get to Manolita café.

'Is this okay?' He holds the door open for her. The décor looks much the same: there's a scattering of couches, tables and backless cube seats in creams and browns. From the street, Sarah catches sight of a new art exhibition. Bold-coloured canvasses featuring musicians and dancers are thoughtfully arranged in themed sections around the cream walls.

'Fine, thanks.' She chooses one of the cube seats closest to the door and waits for Raúl to sit down on the leather sofa. The distance between them when they last met has been overtaken by an unfamiliar formality. Sarah finds it unnerving. She orders two *cafés con leche*.

'About last time,' Raúl begins. 'I'm sorry if it was all a bit too sudden, too much too soon, but I hope we can move past it.'

'Too much too soon? Have you forgotten how many months it's been since the accident? I'm sorry,' she says, taking a moment to catch her breath. 'I don't mean to sound judgmental. I mean, I still don't know how it took you so long to tell me, but that's not why I wanted to see you today.' She takes a sip of the warm milky coffee and pats her mouth with a small square of napkin on the saucer. 'Are you really fully recovered now?'

'Yes, I really am.'

'I'm glad about that.' Sarah studies him while he drinks and wonders if he'll ever get close to what he was before. It's like the light inside him has been extinguished and a cold depression has settled over him.

'Do you think we can move past it? I do still care about you.'

He looks at her, his eyes deadened, as if waiting for her to bring him back to life. Whatever is going on with María, if there's anything at all, isn't enough to save this man. Sarah is overcome with sympathy for him, but she won't show it. She knows the real Raúl, the man she'd planned a life with, would not want her pity.

'I think we can move past it now,' Sarah says finally, 'and I'll always care about you too. But —'

'So can we try again?'

'But what we had is something in the past now, something we can draw a line under today.' She sees his eyes fill with tears and wishes she could give him the ending he thinks he wants. Theirs was a love story, she's certain about that, but one never destined to last. She knows that now.

'I'm not with María. I swear to you, I'm not.'

'And I'm glad about that, too, because you deserve better.'

Sarah places a few euros on top of the bill and links arms with Raúl as they step back into the street. They walk back silently to the *hostal*, both knowing this is the last time they'll walk together, feet dragging under heavy hearts. In time, both of them might realise they had to lose each other to find themselves again. For now, as they separate outside *El Pintor*, only one of them knows.

Jarama, March 1937

~~My spirit is as drenched as our dugouts~~. **I don't have an ounce of spirit left within me.** *Blankets are soaked through by the appalling weather that brings intermittent but incessant rain. Everything is harder in the cold and rain. The enemy is still out there and we can't let our guard down. One reckless move could cost us our lives.*

We'd a few days of sudden attacks which brought me additional worry. One of the worst fears for a man is having to fight against his own brother. Brothers from Ireland are here, on opposing sides of the conflict. It's one thing fighting against comrades and quite another battling your flesh and blood.

They said it was O'Duffy's Brigade in the trenches just a few hundred yards across the Jarama Valley. Sweet Jesus, what's a man to do? I still pray that we never fought brother against brother. I pray it wasn't my brother's face I saw. **I'll never understand what I witnessed, out there in the trenches.** *I hope our Thomas remains safe. I know he sees himself, as many of the men do, as a defender of the faith. I hope his faith has kept him strong, as mine has kept me in the worst moments.*

Every time I close my eyes, I see Charlie's dead face. ~~I can't help feeling I've let him down.~~ **I've let him down. I've failed him.**

I still haven't written to his parents and with every day that passes, it seems a more insurmountable task. **Just another example of my cowardice.** *Morris has offered to help, but the words have to come from me.*

I've had one period of leave when I met Ana in Albacete. It reminded me how real her my love is for her, and hers for me. Ana wouldn't tell me either if she's back at the front or not; she says there are things I don't need to know. I don't agree with her. **I'm a complete fool, not pushing for answers.**

She told me José Luis continues to improve but his place is in ~~Madrigueras~~. **Salamanca.** *I told her about the cross I found in the valley –* ~~I'm sure~~ *it's my brother's.* ~~It's the same as mine and~~ *I'm keeping it safe. She asked me what I thought it meant and I replied that I'd look after it for him. That's all I can say right now.*

Tajuña Valley, June 1937

They've moved us to a place called Mondéjar in the Tajuña Valley, some distance west of Madrid. The proximity to the river is a relief and we are all very glad of it.

I've seen Ana on a few more occasions and she looks ~~well~~. **so beautiful**. *Dare I say it, she also looks rested. I have much respect for her fortitude. She continues to help me improve my Spanish and our exchanges get better each time. When we see each other, we hold hands for as long as we can.*

I still don't sleep more than a few hours at a time and I'm plagued with nightmares. Ana chastises me and says I'm looking more and more exhausted. I don't quite know what I can do about it.

Last time, José Luis came with Ana and showed me some of the notes he's been writing. I didn't understand everything, but I think I was right to call him a scholar. His pages are filled with detailed accounts – I can tell just by the dates and names and places that appear. I'm no match for him. I hope to read his notebook in full one day.

I've eventually written to Charlie's parents. I wasn't sure how much they needed to know about the death of their only son. I concentrated on his bravery and courage and the prayers offered up for him. I didn't tell them that he died ~~abandoned amongst other wounded men~~. **alone**. *My letter is filled with deep sadness and regret, but I hope it finally reaches them. I don't know whether they have only begun to grieve for him,* ~~or if their grief is ongoing like mine~~. **if they'll forever grieve for him, like me**.

I would like to stay here for some time. Although I struggle to sleep, this is a tranquil place. I enjoy being close to the river.

Morris does too. He and I have become good friends.

I fear our time is limited here and they'll move us on again soon. I'm not yet ready for another battle; I don't think the other men are either. The temperatures are soaring and we would do well to acclimatise to the heat first, if one ever gets used to it.

~~I haven't forgotten why I came here~~. **I want to forget why I came here in the first place**.

Day 39: *All that's left behind*

'Sarah, it's for you. It's Eimear.'

The contents of her suitcase lie in disarray across Carmina's bed. Sandals, formal courts, not so formal pumps, midi dresses, long dresses. Most of it doesn't even belong to her. She's raided Carmina's wardrobe with her blessing and still can't decide what's best for a casual wedding on the beach. She still thinks there's no such thing as a casual wedding.

The triviality of her packing struggles hits her hard at the mention of Eimear's name. She grasps the phone from Paco's hand with an unintentional brusqueness.

'Eimear, what's wrong?' A wave of panic thumps her chest. Sarah knows all too well that something's not right.

'I'm afraid I've got some bad news.' Through choked sobs, Eimear tells her how Thomas passed away peacefully in the early hours of the morning, how she was with him until he took his last breath.

'I'm so sorry, Eimear.' The veil of grief descends upon Sarah once more; the reality of her grandfather's recent passing hurts again in places she thought had at least begun to heal.

'I'm so sorry,' she says again. 'I'll pray for him, and for you. Will you let me know about the arrangements for the funeral? I'd like to be there.'

'You don't need to do that.'

'But I'd like to.'

'If you're sure. Thanks, love. There was something else I wanted to tell you. Please, don't take it the wrong way.'

'Oh?'

Eimear clears her throat. 'I think you helped my father to go.'

'Me?' Sarah feels the panic rise inside her. 'What did I do wrong?'

'That's my point, Sarah. You didn't do anything wrong. In fact, quite the opposite – I think you did a lot right.'

'I'm not following.' Paco has moved a chair across to the dresser and helps Sarah lower herself into it. She accepts a glass of water from him and the kiss of condolence he brushes against her cheek.

'My father had been sad for a very long time. I noticed it more when your great-grandmother died, God rest her soul. When he finally told me about his family in Belfast, I should have gone then, tried to find you all. I shouldn't have heeded him. It's a pity we can't change the past.'

'I didn't upset him more, did I?'

Eimear starts crying again and Sarah wonders where the rest of her family are.

'You gave him his brother back. And you let him know that it was okay for him to finally rest. I'm sure that's why he held on all those years, that he was desperate for something of Michael.' She breathes deeply. 'You took his sadness away, Sarah. And he's always been a determined oul' fool, so he made sure he didn't hang around any longer. He was desperate to get to his brother.'

'I don't really know what to say. I just hope he's at peace now, that they both are.'

'I know he is, Sarah. A heart can only stay broken for so long.'

***

'I'm so sorry for your loss, Sarah.'

'How did you know?' A single pillar candle rests on the windowsill, its flame fanned by the cool breeze that feeds the apartment.

Ana crosses herself and waves to Sarah to join her by the window. Her grandfather's papers have been gathered up into a tidy pile and Ana is now slotting them carefully inside a white envelope. There's one page separate from the rest which Ana places to the side of the table.

'I don't want to leave anything important behind, dear, so I've prepared this for you.' She hands the envelope to Sarah. As if reading her mind, she goes on. 'You'll have plenty of time to read the rest, a whole lifetime, in fact. But this part must come to an end soon. I know your grandfather would have wanted you to have these, if you'll accept them.'

'Thank you,' Sarah says quietly. 'It's just that reading these pages here with you makes me feel less alone.'

'Never confuse solitude with loneliness, dear. Now,' she says, taking the single sheet of paper from the table, 'let's share your grandfather's words one last time. Will you read them to me?'

'If my grandfather reads them with us.'

August 1937

~~Respite can no longer heal my wrecked body or soul. Others may judge me, but~~ *I can no longer stay and fight this war. It's time for me to return* ~~home~~*, if they'll allow me.*

We did what we could at Brunete, but we were no match again for the rebel forces. ~~The battle was relentless and we were subjected to constant aerial and artillery bombardment.~~ *Men were mowed down again next to me; the rest of us were dead men walking, destroyed by the rebels and the heat.* ~~Sweet Jesus, the boiling heat and no water.~~

We took far too many casualties and now hardly any of us are left. Those of us who remain are shells of the men we once were. And Morris, they ~~took him out~~ **killed him** *on day one of the battle. He was dead before he hit the ground. Dear God, how many more comrades do I have to watch dying next to me? It'll be my turn soon.*

I took a bullet to the left arm and I'm slowly recuperating. They've sent us back to the Tajuña Valley, but I suspect our days are numbered here. The days seem longer than before.

~~I'm not sure there's a man whose soul~~ **No man's soul** *is weaker* *than mine at this moment. I've made a request to be sent home and now I have to wait for news; I don't know how long for.*

~~*I don't know if Ma and Da will be waiting for me.*~~ **I know Ma and Da won't be waiting for me.** *Our street seems so far away, as if it belongs to someone else.* ~~*I wonder if everything continues just the same there.*~~ **I know nothing is the same there.**

I haven't told Ana that I've asked to go home. It's been a while since I saw her, but time apart doesn't make my love for her wane. I want her to come with me, but I know it isn't possible. She may chastise me for putting myself before our love, but what am I to do? I'm no good to her as a broken man.

I don't want her in the middle of this war. I don't know where she is right now, or how many bullets and fallen comrades she's had to endure. Please God protect my Ana, **always,** *protect these people of Spain from the advancing rebel forces. Please let it stop.*

This is what I'll do. I'll continue to wait for news from headquarters. I'll ~~*take the respite given to me and*~~ *pray we're not moved out to the front again while I wait. I'll not tell Ana until I know for sure.*

If they tell me I must stay, I'll pray to God for guidance and strength to see me through my final days here. If they let me go, I'll find Ana and give her my news. I pray she'll forgive me ~~*and not stop loving me, that war will not bring our love to an end.*~~

~~*I've very little to give her — no worldly possessions, only these pages, and my love.*~~ *I'll ask her to keep hold of these pages until we meet again. For we shall meet again, even if our hearts belong to others; even if it is in death, not life. Love shared can never be erased.*

'Ana, do these words hurt you? Did you feel the same as my grandfather?' Sarah observes the woman's thoughtful expression as she extinguishes the pillar candle.

'I'll always love him,' Ana replies, 'though I know the love itself belongs back then. I know he was always destined to be with someone else.'

'And how did your story end, Ana? Did you love again?'

'Ah,' she says, taking Sarah's hand, 'I never got the chance. Some of us are taken a little earlier than others. The war took my baby – *our* baby – and the dictatorship took me. I never got out of prison alive.'

'Oh, Ana, I'm so sorry.'

'Your grandfather was right.' Ana makes her way to the door and beckons Sarah to follow her. 'Our lives, our identities may change, but love shared cannot be erased.'

'It's time now, Da.'

'I know, Son. But to end here, to know that Ana never got to love anyone else: how can that be? And our baby we never got to love…'

'There are things we'll never be able to explain, Da. Look, they're starting to gather for you, to bring you home.'

'I'm ready, Cormac. More than ready to be reunited with you, my dear Son. And when I cross over, it will also be back to my Annie, to the woman who took my carved-up heart and put it back together all those years ago. She'll be waiting, as she was for you. I will always be full of her love, and she of mine.'

Day 40

'Can you wait for me here, please? Just give me a few minutes, then come and find me. Can you do that?'

'Of course, Sarah.' Paco reaches across and lightly kisses her cheek. 'We're packed up and ready to go. It's time for your heart to heal now.'

'Thank you.'

Evening is preparing to embrace the city as Sarah walks the short distance from the car to the end of the bridge. The last vestiges of daylight slip away in wisped coils behind the spires of the cathedrals. Sarah knows this is goodbye; her feet drag with the weight of her heart.

'Go on, Da, go to her. Say your final goodbye.'

'But you said she couldn't see me. That was the deal.'

'Call it a special dispensation. She'll see you now, if you want her to.'

'Want her to? And she'll welcome me? My God, my heart. Thank you, my dear Son.'

An elderly gentleman appears in the middle of the bridge, illuminated by the delicate ambient lighting of the cathedrals. This man is dressed in his best grey suit and starched white shirt with a white rose buttonhole. He holds a bright yellow daffodil in full bloom between his hands like a sacred offering.

Sarah watches this man process past a guard of honour of suited men and soldiers, young and old, treading his last steps in this world. He stops alongside three figures: two men, one woman, acquaintances of old who each extend a white rose in friendship.

'Granda!' Sarah gasps, 'Granda, is it really you?'

'It's me,' I tell her. 'I never thought I'd see you again, before my departure from this city, from this life. You understand why I had to do what I did, don't you? Why we had to face the ghosts from our past?'

'I do now, Granda,' she says, her eyes luminous with both sadness and hope. 'Thank you. I don't know what else to say, where to start.'

'I wish you could fold into my arms one last time,' I tell her. 'And this is for you – your favourite, as well as mine.' I lay the daffodil on the slice of bridge between us. 'I never wanted you to have a lifetime of regrets.'

'No more regrets,' she whispers, picking up the flower and holding it against her chest, 'and much less fear. You've taught me that we have to release past versions of ourselves, if we are to have any chance of living the present moment. I promise I'll try, Granda.'

'That's as much as any of us can do, love. Will you stay here?'

'I don't know yet. Maybe.'

'You can go wherever life takes you, my precious girl. As for me, I've taken far more from this life than I probably deserved. It's my time to leave ... but I'll never be far from you, if you'll allow it.'

'I know,' Sarah says, wiping her tears, unclasping the crucifix from her neck. 'But before you go, I want you to take this back.'

'No, I can't. That was my gift to you.'

'A gift of love, yes, but I have all I need, right here.' She lays her hand across her heart.

'That's kind, but I don't need it either, not where I'm going. You see, I have friends, family waiting. Look at them, all lined along the bridge. I'd say that's an even better turnout than I had on the day of the funeral!'

Sarah observes the rows of expectant faces, before turning her gaze to José Luis, Charlie and Ana one last time. They are joined by another figure, a man she hasn't seen since she was five years old, a man she's never forgotten. The four of them incline their heads in a solemn farewell and take a step back into the light, into the world to which they must return.

'Let's leave the crucifix here, Sarah, in this city which took its time to establish its place in our hearts. And I leave you here, too, for now; but know that I'll always love you.'

I see Sarah drop the crucifix over the bridge into the flow of the river. I have nothing left to give, nor to say. I feel the tug of the bridge beneath my feet, the voices behind me calling me home; all of it is pulling me to where I must rest now.

Sarah watches as her grandfather's body blurs and dissolves into a fine flare of light; she watches as his light ascends over the gilded expanse of the city and diffuses into tiny shards in the twilight.

She blows a kiss onto the evening breeze. 'Rest in peace, Granda. I love you.'

'Is it time now?'

Sarah looks down into the petalled water of the Tormes where her grandfather's crucifix floats under the arc of the bridge. For the first time since her return, she sees her reflection rippling softly on the surface of the water, next to Paco's. Where it belongs.

And this alone is enough. This is where their story is.

Author's Note

When I first began studying A level Spanish with the most wonderful teacher, Dr Margaret Wright, the Spanish Civil War was an area of history I had not encountered before.

The war took place between 1936 and 1939 and began with a military uprising against Spain's Republican government which failed to take control of the whole country. A three-year civil war ensued between Republicans, aided by the Soviet Union and International Brigades, and the Nationalists under General Francisco Franco, supported by Nazi Germany and Fascist Italy.

The majority of men who left Ireland to participate in the Spanish Civil War did so under the leadership of Eoin O'Duffy, forming part of the Irish Brigade and joining the Nationalist cause. For O'Duffy and his recruits, Franco was seen as a defender of faith and traditions; the war itself as a battle between Christianity and Communism, a Catholic Crusade, a Holy War. Other men joined Frank Ryan to support the Republican effort.

The city of Salamanca was not only the site of Franco's military headquarters during the Spanish Civil War, but remains the home to the General Archive on the war.

In September 1993, while studying Hispanic Studies at Queen's University, Belfast, I was delighted to receive an Erasmus grant to attend the University of Salamanca. It was a year full of new adventures, friendships and experiences which I will never forget.

I would like to acknowledge the following works which proved invaluable while researching and writing this book: Raymond Carr's *Images of the Spanish Civil War* (Allen &

Unwin, 1986); Tim Fanning's *The Salamanca Diaries* (Merrion Press, 2019); Fearghal McGarry's *Frank Ryan* (2nd revised edition: Historical Association of Ireland, University College Dublin Press, 2010); Barry McLoughlin and Emmet O'Connor's *In Spanish Trenches* (University College Dublin Press, 2020); Eoin O'Duffy's *Crusade in Spain* (2nd edition: Reconquista Press, 2019); Murray A. Sperber (ed.), *And I remember Spain: a Spanish Civil War Anthology* (Hart-Davis MacGibbon, 1974); and Robert A. Stradling's *The Irish and the Spanish Civil War, 1936-1939* (Mandolin, 1999).

The Sandstone City is a work of fiction, in part an imagining of the impact of the Spanish Civil War upon a working-class Belfast family, and how choices related to war splinter individuals, families and communities. It is inspired by my fascination with the relationship between past and present versions of the self, and of course by my love for Salamanca, a city reimagined here which will always have a special place in my heart.

Acknowledgements

First and foremost, my heartfelt thanks to Aderyn Press, and publisher and editor extraordinaire, Rebecca F. John. I will be forever grateful for your belief in Michael's story and for giving his voice the best home I could ever have wished for. Thank you so much for all your kindness, care and patience.

Many thanks to the Books Council of Wales for an Author Advance Grant to develop this novel; and to the Arts Council of Northern Ireland and Damian Smyth for a travel award to take *The Sandstone City* to the pink city of Jaipur, India.

To Sian Williams and the team at the South Wales Miners' Library, special thanks for your unwavering generosity in providing access to the Spanish Civil War collection. Cover images are from 'Volunteer for Liberty', courtesy of the South Wales Miners' Library, Swansea University, and the Abraham Lincoln Brigade Archives. Some of the contents of Sarah's box gifted by Michael are also inspired by Spanish Civil War holdings at the South Wales Miners' Library.

Thank you, Kari Brownlie, for the gorgeous cover design, and Julia Forster for your wonderful PR support.

Huge thanks to Alan Bilton, Francesca Rhydderch and the Creative Writing community at Swansea University; and special thanks to Nuria Lorenzo-Dus and Rafa Bocero for your words of wisdom on Spanish language additions.

To my mum, Geraldine, and my siblings – Joanne, Sharon, Stephen, David and Chris – who listened to me talk about Michael relentlessly and provided so much encouragement; and to my Wales-based friends who propped me up – Jacqui, Nathan, Lisa, Jade, Kathryn, John and Kate – thank you all from the bottom of my heart.

Many thanks to all of you who have taken the time to read this story – I appreciate every second you have spent with Michael, Sarah, and their ghosts.

And finally, to the 'Salamanca crew' who loved the city alongside me and with whom I will always share the best memories – thanks a million Jayne, Siobhan, Catherine, Cristina and 'Señor Tacaño', our Jonny B.

Originally from Belfast, Elaine Canning is a public engagement specialist and writer living in Swansea, South Wales. She holds an MA and PhD in Hispanic Studies from Queen's University, Belfast and an MA in Creative Writing from Swansea University. She is currently Head of Special Projects at Swansea University, which include the Rhys Davies National Short Story Competition, as well as Executive Officer of the Dylan Thomas Prize.

She has authored a monograph and papers on Spanish Golden-Age drama and her short stories have appeared in Nation.Cymru and *The Lonely Crowd*. Editor of *Take a Bite: The Rhys Davies Short Story Award Anthology* (Parthian, 2021) and *New World, New Beginnings: Resilience and Connectivity through Poetry* (Parthian 2021), she is also editor of *Maggie O'Farrell: Contemporary Critical Perspectives* (forthcoming, Bloomsbury). *The Sandstone City* is her debut novel.